Swept into the Darkness

Chronicles of the Celestial Book One

LaTaeya Lane

Copyright 2013 by LaTaeya Lane

Swept into the Darkness (Chronicles of the Celestial Book One)

Re-Edited By Dana Goodrow

Cover Design by Phatpuppy Art Creations

ISBN: 978-0615697444

ISBN: 0615697445

CreateSpace, North Charleston, SC

Lucian, this is for you, I love you with all my heart.

ACKNOWLEDGEMENTS

I want to thank my mother Lauriece for all of your love and support. You have inspired me for an entire lifetime. To my grandmother Madear, you will always hold a special place in my heart. Johnny, your presence in my life is more meaningful than you will ever know. My dear husband Leo, your loving spirit has created a light in me that can never be extinguished. Thank you to everyone that played a part in the formation of this book.

Chapter One

The drive to work was always a trip of contemplations. Thinking about my parents burned bright on my mind. It's never easy to survive tragedy and bounce back into the swing of everyday life. I never really paid attention to the low volume radio but the extra noise kept me company. I used to love waking up early to get my day started but lately I wasn't much of a morning person. I lost my father in an accident, and my mother couldn't handle the loss. She had a nervous breakdown and is in a mental hospital, so really I lost both parents in one awful moment. It's a challenge for me to get up and go on with my life like nothing has happened. Just getting out of bed sometimes makes me feel like I am betraying my parents.

This morning I left early so I could have a few minutes to myself before the children came in for the first bell. I spent the drive lost in thought, and was so distracted that I barely noticed that I was pulling into the school parking lot.

Milford Elementary was a traditional-looking school. Normally empty this early, the smell of wax, coffee and stored damp library books lingered in the brightly decorated hallway. My purse and lunch bag scuffed against my long winter coat as I made my way into the main office to sign in for the day. "Good morning, Sydney," said the receptionist as she rifled through papers on the desk. "Good morning!" I replied, then hurried off to my classroom.

The classroom was structured to support the education of young students. Each area had been well defined and looked inviting if you were a six year old. There was a kitchen area, block area, art and music area and even a sand play area, not to mention a discovery science area. They all had toys and other learning tools for children to experience and express themselves through play. After I got settled in, I checked the latest news on the computer. The quiet halls were now crawling with parents, noisy students and teachers trying to get to their room before morning announcements. The kids finally made it by the time the second bell rang. The children went to their cubbies and placed their book bags and other belongings inside. While the children ate breakfast, I went over the day's activities with the teacher, Mrs. Applebum. Our day started with a morning greeting, singing songs and discussing current events. Following that would be morning writing time. I like that part of the morning because it gave me the chance to work one-on-one with some of the children that needed extra help.

The day went by pretty quickly, and the next thing I knew I was home. I lived in my parent's house, which was basically mine now that my mom had been declared mentally ill. As soon as I stepped into the cozy living room a warm calm feeling overcame me and I sighed in relief. The living room was decorated in a European Modern chic style. The sofa and love seat was made of black imported leather, and the lamps and end tables had a marble Italian flair. The carpet, a thick German-inspired piece was a gift to my parents, and the window coverings were dark thick velvet drapes that kept heat in and drafts out during the harsh winters here in the Northeast. The fireplace was made of inlaid brick was that had been painted black and white.

I pulled off my coat and tossed my bag on the wooden chair as the phone rang interrupting my peaceful flow of consciousness. The caller ID read "CHRISTINE"—my best friend. Screening my phone calls was kind of an obsession for me. You would have thought that I worked for the FBI or something.

"Hi Christine!" I said enthusiastically.

"Hey Syd, what's up? How have you been?" She asked. Before I could reply she was inviting me out to have a drink with her at the local Chili's Restaurant. I wasn't much of a drinker these days except for the occasional glass of white wine, but- I hated saying no to my best friend. My idea of a nice relaxing evening was with a character from a great book and a nice hot mug of cocoa. I declined the invitation, but Christine really wanted some company. She insisted she'd bring over a large pie with extra cheese, and a movie.

After our conversation I did a quick assessment of the house to make sure everything was in its place and clean. Now it was my turn. After a hard day working with the kids I felt I needed to take a quick shower and wash my hair. The warm water flowed from the shower and gently beaded down upon my lathered skin, as the tensions of the day lifted off my body. As I rinsed off, I thought about my social life. I loved having Christine over but at times I really wished for some male company.

"A boyfriend," I said aloud. I don't really know why I didn't have a guy around. It's not like I work in the ER as a doctor or nurse on call. I'm not a pilot or flight attendant where most of my time is spent away from home. I was reasonably attractive, or at least I thought I was. I was 5'7" with a petite build, weighing about 125 pounds. I had long jet black hair that's naturally curly, although I recently had it straightened. My eyes were light blue and slightly oval shaped. I also had a small narrow nose and a tiny beauty mark just above my right eye. My lips were full and had a natural pink hue. My skin was soft with a cream complexion. I was happy to say that I had nice sized breasts, 38C to be exact and plump derriere as well. I took care of myself too and often liked to go tanning at the local salon when I got my hair and nails done. I guessed I just hadn't met the right man yet. Until I met the guy that was right for me, I would rather be alone. I wanted to love a man, but a part of me was afraid to because I didn't want to open myself up to that love just to lose it and get hurt. Hopefully my time will come soon.

My shower was quick but efficient. I got dressed and waited for Christine on the sofa while I watched the evening news. I felt a headache coming on, and was having trouble just concentrating. All I could think about was the last trip I went on with Christine, which was the night of the accident. Ever since the car accident I have excruciating headaches. I went into the kitchen and pulled out the drawer that my medication was in. At the moment I was taking prescription pain killers, sleeping pills, and sometimes anti-depressants. I hadn't needed to take those pills in a long time. I tried to deter the pain from gaining force. If it didn't, I was going to have to cancel my date with Christine and go straight to bed. The headaches are almost blinding at times, and literally feel like a hammer is banging inside of my brain. Every time I think about the trip I am reminded of the worst day of my life.

I had just gotten back from a weekend ski trip in Aspen with some girlfriends, including Christine. It was mid-winter and my flight was delayed for several hours due to a terrible snow storm that hit the area. My dad, a surgeon at Milford General Hospital picked me up from the airport after a thirty-hour shift; the staff was low because of the storm so he decided to stick around to help out as much as he could. We were both pretty tired but it never occurred to me that dad was not in any kind of shape to drive. It was 4:45 on a Thursday morning, and it was dark and freezing cold. Sleet came down pretty hard, and made the roads very slick. It looked like dad was doing fine, and I always felt safe when he was behind the wheel. Mom was waiting for us with hot cocoa and I was so excited to see her and tell her about my trip.

The ride was long and I dozed off a few times. I woke abruptly to the sound of skidding tires and a sudden swerving motion. Dad's head was slumped down over the steering wheel, his glasses were crooked and his eyes were closed.

"Dad! Dad! Wake up!" I yelled. I yanked off my seatbelt to shake him with force. The car was spinning out of control. His head bobbed up and down and his eyes lazily open and closed. I grabbed the steering wheel and tried to scoot over as close as I could towards him and reach for the break with my foot. The car was going too fast and bumped and swayed through the light traffic. The car sped up and then everything went black.

A tear rolled down my left cheek as I thought about that terrible night. I wiped my eyes with my hands as I heard the doorbell ring. I gathered myself before I let Christine in. She was perky as usual. Christine's naturally blonde hair was cut in a short bob. It bounced against her neck as she flounced inside with a large pizza box and a bag of movies. Never cold, she liked to sport dark colors for the most part. Today she had on a red short sleeved designer t-shirt and jeans, her arms were inked up with colorful tattoos and her face had quite a few piercings. Her unique fashion sense didn't take away from her beauty.

I happily invited her in and motioned her to go into the kitchen. As I closed the door behind her, the cold wind crept in, reinforcing my decision to lounge around in sweat pants and a cable knit sweater. Christine insisted we crack open the bottle of wine, while we ate the pizza and caught up on some serious girl talk. She told me about the new guy she hired to work at her restoration shop, and mentioned that her business partner and my lifelong friend Angelo was putting in more hours. "I'm actually surprised that Angelo didn't invite himself over for pizza," I said. Angelo, Christine and I hang out all the time. Her brown eyes glistened against the dim kitchen light as she answered, "He wanted to come by but he stayed late at the shop to go over some things with the new employee."

"I have a great plan." She said in her raspy yet feminine voice.

"Mmmm," I replied. I was not in the mood for any of Christine's spur of the moment adventures. My head was really trying to get a hold of me. I shouldn't have had the wine since I'd taken my medicine, but I didn't want to tell her I wasn't feeling well. I didn't want to worry her. She looked too happy.

Now don't get me wrong—I loved adventure, and want adventure but not the kind that Christine wants. I used to have a tremendous hunger for adventure of any kind, but the accident and the death of my father changed everything for me. I can't handle too much transition at one time.

[3]

My friends and I used to go skiing, sky diving, cliff jumping, and bungee jumping; you name it. I'd seen a lot of the world growing up as a child and young adult. My parents loved to travel and experience the world, so I'd been blessed to have travelled to many different places such as Europe, Asia, New Zealand, and Africa. We loved Egypt and went there at least twice a year. I had a great relationship with my parents, and they gave me a freedom that most parents would never give their teenager. I was always a responsible and trust worthy kid. I never took anything for granted. I graduated with high honors at Milford High and my graduation present from my parents was an all-expense paid trip to London. It was an experience of a life-time.

After I lost my parents, my whole life did a 180 degree turn. I stopped traveling, my friends dropped off one by one, church became a distant place that I barely entered and my extended family was torn apart by fights over my mother's care and my parents' estate. Luckily, my parents had their affairs settled before the accident. I was financially secure and didn't have to work. My mother's close friend and business partner, Amy Delilah, had taken full charge of the company. I owned a piece of the company and I helped out when I could, but at first I stayed away. My mother had trained me in marketing and editing, but until recently I felt like I had to do my own thing. My mom kept the doors open for me to return to the company when or if I was ready to.

I thought about my mom and dad, and what kind of plan Christine would propose.

"What's your plan? I abruptly asked her, picking a piece of sausage off of the half bitten slice of pizza.

"I planned a camping trip; hiking, ice fishing, hunting, the whole nine." She smiled.

"What? It's the middle of winter! Who goes camping this time of year?" I frowned. Christine sighed.

"We do. I want us to spend some time together and do things like we used to do. We haven't done anything since…" She paused and gave me a look that read sorrow.

"Since when? I asked her, as my voice trembled. She said nothing. "Since my dad died, and my mother was put away?" I asked struggling to get the words out. Her wide set eyes flickered and her small nose flared a bit.

"Syd… I know you're hurting, and missing your parents, but please don't be upset with me. I'm your best friend and truly love you as my sister. I'm being sincere in my efforts to get you involved in activities again." She gave me a light smile.

"Activities again?" I repeated incredulously. She made me feel like a child that didn't want to get involved in extracurricular activities. I could feel my anger grow. The memory of my parents played on my mind like a video tape stuck on rewind. I couldn't stop thinking of them. I tuned out Christine's voice and went to another place in my memories.

When I awoke after the accident, I was dressed in a white gown and tucked into a hospital bed. The room was bright and felt empty. I heard the steady beeping of a heart monitor, and noticed the IV was hooked up to my right arm. My mouth dry and pasty, I desperately wanted to feel gulps of ice cold water streaming down my throat. I immediately began to panic. I knew there was an accident, but I didn't know how bad it was. I worried about my father. My head started to pound. I felt the side of my head, where the pain was coming from. Massaging the thickness of the bandages with my fingers, my body started to ache all over. This was bad. My heart thudded faster and I heard the increase of the sound on the monitor. I pressed the call button for the nurse. Within seconds she came in with two other doctors.

"Sydney! My goodness... You're awake!" She said with worry and excitement in her voice.

"Where is my mom? My dad was driving, what room is he in? Is he ok? What happened? How did I…" My voice trailed off. The questions flowed freely from my lips.

The dark-haired doctor spoke up. "Miss London, I'm Dr. Randolph."

"Yes Doctor Randolph," I answered him nervously. It was weird looking at everyone stand around the sides of the bed staring at me.

"I see that you remember that you were in an accident. That's good... But…" he paused. I was under the impression that he was trying to tell me something that was not good at all. I made an attempt to brace myself.   "Miss London, this is Nurse Hathaway, and my partner Doctor Anderson." They both nodded their heads and extended their hands. I shook their hands and motioned for Doctor Randolph to continue. I noticed that the energy around them glowed blue. I'd never been a "normal" person. Ever since I was a child I'd had experiences that were hard to explain. For example, I frequently had "flashes" that showed me glimpses of the future. I also remember times when a small light would emerge from my fingers, and I was able to move things using the light. Sometimes I saw things in my visions as well, like shadows and creatures. I could also see an aura around people—usually either a bright blue color or a muddled gray. Sometimes I'd seen a red aura, which for some reason really scared me. I'd tried to ignore these abilities, and there were times when I refused to admit that strange things were happening.

"The accident was extremely bad. The car you and your father were in was completely totaled. Doctor London fell asleep at the wheel, lost control of the car and slammed into a tractor trailer. You weren't wearing a seatbelt, and at the moment of impact you went head-first into the windshield and cracked your skull. You had some bleeding on the left side of your brain." My eyes were wide, and I couldn't believe what I was hearing. "You had emergency surgery to stop the bleeding. Miss London, you slipped into a coma after the operation." He looked so worried.

"How long was I out?" I wanted to know.

"Four and a half months." He replied, as he let out a sigh. "Miss London I am sorry to tell you but your father died in the crash. His body was crushed at the moment the car flipped over. He was pronounced dead on the scene." My heart started to break. The tears began streaming down my face.

"Where is my mom? She was waiting for us at home that night." My voice shook with fear. I couldn't believe that my father was dead. The doctor stared at me for a moment.

"Your mom had a really hard time coming to grips with the death of your father and you being in a coma. She thought you were a lost cause. Mrs. London had a nervous breakdown and tried to kill herself. So your uncles and aunts made the decision to put her in the Loving Hills Mental Rehabilitation Center." My body trembled. I just could not fathom that this was happening to me. My mother is a strong, powerful, sophisticated leader. The CEO of her own publishing company, a business woman and an independent free spirit, she is a God-fearing Christian woman who grew up in a small town just outside of Baton Rouge. This did not sound like my mom. I asked myself a dozen questions and broke down. My mom was committed and dad was gone. What made the whole thing worse was that I never had the chance to get my mom some kind of help and pay my last respects to my father. I couldn't imagine my mom being in one of those places, despite the fact that Loving Hills was one of the best rehab centers in the country. Where the hell were my uncles, aunts and Christine?" Where was she?

The night of the car crash I actually died and was brought back. Doctors said I was dead for about nine minutes or so. Every now and then I thought that when I died, something or someone came back through with me. At home I would hear noises and when I was at work or running errands I often got the notion that someone was watching me, or sometimes even following me. Many people think that when a person has a near-death experience like I did, they're more open and connected to the supernatural, and I believed it. I couldn't call myself psychic, but I was aware that there was something different about me.

The only person that knew about my abilities was Luna Delilah, my good friend and spiritual advisor. Luna and Amy were sisters and have known my parents since before I was born. After I was released from the hospital, my flashes became more frequent and frightening, so I would visit Luna almost every day. At first the visions were really bizarre and I didn't know what they meant, why I was having them, or how to handle what was happening to me. Luna was the only person I could go to who understood what I was going through. During my sessions with her she grew to become such a great friend. She helped me handle and control the flashes. In fact, I hadn't had a flash in months—and unfortunately, hadn't seen Luna in far too long.

When I snapped out of my reverie, Christine looked at me as if she was calling my name for some time. I focused, pretending I was interested in her adventure proposal all over again. I didn't want to hurt her feelings, and I realized that I was being mean to her, but I really didn't want to go anywhere.

After going back and forth with Christine for a while, I finally gave her a maybe on the trip proposal. That was fine with her and she left contended. I cleaned up the mess we made, popped in a CD by The Cure and prepared myself for bed. Getting into my cozy pajamas was the highlight of the evening. I had the music on for a little bit to keep me company while I brushed my hair and engaged in my skin regime. I climbed into bed and looked over at the Daniel Steel novel perched on my nightstand, pondering if I should pick it up or not. My headache was pushing away so I made the choice to ditch reading for the night. All I wanted to do was to go to a happy place in my dreams, for my reality was filled with nightmarish visions of the loss of my parents.

The next morning I woke up feeling worn out. The sun peeped through the chocolate colored curtains. I cheered inside, thankful that today was Saturday. I didn't have the energy to work with the kids today even though my head felt better.

Usually my weekends were filled with errands, such as sorting mail, cleaning the house and doing laundry. Today was going to be different. All I wanted to do was see my mom.

Getting ready didn't take me any time. I could shower, blow dry my hair, dress and have my make up on in about 45 minutes. I love putting on makeup, doing my hair and dressing up. I'm really into high fashion. *Project Runway* and *Top Model* are two of my favorite shows. I'm also a big saver, so I make my fashion choices and spending decisions wisely. I threw on a pair of Jean leggings and a black sparkle top. Designer riding boots topped off my look.

I whipped up some eggs, sausage and waffles and thought about going on that trip with Christine. I wished that Christine had proposed a trip at a nice resort somewhere. I loved room service and being pampered. Getting away might not be that bad after all.

I wasn't sure that camping this time of year was a good idea, but hunting and doing some hiking wouldn't hurt. Maybe we could rent a cabin and do some horseback riding. Riding is one of my favorite things to do. I made my decision. I was going to go on the trip with my friend. I finished my breakfast, cleaned up, and headed out to Loving Hills.

The smell of the freshly painted walls of the Loving Hills Mental Rehabilitation Center hit me as I walked into the building. Despite its cheerful appearance it still made me sad to be here. Walking down the long hall, I felt butterflies flutter in my stomach. I felt excited and nervous at the same time. Suddenly I had a flash of my mom standing by the window. I knew she was at the window.

The flash concerned me—I thought since it had been so long since the last one that I'd recovered from them. I'd been under constant observation since the accident. Doctors were worried that my brain injury may become a long term problem for me. I wouldn't dare mention that I see things and have episodes or flashes. They would think I was crazy, and Doctor Randolph would put me in a room right next to my mom's. We would share lunch and she would give me her Jell-O. She hated Jell-O, but I loved it. I smiled at that strange thought.

The halls were full of doctors, nurses and orderlies, many of them oddly cheerful. It felt like I was pulled into a classic episode of the Twilight Zone. I had already passed the security desk, signed in and presented my identification. Finally arrived at room 13—and yes, I am superstitious. I did everything I could to get them to move my mother to another room but they denied my request. I turned the knob and went inside. I visited my mom frequently and she was accustomed to seeing me often. I usually saw her the same day and time every week but since my headaches became worse I hadn't been able to get there as often. I didn't like to break the routine but I had no choice. When my headaches get really bad, I can't drive, or go to work, not to mention being able to handle my mother's presence. For some reason I was nervous about seeing her today. I stepped into the room and she was standing by the window following the birds movement with her finger pressed against the glass.

"Mom." I softly called to her. She slowly turned and looked at me. I prayed that my mom would be blessed with speech again. Nothing would be better than to see my mother return to the woman she used to be. To hear her speak, see her walk around, communicate and connect with the world again was my greatest wish. She reached out her arms and walked over to me, and I stepped into her embrace. Hugging her tightly, tears rolled down my cheeks. Mom was thin, and pale. Her dark hair was the same color as mine. It was shoulder length and neatly brushed and pulled into a pony tail. I smiled at her and guided her over to the sofa.

I did my best to make the room cozy and home like. The hospital allowed me to bring in a few things, so I put up some nice shades, and brought in a new mattress and sofa. I hung up a few pictures and got a couple of fake potted plants. Everything in her room was safe and cleared as non-threatening. The pictures and plants and even the sofa cushions were glued down for her protection. I was really surprised that they gave me permission to bring in all that stuff. I guess they were pleased that I even cared enough to take the trouble. When most people get sent to places like this their family members don't come back to see them, especially when they are in the shape that my mother was in at first. Since she'd been here she hadn't tried any other attempts to end her life. I sometimes wondered if she really ever tried to commit suicide. My mom was not the type to give up on anything.

I had brought in some of my mom's makeup, the latest issue of InStyle magazine and the most recent Fabio covered romance novel. My mom loves romance novels and adores Fabio. I planned on reading a couple of chapters, a few articles and of course making up her face. I inherited my mother's fashion sense. I told her about my decision to go on the trip with Christine and she just looked at me with a blank face.

The day went by so fast, and I had a nice time. An orderly named Wanda strutted in with a cart of food and announced that visiting hours were almost over. I didn't realize that I spent most of the day there and it was time for dinner already. I kissed my mom on the cheek and ended my visit with an embrace. On my way back home I noticed my cell phone had two missed calls, one from Christine and the other from Luna Delilah. I figured I'd call Luna later and automatically dialed Christine. I thought it was time for me to give her my answer about going on the trip.

"Hey Christine what's up? You called? I went to visit my mom. She looked a little pale, definitely in need of a tan. The next time I go, I'll schedule a meeting with her doctor to see how she's progressing. I just needed to spend some quality time with her today." I was so filled with energy that I barely gave Christine a chance to speak.

"I'm glad you saw Pamela. I know she was happy to see you. I'll go with you when you go see her again." I stopped at a light. I knew the conversation was going to be long so I quickly hooked up my hands free device. There was no sense in me getting pulled over and getting a ticket for talking on my phone while driving.

"Christine," I said taking a deep breath, "I want to let you know that I decided to go with you on the trip. Let's rent a cabin. It's too cold for tents. And even though I'm going with you, I have to take things slow that weekend. I'm still having headaches and I need to be careful." I didn't want to worry her. I didn't want her to pity me, or feel sorry for me, or think that I was weak. I paused. She didn't react as fast as I thought she would.

"Oh, ok, great! I completely understand about the headaches. I just wish you would have told me. I can't believe I brought wine over last night. I'm so sorry. I didn't realize. I'll book a nice place in the Poconos. It's nice this time of year. My parents have a friend that they rent from every winter and fall so I'll call them."

"Remember to book for a weekend, or you can shoot for the weekend that rolls into winter break. I really can't afford to take any more days off work. I have to save the ones I have just in case." She agreed and was eager to get off the phone with me and make the arrangements.

This was a big thing for me. Branching off and going on this trip seemed like a good idea. I was trying to slowly get back to normal and be the person I used to be, but honestly I wasn't sure that would ever happen. I would never be normal. Some may have wondered. "Damn, what's the big fucking deal?" But it is a big deal. Just thinking about the accident caused anger, mostly at myself. I blamed myself for what happened to my parents.

"IT WAS MY FUCKING FAULT THAT MY DAD IS DEAD AND MOM LOST HER MIND AND IS LOCKED UP! IF I HADNT GONE ON THAT TRIP BOTH OF MY PARENTS WOULD BE HERE! WE WOULD BE TOGETHER!" I yelled and cried as I blurted the words out in my car. I frightened myself as I gleamed at my reflection in the rear-view mirror. Thank God I was already parked in the garage. My foundation was runny and discolored with tear stains and my mascara was smudged after I kept rubbing my eyes.

By the time I arrived home it was nightfall almost 6:00 in the evening. The house felt creepy as I walked through, running my hands across the walls to search for the light switch in the garage. Something moved in the darkness, catching my attention and startling me. A nervous feeling fluttered in my stomach. My grandmother's rocking chair creaked. I stayed quiet, still looking for the switch with my hand. I rarely went in the house through this way. I felt for the light switch, and finally found it. I flipped on the switch quickly, but the light didn't dispel the eerie vibe in the atmosphere. I saw a shadow move slowly near a stack of boxes off to the side. The boxes had things in them that belonged to my parents. I surveyed the area trying to catch another glimpse of the moving shadow. My vision quite keen, I kept my back against the wall and made my way toward the door to enter the living room.

I was so scared I couldn't even blink. I wasn't sure what the entity wanted. I eventually made it inside, turned on all the lights in the house and got settled in. Still uneasy, I tried to calm down and convince myself that I'd imagined the strange shadowy figure. I washed off my makeup I didn't have any plans, no boyfriend to go on a date with, no group of girlfriends to be single in the club with. My heart felt heavy.

I thought again about meeting Mr. Right, as I sat on the sofa sipping on a cup of hot cocoa. Suddenly I had another flash, this time of a handsome man with deep, intense eyes that pierced through my brain. I became instantly fascinated by the man and wondered who he was and when he would come into my life. I quickly came back to myself and looked around to see if the shadow would make another appearance. It was time I gave Luna a call.

Chapter Two

Instead of calling Luna I decided to pay her a visit. She was in her early forties, and dressed like a gypsy you would read about in stories as a child. Luna looked like Esmeralda from the Hunch Back of Notre Dame. She had wildly teased dirty blond hair with brown highlights and long, red painted finger nails. Today Luna had on a floor length full skirt with a ruffled, multicolored long-sleeved blouse to match. She always wore black boots that had large silver buckles on the front.

Luna owned a small spiritual advisement center called Guidance of the Garden, where she read fortunes, gave advice, provided Tarot readings and cleaned people and homes of evil spirits. Luna was very powerful, and could also communicate with the dead. She's made a nice living with her gifts. She was the real thing, and has made many people believers in the supernatural. Her abilities were widely known, and she often traveled to other states to help people in need.

Luna led me to the back, behind the counter where people come to introduce themselves and their cases. We went through some long, multicolored beaded drapes. The back room had red and black wall paper with floral designs, and the walls were decorated with old framed photographs of Luna along with, clients, family and friends. Two red sofas sat neatly in place off to the sides and there was a medium sized table resting in the middle of the room, along with a couple of chairs around it. The table had a beautiful purple cloth over it, with embellished crystals sewn into the fabric.

Luna was clearly happy to see me, squeezing me so tightly I could barely breathe.

"I knew you were coming Sydney. How is everything? I believe that your visions have returned to you." She smiled lightly.

"Yes." I quickly replied. "I don't know what to do about it or how to interpret them." I took a deep breath and tried to tell her what happened. We took a seat on one of the sofas. "Before I went to see my mom I saw a flash of her standing by the window watching the birds. Then later on that night I got a flash of a handsome guy. It was just some guy. I don't know him. I don't know what to think about this. I thought that my flashes were over." I let out a sigh and looked at her reaction.

"You know what to think about it," Luna replied, "The time has come to embrace your unique ability, and with proper training you can cultivate it to help others. There is way more to you than meets the eye." She finished her sentence and took my hand.

"But Luna, you know the whole situation. I know I have these abilities, but I really feel they're more of a problem than a gift." My voice was sincere. Luna and I were close friends and she had been a part of my life for many years. I trusted her and also confided in her. She was the only person in the world that knew I can do and see things that were out of the ordinary.

"Please understand—I know how you feel, but just know that you're not alone in this. Even though you may think that, it's not true. I used to believe that I was alone when I discovered that I could communicate with the dead. As time went on, I was introduced to others who have similar abilities. Now I use my gifts to help families move on and gain closure from the loss of loved ones." Her eyes told a long story. I never had any closure regarding the death of my father. Even though I knew she could help me, I couldn't bring myself to try.

"How are these flashes related to me, and why now? Why at this time in my life have they returned to me?" I had to keep asking those questions.

"You'll understand in time, Sydney. You'll get your answer when you are ready to handle it." I gazed upon her face and concentrated on her words. "You're a strong believer and stay true to yourself. You have to realize that there are many other types of powers and forces in this world that are beyond our stream of consciousness—but they do indeed exist. There are other worlds and places beyond our knowledge and understanding. Your situation is very special. I saw the man that is going to come into your life. He is going to bring you change. And the issue with your parents will be…" She stopped then continued. "You will get the closure that you have been searching for." I gasped. I couldn't believe she saw the same man I had seen in my flash.

I thanked Luna for her advice and promised I would keep in touch. I slowly gathered my purse and made my way to the exit. Saying good-bye was hard for me. I felt kind of bad that I hadn't seen or contacted her until my flashes had started back up. I valued my relationships and normally worked hard to maintain them—it was a really big deal to me. And being close to Luna reminded me of being with my mom during the days when she was at her finest.

After leaving Luna's shop, I realized that I had completely forgotten to ask her how things with her daughter were going. Vicky had been sick for the last few months. Luna told me that she was being treated for some type of cancer. I made a mental note to ask about Vicky the next time I saw Luna.

Within a few days Christine and I had booked our trip, and I packed my weekend bag with everything I knew I would need and I doubled checked to make sure I brought my medication. I was a bit nervous. I felt something in my stomach flutter as I peeked into the bag. Christine had already called to say she was on her way to pick me up. My coat and bag rested on the floor near the front door. There was a large tote bag of snacks on the kitchen counter. I made tea sandwiches, turkey, cheese, and tuna on onion rolls. I also packed some chips, rice cakes, and glazed doughnuts. I usually tried to eat healthfully, but when I was on vacation I made an exception. I put some water and a few bottles of iced tea in the small ice chest that I always took on trips, and gathered all my bags by the door to wait. When I looked down at everything resting on the floor, I realized that Christine's trunk was going to be quite full.

Within 10 minutes Christine was pulling up into the drive way in her black 2011 Ford Explorer. I ran out to meet her, leaving my front door wide open. She smiled as she scanned my features and popped open the trunk. She jumped out to help load the car, and kissed me on the cheek. I threw my feather down coat in the backseat—there was no need for me to ride with a bulky coat

[12]

on. My thick cozy white turtle neck sweater, wool pants and, favorite UGG boots were cozy and warm. Christine made a couple of trips back and forth to get all my things. She moved swiftly getting everything into the vehicle. Her energy made me realize how sluggish I was feeling.

We hopped into the Ford at the same time. I heard the click of our seat belts secure in place. I immediately reached for the CD case, thumbing through Christine's collection. I was determined to find some really good music for the drive to the Pocono Mountains. I pulled out Culture Club's greatest hits. It seemed like a perfect way to start the journey.

"Hey Syd, I am so excited about this trip. It's been a long time." Her eyes shined, and I nodded my head, smiling. Christine grabbed a cigarette and lit it. She took a couple of puffs and we pulled off. The driver side of the window was rolled down a little. It was just enough for Christine to flick her ashes. Even though the smoke blew out, a whiff of it got caught my nostrils. Easily to get annoyed, I rolled my eyes without Christine noticing. Christine knows I hate cigarette smoke. I crossed my arms to lock in some of my own body heat. The cool air lingered throughout the vehicle. Christine grabbed her sunglasses that were resting above her head secured to the sun visor. The sun was not too high in the sky today but the freshly powdered snow created a glare. Glancing at the side mirror I was ready to start a conversation. The music played low in the background.

"So Chris, tell me about this weekend," I said, "What are our plans? I'm sorry I haven't been too involved in the planning. There have been a lot of things going on." I took a breath. I was usually the trip planner, when we travelled together. I got a kick out of doing things like researching the destination, booking the transportation and lodging. It was really thrilling to me and helped me get geared up for the trip.

"It's OK Sydney. I know you had to take care of some things. We're staying at that private cabin I told you about, the one that belongs to my parents' friends. They're like family to us so all I had to do was make a phone call. Mr. and Mrs. Rossi have been married for a long time, and are very nice people." She sighed and carefully let out her words. "I don't want to push you into anything. It's better if we take it slow; this is a great thing for you, just going on this trip so our plans aren't etched in stone. The property is pretty big and we can do what we want. There are stables for horseback riding, and trails for hunting and hiking. There are also lots of winter activities; skiing, snowboarding, ice skating—the sky's the limit."

I could hear the excitement in her voice, but for some reason my mind was not on the details of the trip. Thinking about my vision and seeing my mother and Luna played foremost among my thoughts. The features of the man I saw in my vision were quite interesting. Why was I thinking about a stranger? I asked myself.

Christine interrupted my thoughts asking me if I wanted to stop at a rest stop. We had been on the road for over two hours, and I needed to stretch my legs. We were also getting low on gas and had to fill up again. Christine got off at the nearest exit and parked as close to the entrance as she could.

While we were stopped, the skies grew darker and darker and it looked like another snow storm was headed in our direction. We had snacked on a few of the things I brought along the way, but I was still in the mood for a nice, fat, juicy cheese burger. The rest stop was pretty packed. I stood in the long line at "Sonic" and waited to place our orders. Christine was outside gassing up the Ford. I felt a slight headache trying to claw its way to the surface. I rubbed my temples with the tips of my fingers. I suddenly got a flash of a faceless figure with large black feathered wings surrounded by rows of men and women crying and yelling in pain. His body was strong, muscular and tall. He was dressed in dark armor and a dull breastplate as his leg and arm shields protected his gladiator body.

"Oh God, please, help me." I whispered to myself. I held a small bottle of water in my hand. I reached in my purse and grabbed the pills I needed. I threw one back and took a gulp of water. Christine had finished filling up the tank, and joined me in the line. She turned to look in my face, saw that my complexion had turned quite pale, and rubbed my back.

"Are you okay?" she asked worriedly. She knew something was wrong, but I didn't want to plague her with my health issues. I shook my head no and replied that I was fine. We ordered and got our burgers and ate them in the SUV before taking off again.

The drive to the Pocono Mountain's wasn't bad at all. The CD player and good conversation made the time go by extremely fast. We eventually arrived and started to get settled into the cabin. The heat was on full blast too, and that made me very pleased. Before we arrived we stopped at a local market and brought a few items of food and snacks. Nestled in the middle of the deep woods, the cabin made the environment appear mysterious and unfamiliar. It was actually a beautiful country home capturing the cabin feeling. All the décor had authentic country flair: Oak, mahogany, rocking chairs, animal busts and earth tone hues gave the home a warm atmosphere.

By the time we settled in enough to enjoy the place it was early afternoon. I lay in my room on top of the soft pillow top mattress, admiring the room, I thought about the idea of having some hot cocoa and cuddling up with one of the books I packed. Staring out the window, I watched the snow flicker down gently as I got lost in happy thoughts. I felt a presence and turned to see that Christine had stepped into the room holding a pair of hiking boots.

"Are you in the mood for a little hiking?" She asked with a smile. I shrugged my shoulders thinking of an excuse to not go out.

"You don't want to start cooking and relax for the rest of the evening?" I asked.

"Not really. We have plenty of time for that. I wanted to show you around the grounds since you've never been up with me." She held up the boots higher when she spoke—I knew she wouldn't back down. Sliding off the soft bed I went to put on my boots and jacket.

I didn't want Christine to think I was a bad sport, so I thought we'd compromise. "Let's just take a little walk," I said. The evening grew darker with every moment, and the snow started coming down a little heavier. I reluctantly slipped on my coat, gloves and hat, grabbed two bottles of water from the refrigerator and headed out the door with my nap sack, throwing it over my shoulder as we left the house.

The woods whispered to me the moment my feet sank into the snow. I followed Christine carefully, watching each step we made. The whispers grew louder and louder. The trees spoke, reciting tales of old. They knew I was near. I stopped walking, closing my eyes to hear their voices. I have no fear of them. I feel connected to them in so many ways. There are times like this that I feel close to nature and other silent unknown beings. I can't explain it, but I am fully aware of that door that opens to a mysterious world leading the dreamer to a supernatural reality.

We explored the area, and as time swiftly passed, my body craved to be inside under a nice warm blanket. The cold air climbed up my legs and stirred in my bones. The terrain was steep and hilly, and made it difficult to keep my balance. Memories of my father and I hiking as a child took control of my brain.

"Syd, I heard that there is a cool cave somewhere in this area," Christine suggested. "Let's try to find it." I started to get angry and impatient. Looking for a cave was not part of the deal. What was she going to suggest next that we should go jump in the cave? Shit! That would be just like her. I adjusted my scarf and tightened my grip on my gloves. A flash of falling rocks and dirt rippled in my head and butterflies rumbled in my abdomen. We were getting closer to the cave. Christine didn't need to tell me that. I could just feel the location.

"Christine," I called. She turned around to look at me, her light blonde hair peeking out of the blue knit hat that tightly hugged her head. "We should go back; I don't have a good feeling about this. We're not prepared to go wandering in a cave, and it's getting dark." I said looking up at the sky. My case was valid, that feeling of danger came over me. I kept my stride fast to keep up with Christine. She held her head straight and didn't bother to glance at me again. I started to feel a little angry, but tried not to show it.

As we walked we came across an extremely large hole in the ground that obstructed our path. I just wanted to turn around. Christine insisted we jump over to get to the other side. The whole entire area was slick and had patches of ice all over. Christine took a large leap over the hole and managed to get to the other side with no problem. I stared down the hole and grew apprehensive. I stepped closer so I could position myself to make the leap and with that one move, that part of the earth was not stable enough to support my weight and, down I went screaming into the black abyss.

My back crashed against the rocks, and the sharp edges of the hole tore my coat and cut my arms and legs. All I could think about was protecting my head, another blow or injury possibly could turn me into a vegetable. A stream of rocks and dirt fell all around me, just like I had seen in my vision. I yelled in pain as my body hit the bottom hard. I closed my eyes, grabbed head, and prayed that I hadn't suffered another head injury. Blood oozed out of the slashes on my legs, and I realized that my right arm was broken.

[15]

I glanced around the narrow area and realized that I had fallen into a well. My heart raced, and I felt panic settle within me. Tears filled my eyes. It was happening to me again. I knew I should have just told Christine that I was not going to go on this trip. My body pulsated with pain.

"Christine, help!" I called. I'm hurt! But watch out for the edge!"

Christine stood near the edge of the well "Are you ok?" Her voice crashed down to me and I felt the vibration. I took a couple of deep breathes and tried to stay calm. I heard Christine's breathing become erratic. I convinced her to relax and be strong. I knew she had already started to blame herself. Panicking was not going to help the situation.

"Hang on Syd, I just called for help! Someone is coming." I heard her voice but couldn't see her face.

A small beam of light filtered down through the hole, but it didn't provide me with any comfort. I looked around me. My clothes were wet and body ached. The darkness scared me and I wondered what other creatures could be lurking within the shadows. Christine kept talking to me, but after a while my eyes grew heavy and I got very sleepy. For a split second I felt like Alice in Wonderland when she fell down the rabbit hole. That thought almost made me giggle— almost. My head rested against the hard rocks. Breathing the stifling air, I slowly inhaled. Drifting between the dream world and reality, I had no idea what was happening above ground. I could faintly hear Christine apologizing repeatedly, and despite my pain it kind of made me smirk.

A large ball of light appeared from nowhere. Out of the light surfaced the silhouette of a man. My eyes bulged out of the sockets. I could not move a muscle. I fixed my eyes and stared impulsively into the light.

"Hello Sydney, you are not having a good day," the figure said. His voice was cool and soft, and had a light accent. The deep neon blue of the light gleamed at me. I became lost in its beauty.

"You are so beautiful. What are you? How did you get down here?" I asked studying the light.

"You will be out of here shortly. Do not worry. Your ankle is sprained and arm broken, but you will be healed in time." I nodded my head, thanked my visitor and drifted off to sleep.

Getting me out of the well and into the ambulance took some time. Nodding on and off, I really was not too aware of what was going on. When I finally opened my eyes I was lying in a hospital bed, a situation that I was way too familiar with. Christine clutched my hand tightly. I blinked my eyes to stop the tears from forming. The emotions from my previous accident flooded within me. I cleared my throat to speak, but she gave me a saddened expression. I opened my mouth to talk, and Christine pressed her lips, and interrupted me before I could get any words out. I already knew what she was going to say.

"Syd, how are you feeling? I am so sorry for what happened. I should have listened to you." She was very sincere in her apology.

"Christine, you don't have to apologize. It was not your fault," I said as I thought about the brilliant light. "Did you see that man that helped pull me out?"

"What man?" She appeared confused.

"He was in the well with me, after I fell in. I have no idea where he came from."

Christine looked at me strangely, and then shook her head. "There was no one else down in there, sweetie. A couple of guys heard me yelling and came to see if help was on the way, but they didn't go down there. The Pocono Rescue Squad pulled you out. It took a couple of hours."

"That was strange. I would have bet a hundred bucks that a guy was down in that well with me." I gave up trying to convince my best friend that I had company in the well.

"Anyway, the guys that came to see if we needed help stuck around," she said. "They're in the waiting room—and they're pretty hot! One of them keeps asking about you. His name is Gilad." She winked and curled her lips into a smile. I felt like we were in high school for a moment. I kept my mouth shut. "Gilad and his friends are spending winter break here. The guys all go to grad school in Upstate New York. They are staying next door to us. They were hiking in the woods and heard us screaming and ran right over. They actually got there before the rescue squad." Christine had a serious expression on her face. I tried not to smile but truthfully I was bubbling inside. I was strangely interested in seeing who my admirer was.

Being banged up with a broken arm and sprained ankle didn't damper my spirits. My right arm was in a sling and left ankle wrapped tightly in a brace, but I was thankful I still had my good hand to write with. I know it's going to take time to heal. I was looking forward to getting out of the hospital, the sooner the better. I decided that I should notify the school about the accident. Reaching for my bag on the table next to me, I fished my cell phone out and made the call, leaving a message on the main office's voice mail.

During my phone call Christine stepped out of the room to give me some privacy. When she returned she was holding a cup of steaming coffee. A nurse walked in a few seconds later. Her hair was short and cut in boyish hairstyle, but her plump physique was all you noticed. The nurse's face appeared as though she spent hours applying makeup on.

"Miss London, you have a visitor." She said with a bright smile.

"Who is it?" I asked, gently readjusting my position. Christine raised her eyebrows.

"Gilad!" Christine replied. The nurse glanced at the both of us, and said yes in a soft tone. It was quite thoughtful of this guy to want to see if I was ok, but I was curious in how persistent he seemed to be. Why was he so interested in meeting me? I finally told the nurse to send him in, and she and Christine left the room

[17]

A handsome man sashayed into the room. He was a dream to gaze upon. His contoured muscular body bulged from his leather jacket. His thick thighs pulsated through his tight blue jeans. He had a great head of hair, short, thick, black and tousled. It fell perfectly in place with a few loose strands draping in his face. His strong cheek bones and dark green eyes told a story of beauty and battle. I was surprised he didn't have any kind of aura that I could see. I was happy that I combed my hair before he stepped in. The bruises on my face were very noticeable, but no makeup in the world could cover those up. I felt a little embarrassed about being seen this way by a guy, especially one as handsome as Gilad. Then it hit me, this was the same man I had seen in my vision.

"So you are the Miss Sydney London, the young beauty that took a trip down a well," he said, with a bit of sarcasm. His voice was smooth, and had a light accent, but it was hard to place where he was from.

"That's me, the klutz," I replied, glancing out the window for a minute. He extended his hand. I took it with my good hand and firmly shook it. "Thanks for looking out for me and coming here. I really do appreciate it." I smiled at the handsome creature.

"You are very welcome. When my friends and I heard your screams we ran off the trail to find out what was going on." He looked at me with a sparkle in his deep green eyes. His voice was serious and I became lost in every word he said. "I don't want to rush off believe me, but you need your rest. We're staying next door to you guys. I hope you and your friend don't rush home. I would love it if you stayed. I look forward to seeing you around."

"Maybe you will," I smiled. "I'm not sure what our plans are at this moment. I can't really do too much now that I am all banged up, but I'll find out soon." Flirting was not my usual thing but it made me feel pretty even though I was not looking great at that particular moment.

He took my hand and slipped me a piece of paper with his phone number written on it. He was smiling from ear to ear as I watched him leave the room. My eyes could not help but take a peek at his tight rear-end. When did he find time to jot down his number? I wonder what he thought of me.

Despite my fall, I was not planning on going home anytime soon. Our trip of outdoors adventure had been turned into an indoor vacation, but I actually looked forward to doing some reading, and relaxing. With my left hand free, I could also draw a little, since I had packed my drawing pad and travel art set. I'm determined to not let this get me down, but I couldn't believe that I had gotten hurt on the first night of our vacation.

I was released from the hospital the following afternoon. Christine had gathered some wood and had a nice roaring fire going. I was stretched out on the sofa, bundled up with a large blanket, and soft pillows rested beneath my head. It was nice to be out of the stuffy hospital. Chris knelt down by the fire poking and readjusting the wood and paper, obsessed with having the house toasty. We hadn't said anything to each other since the drive back. Talking seemed almost overwhelming for me. My body was weak and tired and I was mentally broken down.

[18]

I had a lot going on my visions were becoming more frequent, and more intense. I couldn't always tell what was real anymore, and this alarmed me greatly. Also, my new fashion accessories, the cast and sling and longing for my parents took a toll on me.

"So what do you think of Gilad?" My voice sounded weak and low. Christine slightly turned her head to let me know she heard me.

"I think he is yummy and really likes you," she said. "He hung around the hospital long after they brought you in and started fixing you up. And he's so handsome. You guys would look good together." Her mouth twitched a little when she spoke.

"Why would you say that we would look good together? I don't even know this guy. Besides it's not like we have anything planned. He just so happened to be in the area. Meeting him was just a chance thing." I started to rant, and my vocal cords began to suffer from all the talking.

"You asked me what I thought and I told you the truth," she snapped. "You act like I said you should go to the bridal registry at Macy's or something." I glared at her. She stood up wiping her hands on her clothes; and waltzed toward the dining area. Christine grabbed a bottle of wine and can of coke off the table, stepping back into the living room quickly. The glasses were already set up on the wooden coffee table.

While she poured the drinks, I took in the environment and appreciated it. I felt so thankful to be in such a beautiful home. I knew the décor must have cost a pretty penny. The owners had invested a lot of time, money and energy into this place.

I sipped the soda out of the straw and followed Christine with my eyes. She paced back and forth for a few minutes and I wondered what she was thinking about. She must have gotten tired, and soon after plopped down on the recliner that was near the television.

"I just thought you guys would make a good couple," she repeated herself. "By the way, I..." She stopped and closed her mouth.

"What?"

"Do you want something to eat?" I knew that wasn't what she had to say, but I decided to let it go.

"No thanks, I'm not hungry," I replied barely parting my lips to speak. She frowned at me. I was annoyed and wanted nothing more than to just go up to bed. I hated to ask Christine for help, so I gently slid off the sofa, reached for the crutch and did my best to maneuver up to my room. She jumped off the recliner and ran to me.

"Where are you going? I will help you," she said softly. I continued to move slowly. I was almost helpless but didn't want to admit that to her.

"I just need to get to my room. I don't feel well," I replied. "I thought it would be best if I went up there. You may want to watch TV or something."

[19]

"Don't be like that Syd. I brought all of the blankets and your stuff down here. It's better for you. Walking up the stairs is too difficult. I know you're mad but you'll get better." She helped me to the recliner. Taking the pillows off of the sofa, she held on to a small handle and pulled. Out came a nice full-sized mattress. I smiled as Christine made the mattress into a nice comfortable bed. The sheets were crisp and the blanket warm and inviting. Christine helped me climb into the bed, fluffed my pillows and propped up my foot. My body felt relief the instant I laid down. I thanked her for making me feel comfortable. Chris sat down on the edge of the sofa bed.

"I know that you're going to be out of commission for a while, and you have every right to be upset about that," she said gently. "I do apologize for what happened to you. And I'm sorry if I wasn't understanding or sensitive concerning the situation. I'm going to let you get some sleep. There's water and juice at your reach, and if you need anything else, just give me a yell." As she slowly walked away from me, her sincere expression made me feel bad about the way I had acted.

While I was in bed I sent my friend Angelo a text message explaining what happened to me. He offered to drive up for the weekend, but I didn't want him on the road since a storm was brewing. We went back and forth for a while, and he promised to cook me dinner when we returned.

The next morning I woke up exhausted. The bed was too comfortable to get out of, so I decided not to. The dull light peered through the blinds. I knew that the snow storm was drawing near and most roads would be closed leading up to the Mountain. The medication I had taken the night before had worn off, and the pain in my leg, and arm began to seep through. My arms, legs, and face were cut up pretty badly, and I was hoping and praying that there wouldn't be scars. I reached under my pillow to get my cell phone and check the time. It was 10:30, and I had missed a call. I checked to see who had called me, and retrieved the slip of paper that Gilad gave me when I was in the hospital to check to see if the numbers matched. Gilad had called but didn't leave me a voice message.

"Should I return the call?" I asked myself aloud. It would be rude if I didn't. I pondered over it for a while, then I found myself pressing the call button. I listened to the phone ring nervously.

"Hello," the deep familiar voice said.

"Hi Gilad, this is Sydney, the women you met yesterday," I said uncertainly.

"Hi Sydney!" he replied excitedly. "I'm so happy that you called me back. It was kind of early when I called but I wanted to check to see how you were feeling." I knew he was smiling on the other end, and then I wondered how he got my number.

"Thanks for being so thoughtful. I really appreciate all that you have done."

"Oh stop. You're welcome. So, if you and your friend don't have anything planned later, will you consider having dinner with us? Do you feel ok enough to get out? I want to see you again but I can come to you if that works better for you." I thought that it was nice for him to invite us over for dinner. Despite my current situation I was determined to not let it get me down. I really wasn't ready to get out but I didn't care at that point.

"Dinner sounds great. It will give me a chance to get off this sofa too. I'll have to ask Christine if she wants to go, but if she doesn't then you can pick me up later."

We talked for another half hour. We discussed a few topics and got to know each other a little better. He lived in Hartford Connecticut, which is a couple of towns east of Milford. Knowing that he lived in the same general area as me made me even more interested in him. After we hung up I immediately felt stronger. I lay in bed for a few more minutes, then placed my cell phone on the end table and proceeded to roll off of the sofa bed. I made an attempt to wash up and get dressed by myself. I needed to talk to Christine.

I decided to start the day fresh with Christine, without all the drama, and hoped that my good mood would rub off on her. I slipped on a simple dress, glad that I had packed some loose-fitting clothing. The temperature in the house was comfortable, so I didn't need to worry about being cold. I managed to brush my teeth and wobble out of the first-floor bathroom towards the closed kitchen door.

The layout of the house was kind of like mine, which made it easier for me to move around. I took my time, getting used to the crutch the hospital gave me. Slowly making my way, I pushed the door open, and the smell of coffee, bacon, eggs and hash browns wafted out. Christine was in the process of cooking. Four pans on top of the stove rested on open flames. She looked at me with bright eyes, and I silently thanked her with a smile.

"Good morning Chris!" I said in a bubbly manner.

"Good morning! You messed up my surprise!" she said happily.

"Thanks for thinking of me! Breakfast smells great. How long have you been up?"

"Not too long." She replied in a relaxed tone.

She put the flames on low and reached for two plates in the cupboard above her head. I hopped over toward the table, pulled out a chair, and slowly sat down. I offered to help her set the table out of sheer courtesy; even though the pain in my leg was getting worse and I really did not want to get up. She smiled and shook her head no, and set the plates out on the table. I was desperate to begin eating so I could pop a painkiller as soon as the last piece of bacon went down. Christine prepared the meal quickly, and we were eating in no time.

"Tonight we're getting a storm, actually a blizzard. It's going to hit around midnight. We may have to stay a little longer than planned," I wasn't comfortable being here during the storm, but I really had no choice. There were no renters scheduled after us, so at least we didn't have to worry about not having a place to stay. Christine mentioned that she was going to the market to pick up more food and other supplies like candles and batteries, so we would be prepared for the storm. I would have liked to go with her, but I would have only slowed her down.

I had to ask her about dinner tonight, but I felt a little bad about having accepted the invitation without checking with her first. I took a deep breath and the words came out.

"Gilad called. He invited us to have dinner with him and his friends tonight around five. I accepted the invitation but I told him that I would ask you first because I didn't know if you were feeling up to it." The room felt small and quiet. I knew she was annoyed with me, but she would never tell me. I waited for her answer.

"Oh, he did call you. Nice. Having dinner with them is a great idea. We won't have to cook tonight. We can bring some wine," Christine said looking at me with a peeved expression. I didn't even respond to it.

Breakfast was finished, dishes were washed and I took my pain medications. Christine headed out to the store to get the things we needed. Since the blizzard was coming, there was no way we could get on the road and get home any time before Sunday, so I decided to stop worrying about it. I sat on the sofa resting and enjoyed the time I had alone. I closed my eyes, and inhaled the air, and then I became lost; literally.

I felt myself feeling weightless, and my essence started floating, then I flew in a whirlwind of a tunnel. My leg and arm were back to normal. The casts were gone and I felt no pain. My body flew up to the heavens and I saw the stars appear. I was able to reach out to them, feeling the heat emerge through my body. Then I saw the planets in their orbits and I even saw new planets I didn't recognize.   From where I was the Earth looked round but damaged, it was not the Earth I knew. Lightning flashed and thunder rumbled in the distance, but strangely I was not afraid. Suddenly, heavenly beings approached me. They appeared to be warriors, both male and female. They were dressed in roman armor with silver and gold as bright as the sun. There were others that huddled around the gleaming warriors, dressed in black, the deepest ebony I could imagine. Their eyes peered at me, and large transparent wings surfaced from their broad backs. The creatures were holding hands and hovering in a circle around the Earth with their heads bowed down to the world. They were magnificent.

One of them looked strangely familiar. He stood among the others, and was handsome and more beautiful than I could even fathom. What was this place? Why I was here, and what was he doing here with them? I had so many questions.

Slowly my consciousness came back to my body. My spirit drifted back through the tunnel of time and space and I slipped into my resting physical manifestation.

The experience was overwhelming. My head started to hurt, and I didn't want to think about what I just seen. I knew that was not a dream. We're my visions growing stronger, and if so, why? Once again tears accumulated in my eyes. I didn't understand what was happening to me. I felt completely vulnerable.

Chapter Three

I took me some time to get ready. I couldn't put on jeans and boots, so I pulled on one of my best velour sweat suits. The pants were wide enough to slip on without hurting my leg. The brace was thick but you couldn't really tell that it was underneath my pants. After I got my clothes on I started doing my hair and makeup. Christine got ready early so she could help me. She helped me wash and dry my hair and even assisted in brushing it. It was so nice and bouncy. Christine applied some of her concealer on my scars and it did improve my appearance drastically. I used my good hand to put on my makeup but Christine also touched up some of the areas. Christine decided to wear a pair of skinny jeans, a blue turtleneck sweater and black snow boots. I was surprised that she didn't sport the biker chick look tonight. Within two hours we were ready. I glanced at my small pocket mirror before we headed out and admired my reflection. My makeup looked great.

The cabin that the boys stayed in was right next to us, so Christine helped me to wobble over to their place. I took my time, and moved slowly. The snow had started to trickle down and the air was quite brisk. I thought going to dinner with a couple of guys that we just met was enough. That was not my typical style. Since Gilad and his friends were a big help, I thought no harm could be done by hanging out with them for a little while. Considering I'd seen Gilad in my vision or whatever it was made me comfortable and uneasy at the same time, if that made any sense. I could not say anything to anyone about what I saw. My guard was up more than ever.

We decided to bring a bottle of White Merlot, but drinking any kind of alcohol hadn't been on my list of things to do tonight. I needed to be careful since I was taking medication. The guys were expecting us right on time and when we stepped in the song "One More Night" was playing by Phil Collins. I smiled as I heard the song and knocked off the excess snow on my boot.

Gilad helped me in as I hobbled inside the warm and cozy living area, and Christine trailed in behind me. The aroma of Italian spices and meats lingered in the atmosphere. Gilad greeted Christine with a smile, kissed me on the cheek and gently hugged me. His embrace was warm and inviting. I reintroduced myself and Christine to the guys that stood off to the side.

Everyone greeted each other happily. Joseph, Cayce, Robert and Gilad were our hosts. Joseph and Cayce had medium builds and light blond hair. They favored so much that I thought they may have been related. Robert was the one that stuck out like a sore thumb with his short, bright red hair and goatee. Cayce shut the door behind us, as we completely stepped in, and I noticed that Joseph and Cayce had bright blue auras, and Robert's aura was dull gray with a trace of red, which made me feel extremely uncomfortable. I took another look at Gilad to see if one appeared around him. I saw nothing.

"Hey guys, thanks again for inviting us!" I said, surveying the environment.

"Anytime," Gilad replied with a smile and nodded his head.

"I hope you guys like White Merlot. We got it at the local discount liquor store a couple miles away from here." Christine said, handing Robert the wine. I glanced down trying not to stare at Gilad and reflected on what I had seen earlier in my vision. Robert made his way into the kitchen carrying the bag and I studied him as well.

Tonight Gilad was dressed in black jeans with a red and black flannel shirt. He looked like a lumberjack. I hate flannel and he really did not look like the flannel shirt type of guy, but I kept those thoughts to myself. The smell of the food was making me hungry. I wanted cut the small talk and haul ass to the table.

"Have a seat girls, Robert is finishing dinner," Gilad said. "It's his turn to cook tonight. He's preparing Italian sausage with spaghetti and meatballs." Gilad pointed to the sofa and helped me get settled. Christine sat next to me. Joseph and Cayce followed, and Gilad opened the wine and filled the glasses. Everyone took a glass except for me. Seconds later Robert came out of the kitchen with a margarita glass in his hand.

"Try this Sydney." He handed the glass to Gilad. "I made this nonalcoholic margarita just for you. I hope you like it." He smiled and I smiled back. Gilad gently gave me the glass. I took one sip and tasted the sweet strawberry, apple and cinnamon flavor.

"Wow! It's great Robert. Thank you," I said as I took another sip.

"Oh don't flatter him too much. He loves that especially since he is going to culinary school," Cayce replied coyly.

"It's ok, he deserves it," I quickly stated.

"I made some appetizers for everyone," Robert voiced, as he stepped out of the kitchen with two platters in each of his hands. Mini beef wellingtons rested on a bed of lettuce, and the bruschetta with hummus and hot peppers looked very tasty. These guys were pretty high maintenance. I was expecting that they would do some grilling; maybe, burgers, hotdogs, and a salad.

"We had that last night," Gilad said, almost automatically.

"What?" I looked confused. Everyone glanced at me, and I paused for a moment. Wait a minute—did he hear what I was thinking? "What did you have last night?" I asked aloud.

"We had burgers, hot dogs, and salad." He made a noise to clear his throat. "Umm, yeah we had that last night." He reached for the small plates and napkins on the table, and picked up a couple and stood up. Piling on the wellingtons and the bruschetta on the plate, he handed a plate to me, and made a plate for himself. Christine and Cayce got a plate of wellingtons too. I ate the appetizer within a few seconds and still wanted more, but I decided not to refill my plate again because I would be too full for dinner. I looked deeply in Gilad's eyes. I wiped my mouth with the napkin, balled it up and placed it on top of the empty white plate. Robert went back into the kitchen, and Cayce followed. I tried to keep my mind focused just in case he had some kind of ability. And I totally did not trust Robert, because he had red around his aura. I had second thoughts about drinking the beverage, but I had no choice.

"I think Robert is really hot," Christine whispered. "I'm going to see if he needs any help in the kitchen." She got up and strutted out of the room to do her usual flirtatious thing.

An hour later, dinner had been served and most of the wine was gone. Everyone was enjoying the conversation at the table. To my surprise Christine didn't appear to be drunk. She had also changed a lot since I had the accident. She seemed to be way more responsible and adult. I was very proud of her.

While the guys cleared the table and washed the dishes, I sat in the kitchen and helped to dry the dishes to the best of my ability. Cayce started making more drinks, and Joseph went to the shed to gather more fire wood. Robert gave Christine the grand tour, which I knew would eventually lead to his bedroom. It had been a long time since Christine broke up with her boyfriend James, and I knew she was lonely for male company. I don't blame her; I miss that kind of company too.

I was watching the news about the snow storm when Gilad approached; rubbing his hands over his jeans as he took a seat. I adjusted my bad leg and got more comfortable by resting my back against a soft sofa cushion.

"So, how are you feeling?" He asked, placing his right arm around me. I felt energy from his body as he scooted close to me.

"I'm really sore," I said. "I would be in a lot of pain if I wasn't taking pain pills." I wasn't trying to complain. I wanted to answer his question honestly. He looked at me hard, sending tingles up my spine. We exchanged life stories, and I discovered that Gilad was from Britain but moved to the U.S when he was very young. I guess that explains the light accent, but his accent didn't sound British to me. He was an up and coming lawyer that worked at a small firm in Manhattan. I was surprised to hear that he worked on a couple of cases that I was familiar with. I knew he had a small apartment in Hartford. I asked him if he liked the commute from Hartford to New York, and he simply said he didn't mind the commute at all. It was nice to know that he was single and had no kids. The more I talked to him the more interested I became, but I still wanted to know more. After I talked to him for a while, I realized that he did have a special ability. I proceeded to fix my lips to ask him about his mind reading ability, but I decided not to instead.

I had such a nice time with Gilad, but we made it an early night. Christine and I were back at our place by 10:00 that night, and by the time we got settled in for the night the snow was really coming down. I lay on the pull-out sofa thinking about Gilad as I tried to fall asleep. I wiggled around, pulling the covers up over me. The bed was a mess after 45 minutes of restlessness. I read for a little while, and before I realized it my eyes grew heavy and I drifted off to sleep.

The hours felt like seconds as I felt my body become light and motionless. I saw myself floating above my sleeping body wearing a black gown. I landed in a heavily wooded area, and my feet were bare and melted into the snow as I slowly moved through the woods. Looking up; the sky was bright and the blue illuminated stars sparkled in the skies. The trees were tall and thick and covered with the soft fresh powdery snow.

I pulled up my gown a little and saw that my brace still clung tightly onto my ankle, and my arm clung to my body secure in its sling. In the distance I saw some kind of creature descending from the heavens. It was a man, emerging from the skies. As he drew closer, I froze, not taking my eyes off of him. The man wore a gold breast plate; his hair was long, straight and dark like mine. Silver, sparkly wings surfaced from his back, and his eyes gleamed silver. He hovered over me, and his gold Roman-style boots touched the snow. His strong jawline could cut stone.

I knew his face. It was the face of my childhood friend Angelo. He looked so different. The Roman Gladiator look made a rush of heat flow down into me. I embraced him and called his name. "What are you doing here, in my dream?" I touched the side of his strong forearm.

"This is who I am," Angelo said. "I wanted to show you. You have been hurt and I have come to heal you and ease the deep pain that has cast a shadow upon you." He spoke softly and took my left hand. I smiled.

"What are you? You look like you came from a different time or something," I said. I brought my voice down to a whisper even though there was not a soul in sight.

"I am an angel." He closed his eyes and looked down. I glanced up and saw a brilliant light encircle us both. I basked in the overwhelming feeling of warmth that came over my body. I was in another place, a place that I'd never been in before, somewhere out of this world. Moments later I felt the coldness of the snow brush against my face. He loosened his grip. I opened my eyes and he guided me to sit. A small iron bench appeared out of nowhere. I gently sat down. I wasn't cold at all, and it felt like I was at home cuddled under the covers in my bed. Angelo was now wearing a shiny bronze cloak with an oversized hood. Part of his muscular thigh was exposed. I couldn't help but notice it.

"You have a purpose in this life Sydney. You are extremely unique," he said, smiling at me. I carefully listened to the sound of his voice. He gently pulled up my gown, and laid his hands on top of my leg brace. Then he touched my arm in the sling. Within a few seconds white sparkles materialized from my injuries. Little by little the cast began to disappear. The pupils of his eyes were glowing. He was radiantly handsome and intriguing. When he was done caressing my arm and leg, both the cast and the sling had vanished along with my injuries. My eyes shone with amazement. I felt better in an instant.

"Thank you. But is this for real?" I whispered lifting my leg and touching my arm. He leaned over to me.

"Yes," he said. "All the answers you seek will be revealed in time." His voice was lightly accented and sweet. He reached out, and delicately held my face, and kissed me. The instant his lips touched mine my body responded. I was tempted to kiss him back—after all, if this was a dream I could do whatever I wanted.

[26]

The next morning when I awoke, all I could think about was my experience. I blinked my eyes to get used to the brightness of the morning. I threw the blankets back and saw that the brace was gone and my leg and arm was completely healed. My happiness was interrupted with a nervous feeling in my stomach. My heart pounded as reality set in.

"That was real?" I said aloud. I became scared of the reality of having to face Christine and explain to her what happened. What would she say? I fractured my arm and sprang my ankle, and it healed overnight. This was crazy! She would never believe the truth. I'd never really been honest with her when it came to my strange abilities, so why should I tell her about this? I gave it a lot of thought and decided to be as honest as I could without exposing myself.

I moved all of my stuff quietly back into the room. Placing the sofa bed back in its correct order, I arranged the cushions in the right positions, then showered and dressed with no problem, silently thanking the angel for healing me.

Thinking about my life in the church and my faith in God, it was astonishing to really see an angel in the flesh. I thought about both Gilad and Angelo all morning: The vision, seeing and speaking to the light in the well, and the dream all had my head spinning. This was getting way too weird. I had actually travelled outside of my body. I remember such adventures when I was a little girl, but all this time I thought they were dreams. I would wake up in the morning dirty, my clothes torn and, with scratches and cuts on my body, and never could explain to my parents what had happened to me. When I told them that I could float away, they never believed me. They just thought that it was my imagination, and after a while I convinced myself that they were right. Once I stopped believing my out-of- body experiences stopped. This time I knew my mind was not playing tricks on me. I knew what happened was completely real. Angelo was really an angel, and I was sure that Gilad was some kind of magical being—I just didn't know what.

It was mid-morning and I was surprised that Christine hadn't gotten up yet. Maybe she had too much to drink after all. It was nice to putter around the house quietly without having to entertaining anyone. When I looked out the window, the storm was blowing over. The ground had to be covered with at least ten inches of snow. I was thankful for being safe inside, and happy that Christine had made arrangements for us to stay longer so we didn't have to travel on the dangerous roads back home. It was nice that it was the weekend before winter break, so I didn't have to worry about work. Butterflies cramped my stomach as I became more concerned about how to explain my sudden recovery to Christine. I knew that she was not going to let it rest. I peeked into her room and saw that she was still cuddled up under the covers. I stepped closer and she lifted her head to look up at me.

"Hey how did you get up here?" She ran her fingers through her short hair. She sat up a little more to get a glimpse of me. "What happened?" Her voice was raspy and unsure.

"Honestly I don't know. I just wanted to check on you," I said as my fingers wrapped around the doorknob. She sat up completely and concentrated on the limbs.

"What the Fuck happened? Your brace! Did you take it off yourself?" She could barely get the words out and I was astonished that she used that type of language. I've used profanity from time to time but it's not really my thing.

"I'm fine!" I said. "I'm telling you the truth. I woke up like this. I don't want to get into it now. I'm about to go down and make some hot cocoa. Do you want some?" She rolled her eyes at me and I knew she was not ready to end the conversation.

"Sure. Thanks. I'll be down soon," she said rubbing her head. I slowly went back down stairs, thinking about everything that had happened. I peered out the large kitchen windows as I made the hot cocoa, and placed a couple pieces of bread in the toaster. I whipped up some eggs and got the container of butter out. My mind was going a mile a minute and I really didn't feel like eating a big breakfast. Christine and I ate breakfast in silence, but I knew she wanted me to explain what really happened.

I couldn't stop thinking about Gilad. He read my thoughts, and I felt violated, but I wanted to see him again and talk to him about everything. Despite the strange events of last night I felt pretty good. My headache was gone as were my aches and pains, thanks to my new healer.

Suddenly I had the urge to contact Angelo, and then I thought about calling Luna. She could give me some advice on all of this. I wonder how Gilad was going to act when he saw me again. In the end, though, when I picked up my cell phone it was Gilad's number I dialed. The phone rang several times before he finally answered.

"Hello Sydney," he said in the sexiest tone. "How are you feeling?"

"Great," I replied.

"That's good to hear, considering how badly you're injured."

"No, I'm fine, really," I snapped. I moved to the sofa so I could sit in front of the warm, cozy fire I had built earlier, and settled in for a long conversation. The longer I talked with Gilad the more I learned about him. He told me more about his career and the charity work he was into. I told him about my job as a teacher assistant and my desire to change careers. A real family man, he mentioned that he had two brothers and a sister who had passed away when he was younger. His parents were divorced, but often got together as travel companions to visit exotic places. As we continued to talk, I felt that Gilad was trying to keep the conversation going to deter me from asking questions he didn't want to answer. I think a part of him knew I was suspicious of him.

I invited Gilad and his friends over to hangout and watch some TV with us later in the day. He and Robert trucked over through the snow wearing jeans, boots and heavy coats. They both looked at me strangely when they noticed that my injuries were healed, but neither said anything about it. Robert and Christine had plans to take a walk to the lake, and hang out at the boys' cabin. Even though it was frozen it was quite a romantic gesture. Christine looked nice wearing jeans, a black sweater and black boots. Christine's light blonde hair bounced as she moved, she was very happy.

Gilad and I were alone in the house. The more time we spent together the more fond I grew of him, but the thought of Angelo rested in the back of my mind. I made another pot of hot cocoa, and suggested that we got to know each other better. We sat by the fire and talked for hours. Even though we hadn't known each other for long, we were already making plans to see each other again after our trip was over. My feelings for this guy were strong and I could not explain what drew me to him. When I got a little uncomfortable with the closeness between us, I popped up, trotted over to the windows and opened the blinds. I stared deeply at the snow falling, almost losing myself in the moment. I thought about the winter wonderland and my experience of last night.

"Hey what are you thinking about?" Gilad's smooth voice vibrated in my ear.

"I was thinking about you," I replied untruthfully.

"What about me?" He asked as I joined him back over by the fire.

"Well, if you're not going to be honest with me, then there's no sense in me bringing it up. If this is going to go any further, you have to be straight forward with me."

"You think about things too much," he said absently. Gilad took my hand, scooting over very close and lightly placing his lips over mine. The longer our lips met, the more intense the kiss became. The sudden push of his soft tongue gently massaged against mine. I was really enjoying our moment. His hand pressed against my back, a spot that I found sensitive to the pressure he applied.

My phone beeped disrupting the moment. Christine left me a text message telling me that she was going to crash at the boys' cabin with Robert for the evening. I enjoyed spending all of this time alone with Gilad, but some part of me questioned whether it was a good idea. I didn't want to move too fast, so I told Gilad that I needed to get some rest. He left after a few hours and told me that he would give me a call.

After Gilad left I had time to think about everything. I thought about the accident and my mother's current condition. Seeing my mother again and getting back to work was my main priority. I also needed to check with Amy to see how the business was going. I was considering going to work at my mom's business full time. I needed to give that some more thought when I returned home. I was supposed to see my doctor when I returned to Milford, but I knew that wasn't necessary now. It was important for me to keep my recovery a secret from the outside world. Only one other person knew the truth about it. Come to think of it, I was surprised that Gilad hadn't asked me how I healed so fast. I thought that was extremely strange.

Chapter Four

L eaving the cabin was a bitter sweet experience for me. The place marked a special time when maybe just once something good came out from something bad. Back in Connecticut, Gilad and I spent time together every day during winter break. I saw my mom, and even had a chance to go by Amy's office to check on things. Angelo and I also hung out during the week, but we never once discussed my experience in the woods.

It was a cold Saturday evening and Gilad and I had plans to watch a movie and order in. Rain and Sleet was in the forecast, and I was expecting Gilad in less than an hour. Things were moving fast between us despite my intentions to take things slow. Gilad was a complete gentleman. Our new relationship kept me so busy that I didn't have time to call Luna Delilah to tell her what happened.

While I waited for Gilad, my previous vision replayed in my mind. My head snapped back from the impact of it. It hit me like thunder, as I saw the Earth again along with the transparent winged creatures holding hands and dressed in armor. The flash was so strong that it made me lose my balance. I rested my back against the kitchen wall, trying to catch my breath. I closed my eyes for a second and picked up the phone. My fears resurfaced as I dialed Luna's number. I wasn't sure if she could really help me, but she was my only council. I explained everything to her in great detail. Her reaction was not what I expected.

"Sydney, I must warn you," Luna said. "Please be careful. I don't know what Gilad is and what he seeks, but I feel that he is after something. Be on your guard. Remember, your visions have changed since he came into your life. They are a warning. You need to start to channel your gifts. You repress them and must not. You must use them in order to reveal the truth about him." She spoke fast, her voice trembling.

"Why must he be something? Why must he be after something? Why can't he just be the man that I care about?" The questions tumbled from my lips. Even though I, too, felt that Gilad was more than he seemed, I was in denial that he was a supernatural being. I had also decided not to tell Luna about the accident on the trip and how Angelo had healed me. It was hard to admit that the men in my life were something more then they presented to me in reality.

"Don't be afraid, my child," Luna said. "Sydney, I need to meet with you tomorrow early in the morning. Come by the shop as soon as you can." She hung up. I listened to the dial tone buzz in my ear. I was tired of warnings. I slammed the phone down on the table and got ready for my date with Gilad.

I quickly slipped into something very sexy and comfortable, a sleek black knee-length dress that was just as cozy as my favorite nightgown. I wore my hair down with loose curls, and put on the beautiful gold necklace that had been a birthday present from my father. The house was nice and warm, so I puttered around bare foot as I tried not to think about Luna's warnings and the strange experiences that happened the last few weeks. I felt my nerves buzzing around as I waited.

The doorbell rang. As I looked through the peephole I saw Gilad stood on the porch waiting for me to open the door. I opened the door smiling, and escorted him into the living room. Gilad gazed into my eyes, and I gave him the eye contact he deserved, but did not lose myself in it. He kissed me gently on the lips.

"How are you?" He asked in a low, pulsating tone.

"I'm fine," I replied. "Everything is ok. I've finally gotten back into the swing of being at work. The kids missed me a lot. "I missed them too but I'm considering leaving my job at the school to work full-time at my mother's business." I waited for his reaction.

"Really? I didn't think you were serious about making such a change."

"I don't understand why you thought I was not being serious," I said, a little upset that he hadn't taken my words seriously. "I've been talking about it since we started going out."

"Don't get upset," he said. "You talk about running the company all the time, but never made a move to really do anything about it. I just..." His voice trailed off and he stopped in mid-sentence. He knew he was not going to win this argument. I didn't have the energy to start a debate with him anyway. What made me more upset was that I had been honest with Gilad in expressing my feelings about my job. Opening up about other aspects in my life was a different story. A headache was coming on so I threw back a pill to deter the pain.

"Are you sure you're feeling ok, honey?" Gilad leaned over and kissed my forehead. I didn't bother to answer his question. I wanted to enjoy a silent moment with him. Before I knew it I was stretched out across the sofa with my head in his lap. My plan to keep things slow moving grew to be more difficult the more we saw each other. We talked more about a new case that he was starting next week, as he rubbed my head. I enjoyed the attention.

Gilad tilted his head down and kissed me, placing his moist, soft tongue inside my mouth. I responded by doing the same, trying to stay in control of the movement. His hands started to travel down near my breasts, gently stroking them and then his fingers moved south. My pelvis throbbed with pleasure. Our clothes were eventually on the floor and our bodies intertwined to meet in the most natural positions. The Earth felt like it moved under us. Voices echoed in my head, whispers, and the sounds of people weeping in pain. I was briefly frightened but did not want to stop, so I ignored the voices and continued.

Our sexual encounter had reconvened back to my bedroom. We lay in bed together, satisfied with our efforts to please each other. I ran my hands up and down his rippled chest, and my body felt totally relaxed. The voices continued to rattle in my brain but I did my best to block them out. My body had been craving this for some time, but I had to admit that I did not feel like myself after we had sex. I wasn't used to having a man next to me. We lay together in silence, as I softly drifted away with his arms wrapped around me. The sound of his heartbeat drummed me to sleep.

My Dreams were no longer dreams. I traveled to other worlds and places in a physical, but spiritual form. It was hard to explain. When my body went to sleep, a part of my spirit would float away somewhere else. Once I crossed over to a plane or world my spirit would re-assume my physical form. I experienced real things. When I was a child, I usually couldn't remember my experiences, but lately I was able to remember. There were times when it was hard for me to distinguish what is real. I did some research on the whole experience, and it is called Astral Projection.

As I slept my self-consciousness had been lifted once again; I floated above the clouds and traveled through the tunnel of space and time. I was not afraid. I just didn't know what to expect from the experience.

I appeared in a beautiful land where I saw Gilad floating along a shadowy body of water. The sun beamed down upon his head. He lifted his head and looked at me. His transparent wings had turned a charcoal black. Gilad hovered over the florescent green grass. As I watched him quietly, the land trembled and the ground underneath split open. My body vibrated. The quake grew in intensity. White steam and hot red lava fiercely poured out of the opening in the ground into which Gilad descended without warning. I screamed and called out for him.

"Where am I?" I asked myself. The skies darkened and the land changed into a place of darkness. A thick black arm and hand surfaced from the dirt. It stretched its grimy fingers towards me, its dark green nails full of infection. Was this hand Gilad's? I didn't want to know, and I stood there in the dark, alone and fearful of what I saw. I wanted to wake up, and fast. I closed my eyes. My heart pounded. All I could think about was leaving this place. I thought this was a warning and the signs pointed that Gilad was bad news.

My eyes blinked open, and I glanced around to survey my surroundings. Everything was in its rightful place. A sigh of relief escaped from my lips. The sheet draped over Gilad's most intimate parts, and his arm lay dangling off the side of the bed. His chest was rising and falling as if he were in a deep slumber. I abruptly sat up in bed, reaching for the thick chocolate comforter to cover me for more warmth. It was time for me to start asking questions and getting some real answers.

"Gilad what's going on?" I asked. He opened his eyes and gazed at me in a sluggish manner. He didn't want to be disturbed, but that didn't faze me. "What's with you? Why are you in my dreams?" I asked as my face grew angry.

"Am I really? Well, good morning to you too," he responded nervously. He had things to tell me and it was time for those things to come out. I became impatient and felt the words utter from my lips.

"Stop pretending," I said. "Who are you? You knew that Christine and I would be in the Pocono's didn't you? What do you want from me? I know that you are not HUMAN!" I yelled, almost regretting my fast acting lips. He rose up out of his comfortable position.

"What makes you think I'm not human?" He was careful with his words.

"I know things," I said. I have seen things happen to you." He was so surprised that his expression read panic. "I know that you have secrets, dark secrets and abilities." I watched him closely, and looked directly into his eyes. He smirked.

"Come on. What do you think this is?"

"All I want is for you to be honest with me," I said. "I'm not stupid." I waited for an answer. He shrugged his shoulders and threw up his hands.

"I tried to make you forget," he said. "I guess what they say about you is true. Will you still have feelings for me if I tell you?"

"Tell me now, or whatever we have is over!" My voice vibrated. "I've seen what you can do. And why would you try to make me forget? How did you try to make me forget?" He stared down at the sheets then looked back up to me. "I saw you levitate once when you were fixing the light bulb in my bathroom the other day. You can hear my thoughts sometimes, and I can't see your aura. We still never talked about that day at your cabin, after you heard what I was thinking," I continued. "There is no telling what else you can do. I see you in my dreams and in that place beyond my dreams. Some of the things I've seen really scare me." His eyes glazed over a bit and appeared to change to a light gray color. I gasped. "Your eyes just changed color right before me," I softly replied.

"Will you leave me once I tell you everything?" he asked. The sound of his voice had a sincere measure in it, and something inside me knew what he was feeling. He was almost relieved.

"I just don't know anymore," I said. "I care about you, but if you can't be honest with me we can't move on." Gilad bit the bottom of his lip, and took a deep breath as he ran his slender fingers through his dark, wild hair.

"I am an Angel," he said.

"Thank you. I only wanted you to admit it. I already had my suspicions, but why me, out of all the other women you could have why do you want me?"

"I am in love with you," Gilad said. "I am drawn to you. Tell me what you saw in your visions."

"I don't want to talk about that right now," I replied. "What did you mean when you said that you're drawn to me?"

"Can we save this conversation for another time? Since you don't want to answer my questions why should I answer yours? I have a long commute into New York today anyway." He slid out of bed and went straight into the bathroom.

"This conversation is not over!" I yelled, as he shut the door behind him. I was not willing to expose that part of myself when it came to my abilities. He hadn't earned enough of my trust to deserve knowing all of my secrets. The fact that he actually confessed and revealed his true identity made me even more nervous. I thought it was strange that he didn't even reply to my comment about his aura. This was my first time knowingly being involved with a celestial being. Angelo's situation was different, and I had many questions for him as well. I knew Angels existed, but their direct involvement in my life made me wonder. When I was younger I thought I could see them hovering around people. As I grew older I stopped seeing them for a while but, after the accident I started to see them again. I heard there are different types of angels, and I had no idea which kind Gilad was. I rolled out of bed with those thoughts and went to wash up in the down stairs-bathroom.

I went to the kitchen, and thought about Gilad, and why he tried to convince me to tell him what I saw. I was curious to learn why. There was still much to talk about, but I decided to save it for another time, like he suggested. I made waffles, eggs and few pieces of turkey bacon as I tried to take in our conversation. I needed to get Gilad out of my dreams and visions. I had to see Luna. So many things were going on at the same time. My mother plagued my thoughts as I made coffee for Gilad and hot cocoa for myself. My guy took a long time to shower and get dressed so I drank my cocoa, and waited patiently for him to join me at the table.

Gilad eventually came down dressed in a dark suit and tie. I wondered where the suit came from. When he came over last night I didn't remember seeing an overnight bag. I wanted to see him in his true form. That image circulated in my mind, but I didn't know how to ask him, so I just gave him a kiss and invited him to sit in front of the steaming plate of food.

"The food smells great Sydney," Gilad said with a smile.

"Thanks," I replied back.

"So what are you planning to do today?" he asked taking a sip of orange juice.

"Nothing," I muttered, taking a bite of my waffles. I planned on keeping today's activities to myself. "What about you?" I asked continuing the dialog.

"Remember I told you upstairs that I have to go into the city today. I have an important meeting. Would you like to see a movie and have dinner later on tonight?"

"You have a meeting on a Sunday? That's different. Sure dinner sounds fine," I replied as I shrugged my shoulders. A strange silence came over us for a moment.

"What movie do you want to see?" he asked, gripping the handle of the coffee mug that rested next to the glass of orange juice.

"Death Trap," I softly said with a grin.

"So you're into horror movies?" he replied, sounding surprised.

"Yes! I love that kind of thing, especially classic horror movies by John Carpenter, Clive Barker, and Wes Craven," I said. "They're the greatest directors of horror." I quickly stated and finished my breakfast.

[34]

I started getting ready. We set a date for the evening, said our goodbyes and officially started our day apart. I showered and got ready as quickly as I could and headed out the door to see Luna. I didn't realize it had snowed a little bit, so I eased out of the garage and on to the slick driveway. Everyone on the road took it easy and I did the same. I thought about Christine as I drove. I hadn't heard from her in about three days, which wasn't like her. I made a mental note to call and check on her after my appointment with Luna.

Instead of meeting her at the shop as planned, we met at the local diner. Luna had a mug of coffee in her hands as she waited for me. Her dirty blonde hair was wildly tousled all over her head. She kept her "Esmeralda" look exciting. She stood up as I approached the table, and I greeted her with a hug and ordered a cup of hot cocoa. The oversized white mug came filled with cocoa and topped with marshmallows and whipped cream. It tasted wonderful. The sensation of the warmth made me feel cozy. When the waitress walked away, I got a strong vibe that she thought she was pregnant—the consequences of a one night stand. The emotions I got from this girl were overwhelming, but I think I handled myself pretty well. That information was personal, but it still made me quite uncomfortable to know.

"Did you feel that?" I asked Luna. She nodded her head in response and appeared sorrowful.

"We must honor their privacy," Luna said, paused, and then continued. "So what have you learned about your new friend?"

"He's handsome, gentle, scary and fascinating at the same time." I leaned in closer, so she could hear me. "He is a supernatural creature, a being from another world. I think I'm falling for him but there's something about him I don't trust. My dreams…" My voice trailed off.

"You astral project when you sleep," Luna said. "I feel a great power surging from your aura. Your gifts are increasing. Something is in you that I've never sensed before, something ancient, something that belongs to you that was lost but now returned." Luna deeply exhaled as her open hand was extended across the table directly facing me.

"What do you mean?" I asked. She shook her head.

"I don't know. It's what I read from you. What were you going to tell me about your visions?" Her hand retreated back to the mug.

"That my dreams and visions have intensified, and my astral projection experiences are intense. Sometimes Gilad is there when I don't want him to be. My connection to other people has also grown." The tone in my voice was low and steady.

"Do you know exactly what he is?" Luna asked. "This is important because he may have some kind of plan." Luna took another deep breath.

"He's an angel. I saw his true form when I went down into the astral plane. I think it was the astral plane. I feel that he may be a dark angel. He revealed his identity but it took some

[35]

time for him to come out with it. He told me that he loves me." We were both silent after I finished my sentence. Luna's mouth dropped.

"What is he doing on Earth? What is his back story?"

"If there is one, I don't know it yet," I replied. "Apparently he lives life as a regular human. He actually came into my life after I fell down a well on a trip I went on with Christine. I was in bad shape, with a few injuries. Something else weird happened," I said as I paused, and gathered myself. "When I was in the well I was visited by a being of light that spoke to me. When I was rescued and released from the hospital an angel healed me in my astral form. I guess the astral plane and the real world are connected in some way." There was still a lot for me to learn about my abilities and the reasons I had them in the first place.

"Luna, it's so hard for me to accept that Gilad isn't human. What should I do?" I asked, frowning. Luna's eyes glared for a second. Before she could reply, I interrupted her to speak. "Maybe it doesn't matter why he is here. Maybe he's here just to make me realize that there is a love out there for me." Luna twisted her mouth and gaped at me.

"You know better than that," Luna said. "Please don't be naïve. He is a..." She stopped. "I would be very much interested in meeting him face to face. Is there any way that can be arranged?" I shrugged my shoulders. I was not sure if that was a good idea. "My only problem with meeting him is that he would be made aware of my gifts as well. Angels are extremely powerful and influential. They have many sides and are far different from humans. They try to blend in with humans but other Supernaturals know that they are not human. Angels can also detect others that have supernatural abilities. I assume that you've seen him use some of his gifts." She grinned, and I nodded.

"He heard my thoughts the first night we spent time together," I said. "It was a slip up though. He knows what I am thinking sometimes. I think he can only do it when people are emotionally vulnerable. I caught him levitating when he was trying to fix my bathroom light a few days ago." I tilted my head slightly to observe if anyone had heard me. The subject matter we discussed should have been better expressed in private. "I believe he has other powers but I don't know what they are yet."

"Who healed you in your astral form?" She asked looking into my eyes. I hesitated for a moment.

"It was a being of light. It was one of my best friends who I've known practically all of my life. I can't even explain how he appeared to me. The whole thing was just very bizarre," I explained.

"How do you feel about that?"

"I don't like the fact that that he has hid his true identity from me for all these years, but I know Angelo would never harm me, I know that for sure. He is a wonderful guy." I said, smiling as I thought about him and what he told me.

[36]

"Okay, just keep an eye on Gilad," she said. "Don't put all of your trust in him, and please don't give in to his sexual advances." Luna looked at me then continued, "The sexual connection can be very dangerous," she warned, as she grinned, and I grinned back making every attempt to not blush.

"Luna, that's going to be so difficult! We're in a new relationship it's part of the package. Plus, it's so hard to resist him. I can feel the energy pull from him, and his will is very strong. Don't worry: I promise that I'll watch my back." I paused and thought for a second.
"My feelings for him are strong and I cannot deny that." I felt Luna become nervous, as she listened to me carefully.

We ended our meeting with another hug and made plans to contact each other at a later date. I strolled back to my little Ford, fished my cell phone out of my purse and punched the speed dial button to call Christine. I sat patiently in my car, while the phone rang and rang. The voicemail prompted me to leave a message. I hate leaving messages.

"Hey Christine, It's me Syd," I said. "How are you? Give me a ring as soon as you can. We haven't spoken in a couple of days and I wanted to make sure you're okay." I pressed the red button to end the call, then dialed her house line and also got no answer. I pulled out of the parking lot, and kept up with the traffic flow. Still being mindful of the slick roads, I took my time driving slowly. I decided to go by the restoration shop hoping that Christine had gone into work today.

The restoration shop Resurrection, didn't look too crowded for a Sunday morning. On weekends many people brought their antiques and other special treasures in to have them restored to their original state. I surveyed the outside of the shop as I parked right in front of the newly renovated mini strip mall in down town Milford. I jumped out of car and reached for my purse, avoiding the small bank of snow that obstructed my passage to the door. I was planning on being inside only for a couple of minutes.

The bell rang the second I opened the large black glass door. I stepped into the shop, and caught a whiff of exotic incense. Stomping my feet on the dark rug, I knocked off the excess snow that rested on my boots. Slowly I maneuvered through the entryway. One large open space revealed wall to wall antiques. From old furniture, art, toys, period pieces and everything else in-between, this place displayed parts of history that everyone could appreciate. A dark curtain near the back covered the entrance to narrow steps that lead to a large back room where Christine and the staff worked on restoring the unique treasures. There was a large glass counter set up in the front that displayed gold, silver and other small valuable knick knacks. All the items on display were either for sale or ready for customers to pick up. Sometimes I came to look around to check for any new items that I may want for the house. I noticed a couple of older ladies checking out the china display that was mounted on the wall. A younger woman was at the counter talking to Brittney, an employee there, about purchasing some gold jewelry. I gave Brittney a glance and she smiled at me, and then nodded. She had been doing quite well managing things at the front counter.

I looked around to see if Angelo was in my sight. He must have known I was there, because he busted through the black curtain with his eyes fixed on me. My childhood friend walked up to me wearing an apron with paint all over it. He wore a mask that was pulled down, dangling from his neck. Angelo was tall, nicely built, and had dark blue eyes and dark shoulder length hair that was pulled back into a neat ponytail. Under his apron, he had on stonewashed jeans and a tight black t-shirt that accentuated his toned body. He was so beautiful. His blue eyes pierced into me. I smiled, but couldn't hide my worried expression.

"Hello Sydney, I've missed you." His soft accented tone was music to my ears. He hugged me, lifting my body gently off of the floor. My feet dangled in the air. As he held me in his arms I took in his familiar scent of unspoken love. The aroma sent sensations throughout me. He placed me back down, and gripped my shoulders. I felt that he was concerned about something but didn't want to show it in the presence of the customers. I glanced over to see if Christine was anywhere.

"Angelo, how are you?" I asked, dropping my head. I stared at the floor tiles pondering over the supernatural experience we had shared.

"How are you feeling?" he asked.

"I'm ok," I said. "Is Christine working in the back?" I asked with a lump in my throat.

"No. She's not here. I thought she took off on another trip or something. I know she was seeing someone. Have you talked to her?" He asked, speaking at a low tone and moving even closer to me.

"No," I said weakly. "We need to talk Angelo. Finish up what you're doing. I'll wait for you." He nodded and went back through the curtain up the steps.

I stood outside the door, clutching my coat as a brisk breeze swept down on me. I secured my scarf tighter around my neck. Walking into the nearby bookstore made me feel like I was in my dad's library at home. I shuffled down the aisles, scanning the various literary genres. The emotions of other customers pulsated through my body and spirit; anger, sadness, excitement, pain, happiness, and desire. Feeling other people's emotions had an exhausting effect on me. It was unpredictable. I quickly felt myself start to panic because this was the first time that I read so many different emotions at once.

I stopped for a moment, closed my eyes and got control of myself. I realized that I had stopped in the middle of the New Age section. Rows of books resting on the shelves were a familiar comfort to me. I moved the surge of emotional energy in the pit of my stomach. I brought it to a place that I could control. I opened my eyes, and noticed a book about angels called "Angels Among Us," written by an author I'd never heard of. I grabbed it off of the shelf, and studied the old leather bound cover.

"Interesting," I said aloud. I looked through the book for a couple of minutes, when my phone beeped a text message.

"I bet you're looking for a book in Patsy's Prose," Angelo's message said.

"Of course I am. Be right out," I texted back.

I brought the book to the counter where the owner, Patsy, stood. She smiled as she looked at the book.

"Hi Sweetie, how have you been?" she said. "You haven't been in here for a while." Patsy's gray hair was tied up in a tight bun. She looked at me through her rectangular glasses, which looked just like the classic grandma glasses with the pearl chains dangling behind her ears.

"Hi Miss Patsy," I said. "Yes I know it's been a while. I'm still reading a couple of books. I wanted to see if you had anything new and came across this old book. It looks intriguing so I picked it up." I grabbed my Patsy's Membership Card and she scanned it. Only members were able to borrow books. Patsy had a wide selection of books to choose from. Her little store was pretty cool, and she even had a lot of books that the Milford public library didn't have.

"Enjoy, and keep it as long as you like. You're one of my most loyal customers," Patsy said placing the book in a paper bag. I thanked her and walked back out into the elements.

Angelo was standing outside in front of the building. I walked directly up to him.

"I can't believe that you thought that Christine had gone on another trip," I said.

"You know Christine doesn't tell me everything. She hasn't been to work for about four days now. I called a few times and didn't reach her. I just assumed."

"The last time I heard from her was about three days ago." I informed him. "Do you know she's been going out with a guy we met on our trip?"

"Yea, I heard you were too," he replied in a salty tone.

"It's new, and different. No big deal," I said shrugging my shoulders. I quickly changed the subject back to Christine. "It's not like her to not call. We have to go by her house and check on her." I became more nervous over the issue that Christine hadn't contacted us.

"You're right. Let's take my car." He ran back inside, got his coat and told Brittney he had to leave for a short while. He came back out with a set of keys in his hand.

We hopped into his black Excursion, which was roomy and fully loaded with everything you would need for long trips on the road. Christine only lived about 10 minutes away from the shop but it seemed like the trip took forever. Angelo was very quiet, and for the first time I realized that I couldn't really read any emotions from him. His aura was also different: it was golden with a hint of white sparkles. I had never really noticed it because we've known each other forever. His face was blank as he kept his eyes glued on the slick roads.

Out here in Milford Connecticut, there are a lot of southern inspired homes. Christine's house is a nice white two-story, southern styled home with a little early American elegance to it.

The shutters were a deep cobalt blue. Her black Explorer was parked in the iced-covered driveway.

"It looks like she's home!" I said, and I jetted out of SUV before Angelo could even stop and park. He rolled down the window and yelled something but I didn't bother to look back. I almost slipped on the iced covered walkway leading up to the front entrance. Angelo parked his car and made it to the door in a split second. A whiff of my hair got swept up in the wind. I glanced at him with an expression of wonder, then pressed the bell and heard the ringing echo from the inside of the foyer. After no response, I started to pound on the door. Angelo stood behind me and we waited for about 5 minutes. I didn't want to barge into the house, but I didn't get a good vibe from this situation. Christine keeps a spare key under the welcome mat outside and I bent down and retrieved it, put the key into the door and turned the knob to open the door. I gave Angelo an apprehensive glance and proceeded to go through the door. A sudden swarm of dark flies obstructed my vision. I waved my hand to block them away from my face, as Angelo did the same.

"Christine! Christine! Are you here?" my voice rumbled. My stomach turned in knots thinking about the nasty flies. The place was a wreck, and smelled terrible. I left the door ajar so some fresh air could get in, and noticed a pile of unopened mail on the floor near the mail slot. The mail appeared to be pushed aside; as if someone had moved it on their way out. We scurried through the entry-way that leads to the grand kitchen, then into the living room. There was no sign of Christine. In a panic I ran upstairs. Angelo followed me swiftly. The second level was dark and smelled really bad. All the doors were closed, so I went from room to room to see if there was any sign of my friend.

"I don't like this Sydney. This does not look good," Angelo whispered, shaking his head.

"I know Angelo. Maybe she hasn't had time to do any cleaning. She could be in the shower getting ready for a date or something," I said hopefully.

"We both know she pays a cleaning company to come twice a week. You don't believe what you just said. I know how you feel." Angelo placed his hand on my shoulder. I ignored his last sentence and ran down the hall opening all the doors that I hadn't got to yet. I peered into them, looking as intently as I could. My heart began to pound so hard that it hurt. Angelo and I approached the bathroom door. A loud buzzing noise drummed as I placed my ear to the ingress. Slowly turning the knob, I opened the door. It creaked loudly. Another large swarm of flies slapped our faces as we stepped into the putrid bathroom. I automatically gasped, covering my mouth and nose to avoid the odor and flies. Water dripped from the tub, and the floor was covered with at least four inches of murky water. I walked up to it slowly glaring at the opaque shower curtain which was half wrapped around a heavy figure. I reached out to open the curtain to reveal who was wrapped in it and the second I was about to touch it, Angelo yelled.

"Don't touch anything! This is officially a crime scene," he said. We backed up, still covering our mouths and noses with our hands. My body trembled all over. Resting my back against the wall in the hall I watched Angelo dial 911 from his cell phone.

Chapter Five

Christine's beautiful home had turned into a scene from C.S.I. The place was crawling with police, detectives and forensic specialists. My heart sank as I saw them wheel out a body on a covered stretcher. I stopped the coroner immediately. Angelo stood close to me.

"May I see? I need to know if it's really her," I said, as the tears filled my eyes. It was hard to fight them back. Angelo tried to keep me from seeing but I pulled away from him. The coroner tugged back the sheet to reveal her face. There she was, lying on a stretcher lifeless. Her face was swollen, and pale, eyes dark with blue and purple circles around them. Her short blonde hair was dull and matted. This was just too much for me. I held my hand out to touch her forehead and suddenly...

A flash of light appeared and I was back inside Christine's house. The bathroom appeared normal, as I saw my best friend prepare to take a bath. The tub was almost full. She turned off the running water, removed her robe and carefully stepped into the tub. I felt like I was invading her privacy, but this was a vision. Suddenly, a dark, masculine figure appeared. A cloak of mist floated behind the figure. I was frightened, but did not want to lose my concentration.

The dark figure grabbed Christine's hand and pulled her forcefully out of the tub. She screamed with fear and yelled for him to stop. Struggling with all her might, Christine stumbled, almost hitting the floor. The man bit into her neck, drinking her blood with deep passion. Blood oozed from her torn flesh and the tissue and muscle was exposed from her collar. It was an angry and deadly wound. My eyes widened at the horrific sight as I watched the monster drain the life out of my friend. His misty cloak swayed back and forth as he held her up to his mouth. He gnawed into her with intense hunger, and soon released her lifeless body into the tub filled with water. The corpse floated motionless as the water rippled. Distracted for a second the figure turned around and I saw the monster's distorted face. What was this creature? I asked myself, shaking.

I came back to reality the instant Angelo grabbed my arm.

"What are you doing? Are you okay?" he asked, pulling me away from the body. I started crying uncontrollably.

"Something killed her," I softly told him as he held me up and walked me toward his car. My head pounded when I thought about Christine being murdered. I fished my pills out of my bag, threw them back and felt the small hard pills go down my throat. I didn't even bother to grab the water bottle that was in the cup holder. My energy went down, and I felt faint and sick. Angelo stood outside of the car and spoke to the police that questioned him. I knew most of the police officers on the force. Milford was a small community that wasn't accustomed to any type of crime. I clutched my head and inhaled deeply. I couldn't even remember getting back into the SUV.

[41]

"Your headache is just going to get worse if you don't calm down," Angelo said, as he stuck his head in through the window. The police wanted me to make an official statement down at the station, but I was just too distraught to go through that. Angelo convinced detective Luke to take my statement right then and there. I answered a few questions while I sat in the car. I gave them all they needed in about 20 minutes, and then we left.

We pulled into the driveway of my place, and Angelo helped me out of the car and into the house. I felt completely numb. My heart and mind was broken over the loss of my friend. I thought of Christine as the sister I never had. She was my family.

I dragged myself into the living room, my body weak with grief.

"I can stay with you." Angelo offered, speaking softly. I sat on the sofa, with my hands on my knees. I couldn't stop thinking about my vision.

"It's okay. I have some things to go over. I'll be fine." I looked at Angelo. He sat next to me, and put his arm around me.

"I will have someone drop off your car later today," Angelo said. "I'm going to go pick up some food, and come back over to keep you company." He held my hand.

"I have plans to hang out with Gilad tonight. I think I need to cancel them," I said. "The second I tell him what happened he's going to come over anyway, but a part of me feels like I need to be with you."

"Then be with me. You don't have to explain yourself. I would hope our relationship comes before a guy you just met." Where did that come from, I thought to myself. I was not in any mood to talk about our non-existent romantic relationship.

"Gilad and I are dating. But I do need you, and I want you here. Right now I have to be alone to sort this out. I plan on going to visit Christine's parents' first thing in the morning. Pick me up at nine tomorrow."

Angelo kissed me on the cheek, and I stretched out across the sofa. He stroked my back, as I drifted off to sleep. I was afraid to go to sleep because I didn't know what I was going to experience. I had no desire to astral travel today. This time I was way too exhausted to do anything but actually sleep.

When I opened my eyes, and sat up, I noticed that Angelo was gone. It was almost 7:00 in the evening and Gilad was expected to be here within the hour. I was in no mood to do anything or go anywhere. I sighed deeply and pulled myself off of the sofa to take a warm shower. The water felt so good that I didn't want the shower to end. The warmth of the flowing water beating gently on my skin was alluring and relaxing. It took me about 20 minutes. I slipped into my warm cozy pajamas, with small brown teddy bears all over; it was a set that Christine had given to me for my birthday a few years ago. Putting on makeup was not going to improve my mood so I didn't even bother.

[42]

I took one last look at my reflection before I left my room. I looked like I hadn't slept in days. I threw on my old plush robe and started down the stairs. The doorbell rang as I approached the bottom of the steps. I opened the door. Gilad was dressed in black jeans with a light blue button-down shirt. He had on a suit jacket and shiny black loafers to compliment the look. His dark tousled hair was neatly slicked back with some kind of pomade.

"What's going on?" he asked, as his smile turned into a concerned look. "I thought we had a date this evening?" He looked me up and down.

"We did but…" My voice faded away. I could not manage to curl my lips up to force a smile, instead, I started to cry.

"What's wrong?" he asked, stepping in and reaching for me. I buried my face in his jacket. The door was still open, but he was not bothered by the coldness of the evening, and neither was I. He placed his hand on the side of my tear-stained face.

"Someone killed Christine. I found her body earlier today," I sobbed. I broke out of his embrace, guided him into the warmth of my home and closed the door behind him.

"What? Why didn't you call me? You know I would have been there for you," Gilad said.

"I don't know," I said. "I was just too distraught." He wiped my tears. I thought about his abilities, the ones I knew of and the ones he had yet to reveal to me. He stepped closer to me. I gripped on to his arm tightly.

"Gilad… Is it possible for us to go to the morgue and see her?" I knew it was a strange and morbid question but I didn't care.

"Why? That's not a place for you. Sydney I understand that this is a lot to handle but now you must come to grips with her death. You have to accept it. It's not healthy for you not to." His voice was deep and sweet. I found it strange that he didn't show any remorse or express his condolences.

"You can bring her back," I said sharply without thinking. He had an intense look on his face. I couldn't tell what he was thinking.

"I can't," he said, not really giving my remark any thought. I started crying again.

"Yes you can. I know what you can do." I said, sniffing. "Gilad you're an angel, a spirit being that has manifested in a physical form. You've come to this realm for some kind of mission and maybe this was your mission." My voice sounded desperate and my words were strong.

"Sydney, I may be an angel but honestly I don't possess that kind of power. There are limits to what I can do but…" Gilad's voice trailed off.

"But what?" I snapped.

[43]

"You still may be able to save her. There are others that can bring her back, others that have the type of power you need."

"She was all I had left of my old life. You know my mom isn't sane." We were both quiet. I plopped down on my dad's oversized recliner. The silent moments were long and tense between us. The man I cared about sat on the floor next me.

"There are major risks involved in what you want to do," he said. "I can't begin to tell you what you're in for." I looked at his lips, trying to decipher his words.

"There are risks involved with anything Gilad. I'm tired of losing the people I love. I am tired of being alone and having no one." I pulled my hair into a pony tail and secured it with an elastic band. "What's left of my family doesn't give a shit about me, my old friends are gone and my dad is dead and he's not coming back. There is no telling if my mom will ever get back to normal. All I have is Christine," My tone swelled with anger. "Gilad, the relationship you and I have is new. Nothing in my life is guaranteed." I took a couple of deep breaths, and tried to gather myself.

"Sydney! I AM NOT GOING ANY WHERE!" he yelled. I jumped off of the recliner and stormed into the kitchen, Gilad trailing behind me like a small boy. I opened the refrigerator to reach for a can of soda. He turned me around grabbed my face and planted a soft kiss on my lips. I then gave myself to him with a powerful force that I never realized was part of my sexual personality. When it was over I was surprised that this became my one and only experience of having sex on the kitchen floor. Something about me was slowly changing. Whatever it was, it surfaced from a secret place that resonated deep within my spirit.

Gilad stayed with me for a while. He lounged around my house in his boxers, preparing baked ziti and salad. He had a special culinary talent. Maybe it was divine inspiration. My mind wondered as I took another shower in my private bathroom that was located in the master bed room of my home. I felt relieved, but was more determined to plead my case to Gilad in an effort to bring my friend back from the dead. It was bizarre that the idea was now a possible option, no longer imaginary, but real.

We finished dinner and he washed the dishes and put them away. I was ready to start the conversation again. I sat at the table in the kitchen watching Gilad clear the counter of spices. I wondered how we could pull off something like bringing the dead back to life. I had never dabbled in witchcraft or voodoo, so I had no idea how could Gilad make this happen? Was it truly possible? It seemed like the type of thing you see in the movies or read in books.

I got up and put some milk in a small pot on top of the stove. I was craving a nice cup of hot cocoa. Before I could strike up the conversation, the doorbell rang. The shock of the door made my stomach flutter for a minute. Gilad rushed to retrieve his clothes. Seconds later he returned with his jeans on halfway and buttoning up his shirt.

I knew it was Angelo. This would be the guys' first meeting. I felt a little uncomfortable having Angelo meet Gilad this way. I answered the door reluctantly hoping my childhood friend would approve. Angelo was not bundled up enough for a blustering night in January.

[44]

"How are you holding up?" he asked with a somber demeanor. I invited him in, feeling a strange vibe from both of the men. I introduced them and they hesitantly shook hands.

"I'm doing a little better," I said, as I saw that Angelo had a bag of takeout in his hand. I knew that he wasn't going to listen when I told him not to worry about dinner. He used dinner as an excuse to come back over to meet Gilad.

There was an uncomfortable moment of silence as Angelo looked over Gilad and said, "Do you know that Christine was last spotted with Robert who apparently is a friend of yours?" My eyes grew wide as I listened to the anger in Angelo's voice.

"What are you talking about, guy? Gilad retorted. "How do you know she was with Robert? And how do you know he's my friend?" Gilad looked like he wanted to ask a dozen questions.

"I know because it's all on the news, some witnesses came forward and said they saw her going out with Robert the morning before she went missing."

"That's interesting because Sydney told me that she was found in her home, so it really doesn't matter who she went out with." Gilad countered. I glared at him suspiciously. His words disturbed me. They were so insensitive, and his tone so hurtful that I almost threw up.

"How can you say that?" I walked out of the living room and into the kitchen not sure what I felt about the guy I called my boyfriend. My body trembled. I sat down in the wooden chair trying to maintain my composure. I didn't want to lose my temper while company was in the living room. Angelo appeared behind me. He lightly touched the nape of my neck. I closed my eyes.

"Did they really have a report on the news?" I asked, not turning around.

"Yes. Her murder is officially a homicide. Her parents made a statement on the news. They're going to report the story again. The whole town is in an uproar about this murder. The police aren't sure what they are dealing with so they posted a curfew. By midnight everyone has to be off of the streets or the cops will take them in. I suggest that Gilad goes home since he doesn't live in this town."

I looked over my shoulder to see Angelo's face. He stood like a statue. "I'm so sorry about everything Sydney. I didn't realize that things in your life would become this complicated. I need to tell you something. I can't hide anymore." I stood up from the chair to meet Angelo's eyes. What was going on? I didn't know how to react to him, and I gave him a gesture to go on with what he had to say. The second Angelo parted his lips to speak; the kitchen door swung open and, Gilad walked in.

"Is everything ok sweetie?" His voice was low. I stared at him and nodded in response. Things were happening so fast, I hadn't had the chance to tell Gilad about my close friendship with Angelo. He was suspicious. He shifted his glare back and forth to read us.

[45]

"We're fine. Angelo is a great friend of mine. We've been friends since kindergarten. He came over to see how I was doing. We just need a moment to talk in private." Gilad was clearly uncomfortable with that, but I was not about to let Angelo leave. Gilad plastered a fake smile on his face and stepped out of the kitchen.

"What did you want to tell me?" I asked Angelo.

"It is very important. But before I do this I need to know if you'll be able to handle it. I also don't want you to feel that I've lied to you. I need to know if you'll still love me and want me in your life." He was so sincere I had never seen his face fixed in such a way. My heart rate soared as I prepared for the battle ahead. I let out a deep forceful sigh. I had a feeling this had something to do with our previous supernatural encounter.

"Out with it." I softly whispered.

"I can feel what you feel. I know what you want and have asked for."

"What are you talking about Angelo?" I asked, impatiently. "Look, I need to get some rest. Come with me tomorrow morning to Christine's parents' house. I don't think I'm ready tonight for what you have to tell me. I'm not ignoring you but I just can't do this now." I wanted to cry my eyes out.

"I understand." He kissed me on the cheek and I escorted him to the door. He gave me a tight hug and brushed his hand down my back. I saw the jealousy in Gilad eyes when we broke our embrace. As he blew me a kiss I noticed my car was parked in front of my house. I smiled at Angelo's thoughtfulness.

The snow started to come down pretty heavily. I made another cup of hot cocoa and sat on the swing of my back porch under the large heat lamp bundled up in a thick fleece blanket to get a better look at the weather. Milford was supposed to get about five inches of snow overnight. The swing rocked back and forth, and squeaking a little. My father and uncles built the swing when I was just a little girl. The back yard was covered with fresh snow. A small storm was headed towards Milford.

Gilad walked out, letting the back door slam behind him. He sat next to me and tried to snuggle under the blanket with me. I protested a little, still angered over his remarks about Christine. I didn't let him know how I really felt because a part of me didn't trust Gilad.

"I've been thinking about what you said, and I think we can bring back your friend," Gilad said quietly.

"I thought you said you didn't have that kind of power."

"I don't, but there are other angels that can help us." My phone buzzed in the side pocket of my pajama pants. I ignored it, and kept listening to Gilad. I just wanted to get to the bottom of this suspicious situation. Everything about it was suspicious: Gilad coming into my life, my accident on the trip, and Christine's murder.

[46]

"So tell me. How do we do this? I took a huge gulp of cocoa.

"You took my news without real surprise. You accepted me and my ability. You ask me questions that no normal human would ever ask."

"So?" I uttered.

"Don't you think that's strange?" He leaned over to get a better look at me.

"I'm not the typical girl next door."

"That I know," he said in a flirtatious tone, raising his right eyebrow. "*You* have to realize that *you* will be exposed to worlds and dimensions that no human has ever crossed before. *You* will have to access parts of *you* that have lain dormant inside of *you*. Before *you* do anything *you* must first accept and give into who *you* are completely." Gilad's eyes glowed. I hate when people try to tell you things. He was beating around the bush and making things more complicated. And, what was up with all the emphasis on the word "You?"

"Just tell me what I need to do," I said impatiently.

"You have to go to the Guardian of Spirits. Her name is Hope and she dwells in a cave within the ruins of a desolate dimension called the Borderline of Souls. It's a place where the dead live, where spirits go before they move on. Hope has dominion over those spirits. Your time is limited though. You only have five days from the day Christine becomes a spirit to bring her back. After that her spirit makes the final journey to her eternal destination.

"This will not be easy, Sydney. You must go to Hope to make an offering and present a valid case for why you have come to take Christine back to the world of the living." I narrowed my eyes at his words. This was some deep shit.

"What can I offer? What earthly good or product could I give her that would be worthy enough in her sight?" Gilad grew silent, bowing his head, slightly.

"You can offer another spirit in exchange," he replied. Everything became still. Nothing in the air moved, not even the snowflakes reached the ground. It was like time had stopped for a split second.

"I could only offer up my own spirit," I replied, and for a moment I thought about what it would be like if I were dead.

"You can get a spirit from the Pit of Lost Souls. The pit is a place where people go when they've lost their way during their travels to the Borderline of Souls," Gilad whispered. I didn't realize what I was getting into, but time was against me. I had a lot to learn, and fast. I was determined to do this.

"Where is the pit and how do I get there?" I cleared my throat and kept a straight face.

"The pit is in the dimension of Amu. The only way you can get to any dimension is through the portal of time and space."

[47]

Whoa, I thought. That sounded familiar. I had traveled through time and space by astral projection. That was my little secret. Did Gilad know my secret?

"Are you kidding?" I asked.

"You may not want to hear this, or want to believe me, but Sydney you have the power to do this. You've been to other worlds and dimensions. Did you think I would forget? When you saw me in your "dreams", they weren't dreams. I think you know that too."

"You must channel your power and connect to it when you go to that state in your mind," he said. "Your mind is an extremely high-functioning entity. Your abilities are remarkable. I'll go with you. You don't know what to expect. You haven't been to the darkness." Gilad had never spoken this way before. It was scary.

"When you go to sleep, I'll link up with you in your astral form and show you the way. A part of our bodies have to meet in order for it to work. It must be skin to skin contact, so you have to prepare," Gilad said. "Astral Projection is also a form of teleportation. Your body will feel the effects, so always make sure you eat a full meal before you go down." Gilad looked very serious. My mug was empty and I was ready to go into the warm house. I stood up with the blanket still wrapped around me and waddled inside. Gilad followed, locked the door and doubled-checked for security.

It was getting late, so I went up to my room to get settled for bed. I didn't ask Gilad if he wanted to spend the night. I assumed he would since the storm was already hitting the area and the curfew started.

My mind was in overload. I called my principal and notified her about Christine's death. She was very understanding when I officially told her that would be taking a leave of absence. My life was in such a turmoil that I couldn't handle going back to work with the students. It wouldn't be fair to them if I couldn't focus on them and their education. I realized the leave of absence would eventually lead to sending in my notice. The longer I stayed away from school, the more I wanted to work at my mom's company. She deserves for me to have an active role in the business. I pulled back the comforter and sheets and slithered under the covers. A few moments later Gilad tossed his clothes on the brown recliner and joined me.

"Who was that on the phone?" he asked.

"My Boss. I'm really going to leave the school district," I replied. "I told her I needed a leave of absence to deal with Christine's death. During this time off, I'll write and send my official letter of resignation. There is no way that I would be any good to the kids. They're great and they need someone that can really be devoted to them. At least working at the publishing company, Amy is there and I'll have the freedom to come and go as I please. Plus, all I keep thinking about is Christine. Who knows how long this whole task is going to take." I fixed my pillow and sat up in the bed. Gilad was brushing his fingers up and down my arm. The sensation tingled and made goose bumps surface on my soft skin.

"That's a good decision," he said. "I'll be here to fully support you, Sydney." He smiled as I looked at him. I leaned over to meet his luscious lips, then rolled over and took a deep breath.

The stress of this whole situation was making my condition worse. My head started to throb lightly. I took a pain killer and sipped a little water. Since I first slept with Gilad the voices in my head had become more potent. Maybe it was time for me to go back to my doctor, but I was sure that he wouldn't be able to help me. I placed the glass of water back on the night table. My body needed to rest.

I slid back down into the bed and pulled the covers up to my chin. Gilad scooted closer to me poking me, with his penis. Sadness overcame me and my mind wondered once again. I thought about the spirit and what it was really capable of. Was Christine able to feel? Did she know she was dead? What did she look like now? Was she floating around in an abyss?

Christine's death brought back all the pain I felt for my father and mother. The hurt resurfaced, not that it had diminished in any type of way. Gilad knew I was crying. He pulled me to him and held me. I relaxed my head under his chin, my face touching his bare chest. A part of me started to doubt myself. I wasn't sure if I was strong enough to face the mission we were about to undertake. To cross that boundary and go to another world in my astral form without the dream connection is foreign. I was too tired to keep thinking about it, but had one more question: What in the world am I?

After Gilad finally dozed off, I slipped out of bed to retrieve my cell phone. I wanted to privately check my messages. I made it down the steps quietly. The hardwood floors were cold against my bare feet. I tried not to make too much noise when I scurried through the house. The fire finally died out, and the air in the living room was a little chilly. I looked at my phone and saw the message indicator flashing. I had three missed calls and three text messages. The missed calls were from Angelo. I assumed the text messages were from him too.

Call Me! the first message read.

Danger! the second one read.

Don't trust Gilad. Call me as soon as you get this! the third message read.

Butterflies fluttered within me. It was hard to ignore messages like that when the man you're supposed to watch out for is under the covers asleep in your bed. I hope that Angelo hadn't thought I was ignoring him. The mood of the house became creepy. I inspected everywhere for strange distractions. A small amount of light from the porch light peered through the slits of the blinds making tiny light trails on the floor. Tip-toeing toward my father's study, I opened the doors slowly, careful not to make a sound. Closing them, I stepped over to the small lamp, and touched it once to turn it on. The dim light gave me enough illumination to see everything in the room. My father's books and papers were scattered everywhere, just as he left it before he died. I came in once a week to dust and straighten up but tried hard to not damage or disrupt my father's essence. Clutching my cell phone tightly in my hand I pressed the button to call Angelo.

"Hello," his deep voice sounded alert and edgy. There was no way that he had been asleep.

"Angelo what's wrong? Boy you sure know how to make a girl nervous."

"I'm coming over right now. There's something I must tell you." Before I could reply to his comment or protest against him barging over here in the middle of night, POOF he was standing right in front of me, surrounded by a cloud of white sparkly dust. I dropped my phone in sheer shock and placed my hands up to my mouth to cover my shriek. The Oriental rug my father had put in muffled the sound of the phone hitting the floor.

"What the…! What is this?" Please don't kill me!" I said, my voice shaking. There was no weapon that I could reach for. I was too scared to move. The bright light around him diminished and Angelo stood tall.

"Sydney, it's me, Angelo. Don't be afraid. Of course I'm not going to kill you." He smiled and looked absolutely beautiful. "Things are getting out of control. You're in danger. I'm sorry you had to find out like this, but I had to reveal my true identity in order to protect you, the way I'm supposed to. The threat of darkness is upon you." His eyes glowed light blue and his skin was illuminated. I had never seen my childhood friend like this before in the flesh. He wore the same clothes he had on when he came over to check on me, but he appeared so different. I looked at him suspiciously. "I mean you no harm. I'm an angel called a Watcher. I watch over very special people like you. People that have been chosen to do good things. I take on this physical form to guide and protect the chosen."

"Why am I chosen? What is the danger? And before you answer any of my questions why the hell didn't you tell me this before?" I started to cry as my voice became weak.

"It wasn't like I had any choice."

"Then you know my secrets?"

"Yes," he said looking down.

"They were mine and only mine to keep. You're not what I thought you were. How is it that you grew up with me?"

"I was sent here specifically for you. I had to live as a child and experience growing up because of you."

"What does that even mean?" I asked. "Are you serious? "Angelo, are you my guardian angel?" I chuckled for a few seconds, not believing what I had just asked. "So everything I experienced in my vision was real?" I wiped my face and crossed my arms.

"Yes," he replied gently. "I know we don't have much time. I'll tell you everything you need to know when I have a chance. Gilad will be awake soon. Don't trust him at all. He is a fallen angel and is evil. He wants you. He is a bringer of darkness and after your power. I know he was involved with Christine's death." I trembled from hearing that information.

[50]

"How can I trust you?" I asked Angelo.

"You can because…" He stopped and touched my hand. A flash of us at different stages in our childhood crossed my mind. I saw his face as we played together. At five he stood up for me when I was teased. When we were 10 he saved me from drowning at Lake Millett. At 15 he stopped the kitchen light fixture from crashing down on my head. In college he threw away a drink to avoid me taking the date rape drug. And when my father's car crashed, he pulled me out of the vehicle before the first responders made it to the scene. My eyes filled with tears as I came back from the vision gasping for air and trying to collect myself. I'd forgotten those things happened, but I was able to remember them clearly now.

"You've saved me so many times. You helped me through my life. How did you?" I couldn't get the words out. But he knew what I was trying to ask.

"I had to readjust your memory. I couldn't let you know that I did those things. I couldn't risk exposure." His face was very serious.

"All this is very interesting, so both you and Gilad tell me you're angels, and then you tell me about Guardians and Pits of Lost Souls! This is amazing! I knew there was something more to this world," I wondered aloud. The excitement in my voice increased.

"Whoa, wait a minute. He told you about the Guardian?"

"Yes. I asked him about bringing back Christine. He said he couldn't do it but there are others that have the power but—there's a catch. In order for me to bring her back to the living I must offer up another soul in return. I must travel to a dimension to acquire a random soul and exchange it for Christine's. He says he'll lead me there."

"All that he says so far is true, but he left out one important detail."

"What?" I asked, throwing up my hands.

"It is forbidden to bring a soul back from the dead. He's leading you into some kind of trap. He will try and lure you to the other side. You must believe me. You must trust me and know that I'm in love with you." A warm feeling pierced through me, and I couldn't speak. His eyes shined with great beauty. I have always had feelings for Angelo, but now this changes everything. I didn't want to get sidetracked with my own emotions. Deep down I believed. I believed in the great magic that makes this world and others so special.

"The important thing is that I have to do this. I have to bring her back. Don't tell me not to. If it wasn't possible then why would he tell me it was? And if you were doing what you were supposed to, then with all due respect, why didn't you save my father and where were you when my mom lost her mind? Why didn't you save me then?" I forgot that I had to keep my voice low. Anger settled over me.

"Shhhhh," he cautioned. "Some things are beyond my control. Life is not about quick fixes, Sydney. It's about taking chances and experiencing everything in a positive way, but you have to meet challenges, face your fears and overcome obstacles. It's about growing and learning in a way that makes you stronger despite the possible hardships along the way." His eyes glowed silver. This conversation was way too much for me to handle in my fragile state. I wanted to go back to bed but I also needed to hear what Angelo had to say. Something made me believe him even though I questioned him moments earlier.

"Go to bed," he said. "I feel that you're exhausted. I will speak with you tomorrow. Go and start your mission to save your friend. I will follow you, out of sight, so that I can watch your back."

"Wait!" I commanded. "Before you go, please tell me, how do you know Gilad's intentions?" I thought it was a valid question.

"I just do," he replied vanishing into thin air. I wondered where he had gone. I silently went back upstairs and climbed into bed without Gilad even noticing I had left the room.

Chapter Six

I managed to shower and dress while Gilad was still in bed snoring away. I wanted to avoid any kind of interaction with him until I found out who he really was, and at least processed this thing with him and Angelo. I plowed through the snow, walking away from my house. I sent Angelo a text telling him to pick me up down the street. I knew he would understand without questioning me. When he quickly pulled up, I saw him in a different light. I almost felt like I didn't know him after last night, but I didn't want to feel that way. I jumped into his SUV and greeted him with a smile.

It was strange to watch Angelo drive now that I knew the truth. We'd been friends for as long as I could remember, but I always looked at him as my next door neighbor who grew to become a great lifelong friend. I couldn't believe that he told me that he loved me last night. While I had to admit that I felt a new sexual tension between us—his human form was distractingly attractive—I was afraid to think about risking our friendship. Even though I knew his secret, the situation felt too precarious for me to deal with. Had he forgotten that I was dating Gilad? And why would he wait all these years to tell me he loved me? I'd had about enough these last few weeks of uncovering concealed truths.

Angelo explained again how he had been assigned to watch over me since I was born, and that as time went on it became difficult to watch and protect me without arousing suspicion.

"What makes you so different from Gilad?" I asked, glancing out of the window.

"I'm not a Fallen One. I'm a guardian that watches and protects good," he replied. I help look after those that are benevolent. I have favor in the eyes of the Ultimate Power. I'm not a traitor and don't take advantage of my abilities. Fallen Ones are the angels that have betrayed the Ultimate Power of Good. They were punished for their betrayal, and banished from the Heavenly Realm. They were sent to a place where they could be reminded of their treacherous ways, off where they could envy the ones they most desired from a distance, humans. Gilad was my brother in spirit; he was once good but lusted to be worshiped. He knows what you are and will do anything to make his cause a worthy one." I stared at Angelo, taking in everything he said. He had no reason to lie to me. He had nothing to gain.

"That explains a lot. But it doesn't explain what I am and what I have to do with all of this." Angelo was quiet for a moment. "Does it make sense for us to go to Christine's parents' home if we're going to bring her back to the living? How does that work? There's a murder investigation. The crime was reported on the news, and her body is at the morgue. So many people know about it, and funeral arrangements are being made."

"It makes sense for now. We must follow the natural flow of what's happening in life. Once you obtain her soul and it's restored in her body, time and the minds of everyone affected will naturally readjust and adapt to the change. It will be as if she never died. She will assume her old life.

"Will I remember?"

"Yes of course. But she won't. It's not good for a person to know or realize that they've passed on and returned to the living, because many will regret that they came back, while others will look at it as a second chance. It can go either way."

"Why are all the rules changed all of a sudden? First I died and you brought me back. I think something came back with me. For a long time after the accident I felt a dark presence. I couldn't sleep or stand to be alone in my own home. Thank God I haven't experienced that type of disturbance in a while, but I do see dark entities from time to time. It can be really scary. Is that what I'll be risking if I go through with this? Is that what Christine possibly has to deal with if she comes back here?" As I spoke the fear in my voice increased.

"Your situation was different, *you* are different. I told you. You're not the average human, so I have no idea what's going to happen with Christine once she rejoins the living. Anything is possible." I looked at his face then turned to peer out of the window at the few cars that slowly travelled on the road.

"I hate this cryptic shit. Why am I not the average human? I'm tired of your half-answers that don't tell me anything. What makes me not the average human? And why would you say such a thing? Just because I don't know doesn't mean that you're supposed to keep it hidden from me." I grew so angry that I wanted to jump out of the car and get away from Angelo.

Everything was quiet as we pulled up to the large home. A strong feeling of despair encapsulated my spirit when I saw several cars parked in the area.

"Angelo, the family is very hurt over this. We have to make this short and sweet," I said as I decided to let go of my angry feelings.

Angelo nodded his head in agreement. He parked the truck and scurried out of the vehicle, coming to the passenger side and opening the door for me. My boots melted into the snow as we walked up to the house. Silvia, Christine's mom, opened the door suddenly as we approached, and noticed us immediately. From a distance she appeared tired as she stood on the porch with a knitted shawl around her shoulders and a cigarette sticking out of the side of her mouth. I could only imagine what she looked like up close.

"Silvia!" I called. I went up the wooden steps, and saw a single tear roll down her cheek. I held my arms out and gave her a hug. I felt relief flutter within her.

"Sydney, I'm so happy you could make it. I appreciate your support, Angelo," she said with a crooked smile. She broke our hug and reached for Angelo.

"We're so sorry for your loss. If there's anything we can do, please let us know." Angelo was so comforting to her. Silvia invited us into the living room to have tea and small cakes that were Christine's favorite snack. As I sat on the soft vintage sofa, I noticed family members were coming and going, expressing condolences. Silvia and her husband Howard did everything to be gracious hosts, despite the pain they were going through. They told us about the upcoming funeral arrangements, and we discussed the murder and the investigation. We talked about possible leads and Christine's new relationship with Robert. I answered Silvia's questions but only relayed what was already public knowledge, which wasn't much. I felt saddened and guilty for not being completely honest with her—she had been such a great support after my father passed away and my mom went to Loving Hills—but I promised to do whatever I could to help. As we were leaving, Silvia told us that since this was a murder investigation, there would have to be an autopsy.

I panicked at that thought of the medical examiner cutting up Christine's body. Angelo said that he would work his magic to buy us some time. There was something about him that made me fully trust and believe in him. Everything he told me had to be true. Our past connection and our current relationship gave me a reason to never doubt him. Angelo was a kind and gentle spirit. On the way back to my place I ranted and raved about his identity and even apologized for questioning him.

Within the hour we were back at my house. I wondered how Silvia would react if she knew that I was willing to go to any lengths to save her daughter. My mind raced over what to do. Gilad had left a note on the refrigerator door saying that he had to spend the day in the City and would return this evening. He promised to call me when he got to work. It was hard for me to believe him, but I was happy that he was out of the way so I could discuss our plan with Angelo. Angelo was the one I wanted to travel to another world with, not a man I barely knew and hardly trusted.

We settled on the sofa and got comfortable. We faced each other, and Angelo took my hand, gazing into my eyes.

"Listen, you have to focus," he said. "You have to clear your mind and take your spirit to that place when you're about to drift off to sleep. I know you've never used your astral projection power outside of the dream state, but it's not as hard as you think. You'll eventually have the power to do it at will, but for now just relax and take a deep breath. Take yourself to that place beyond yourself and your dreams. Listen to the sound of my voice. Hold on to it, block out anything and everything else around you. When you get there, you will be in another dimension. The environment will be different, just follow me. Remember your mind and emotions are extremely influential. Embrace the world around you. Do not be captivated by the temptations of the travel experience." I listened to his voice and the sound of his breathing. I followed his lead and we breathed deeply in unison. I completely relaxed, and lost myself in the familiar sound of his soft, loving voice. I felt the energy building inside me and my spirit projected from my physical body, and lifted from its resting place within me. I stayed calm, feeling Angelo's touch comforted me.

Rising higher and higher, I found myself floating above my body, then above the house, followed by the clouds, zooming through a whirlwind of a portal. The stars and constellations surrounded me. Angelo's entity hovered alongside of mine. Clouds of dust and cosmic gasses lingered all around. Trying hard to keep my focus, I observed everything around me. As we passed through the portal our travels stopped suddenly. I looked down and saw myself hovering over a beautiful garden full of all kinds of trees moving in slow motion. The grass was deep green, and thousands of plants and flowers covered the area. It was like a painting had come to life. Then in the near distance I saw little girl running and playing. She was dressed in a light blue gown, her hair dark as night and skin as pale and smooth as cream. I danced and frolicked to music that only I could hear. Her feet were bare and as she took a step, a dark purple rose popped up to fill an empty area. The beauty of this place was beyond words. Angelo appeared next to me draped in a golden cloak, glowing with all his glory. He was more beautiful than I could ever describe. Silver white wings, like the wings of a dove, stretched out about 7 to 10 feet behind him.

I was soon distracted by another figure running in the distance. She looked like me and was dressed in the same gown as my child-like version. Seconds later a man appeared running, tall and handsome. The three clasped hands enjoying the happiness they shared. Tears rolled down my face as I realized who the man and woman were.

"Angelo," I said blinking as the tears fell. "This is not a memory." I replied.

"No it's not." His voice lightly echoed. "This was your life as a child and your future of happiness. There will be a day when you will be with your parents again, and you shall dwell in The Garden of Eden." He smiled displaying his gleaming white teeth. I could not believe what I was seeing. I tried to compose myself.

"I am so sorry that I made you feel like I was not there for you. You have a right to your feelings. I owed you this. I had to show you. I understand it has been hard. You'll find the peace you've been searching for." Angelo spoke so smoothly that the words rolled off his tongue. I stepped up to him, clutched my arms around his body and embraced him. I closed my eyes and felt the glow of body heat and love combined. He touched my head with the tips of his slender fingers and all of a sudden a rush a relief surged through my brain. I smiled and basked in the warmth of his goodness, and… Poof! I opened my eyes and abruptly sat up, inhaling deeply.

"How do you feel?" Angelo patted me on the shoulder.

"I feel good. You gave me something that I thought I'd never have again. Thank you Angelo, the experience was like no other. Seeing my parents makes me hopeful again."

"I'm glad that you're in a good mood. We only have four more days to save Christine. I bought us a little time, but only a little. Just so you know you can practice your gift at home alone. All you have to do is go to that place within yourself to channel your ability. Go as deep as you can, bring it up and beyond. You'll feel yourself floating like before." My eyes were centered on his. "Listen, before this is over you're going to have to kill Gilad before he attempts to draw you into the darkness. Stay on guard."

"Are you crazy?" I said, as my eyes widened. "I didn't think it would lead to me having to kill anyone." I paused and thought for a second. "I know killing him won't be simple." I could not believe I just blurted out those words.

"There is a weapon that can extinguish the life of a Fallen Angel: a special dagger called The Dagger of Doshon. This dagger is kept in a crypt underground in the dimension of the Neatherwood, and is guarded by Keepers of the Deep. The location of the crypt is unknown, but if we combine our powers we can sense the location. And Sydney, don't regret his demise; if you want to survive this then it must be done." I took in what he said but it didn't sit right with me. My mouth dropped. I was surprised something didn't fly in it.

"Do you really think it will come to me having to kill someone? I can't imagine myself doing something like that. Maybe you have Gilad all wrong. He hasn't done anything to me to make me believe that he's evil, and that is the truth Angelo."

"I just can't understand why you can't see through his evil," Angelo said in frustration. I shrugged my shoulders. I wasn't in the mood to go over this again about Gilad. "Maybe he has it masked or something?" he said thinking out loud. "I know you can sense evil and see the auras of humans and other beings. That can be the only explanation."

"It's hard for me to fully believe that he's this evil entity that you claim him to be. You say he was your brother in spirit before he fell—maybe he's changed. I think everyone deserves a second chance, don't you?"

"Why do you keep fighting me with this? You don't know the half of it. Gilad has a bad reputation. I know everything about him. He's killed many innocent people, started wars, encouraged wicked behavior, and made good people lose their faith and hope in life. There's a reason why he hasn't tried anything with you. He wants to gain your complete trust and when you finally let your guard down he'll do exactly what I'm saying he will do. I know how you feel about him. I know you have your suspicions. Why can't you just come to grips with it?" he said, exasperated. I hesitated there were so many things going on with me that I couldn't confess how I feel about Gilad. The truth was that I was torn between the belief that he really did love me and the suspicion that I couldn't trust him. I felt that there was something deeper that I didn't know about him. My eyes grew big. Maybe I was under some kind of spell.

"Did he really kill people?" I asked.

"Yes. You have to stay away from him. It's hard for me to protect you when you lie in the arms of evil." His words frightened me.

I hesitated for a moment. After processing this new information about Gilad, I decided to tell him some things that I was holding back.

"There have been some moments lately when I feel that someone is watching me, and when I turn around to see who it is, no one is there. It's happened a few times, but I really didn't think it was important to bring up, until now."

"I'm glad you told me," he said. "That's important information, but I don't like it. If someone is watching you and you can't see them, it probably means they have the power of invisibility. There are a number of creatures that have that power. Break up with him. You have no reason to continue the relationship with him anyway. I am here for you and I know you don't love him." His beautiful pupils dilated and sparkled. I ran my hands through my hair, as Angelo stood up and waited for my response. I kicked off my boots and folded my legs across the sofa. Angelo towered over me as he looked down into my eyes. I gave him a smirk that read "I know what you're thinking."

"You can't honestly tell me that you love him," he protested. "I know who you love. I know your deepest dreams and desires. I know your fears." His smooth voice made me tingle inside. I continued to stare at him, smiling just a little so that my lips slightly curled. I knew where this conversation was going, so I quickly changed the subject.

"We still don't know who killed Christine. All I saw in my vision was the distorted face of a dark figure drain the life out of her." Then the burning question that I have been dying to ask surfaced upon my lips. "Angelo, do vampires really exist?" He fixed his silver eyes on me and knelt down in front of me.

"Yes of course they do," he replied in a deep tone like I was supposed to know for sure. "Why?"

"Well I was thinking. When I saw the murder in my vision and saw the wound on Christine's neck, I thought to myself that there is no way that a human could have done that. Her neck was torn like a vicious animal. She has no pets and the cops did not mention any kind of animal attack. I believe that a supernatural creature of some kind, possibly a vampire, killed her." I paused, then blurted, "I think the guy she was dating, Robert, may have had something to do with her murder—if not the prime suspect, then as an accomplice." I felt like I was part of a mystery television series.

"How long had Christine and Robert been going out?" he asked, and I looked up at the ceiling at an imaginary calendar.

"They'd been going out ever since we met them on the Pocono trip, like I told you." I looked back at Angelo. He left me in the living room and waltzed into the kitchen. Moments later he came back with a bag of chips and two sodas. He sat next me silently and placed the bowl between us. I grabbed a couple of chips; stuffing them in my mouth, I proceeded with the conversation. "I wish you could meet Robert. Since Gilad is an angel, it's possible that Robert is too, but I really believe that a vampire killed her."

"Your theory is quite interesting. The Fallen associate with other magical creatures, and have human followers. They band together with others to form alliances to strengthen their cause. Since I've never met Robert I could not determine his humanity. Did you see an aura when you met him?"

"Yes I did. It was a dull gray with a hint of red around it."

"Interesting," he said. "That means he's human that is in the process of turning demonic." Concern increased in his voice. "Angels have the power to sense each other but very powerful ones like Gilad and I have the power to mask our scent to keep others from recognizing us." He shoved a hand full of chips into his mouth.

[58]

"So is that how you and Gilad can be in the same room together without ripping each other apart?

"Actually yes, my scent is masked and so is his, but I know the human form that he uses, so I recognized him. For some reason he loves that version of his human self. I have heard of Gilad, but he has never seen me in my present form. All this time I have been here, protecting you, I've used my power of shrouding to mask my identity from other enchanted beings. Not every angel has the same powers." Angelo deeply explained. I chugged a diet Mountain Dew, one of my favorite soft drinks. Thinking about what Angelo said, I realized that every day I learned something new about the world of angels.

"If Robert is turning demonic then we can rule him out as a suspect, especially if I think a vamp is responsible," I said. "In my vision I saw the creature hover I, felt the influence of his power. It wore a long misty cloak that rippled in the air. It was faceless too, it didn't have a face like we do, and it was shadowy and distorted. But it looked in my direction when it heard a strange noise. For a moment I thought it sensed me."

"Angels defiantly hover, but other creatures like vampires do too." Angelo informed me. "Just in case you don't know it, you also have the ability to replay the vision and make new discoveries about it."

"That's what I did when I touched Christine. That's how I saw the creature. It was my first time experiencing that. Are you saying that I can go back and replay a vision?"

"Yes," Angelo replied.

"How is it that you know so much about me and my abilities?"

"I told you, I've been watching and protecting you since you were born. I'm supposed to know everything about you." I grew perplexed about the situation I was putting myself in.

The morning had turned into afternoon, and Gilad was expected to return soon. I needed to figure out what kind of plan Angelo had to help me retrieve Christine's soul.

"How are you going to travel with Gilad and me without being noticed?" When the question slipped out of my mouth I immediately felt stupid. He just told me that he has the power to mask his presence. I laughed a little and made an apologetic face.

"I can transform into any object I want. I'll go as a charm around your neck. That way I can be as close to you as I possibly can." I started laughing uncontrollably. Angelo was quiet and stood still.

"Are you serious?" I asked, trying to make a straight face. He nodded in response.

"I'm so sorry," he said. "It's probably hard for you to understand me when you have not seen me use my gifts." He jumped off the sofa and stood stiff as a board, glanced at an object by the fireplace, closed his eyes, and within a split second particles of blue sparkles disintegrated into the air and a white cloud of mist formulated near the floor by my feet. When the mist cleared, the Japanese vase that my mother purchased from a yard sale was sitting on the floor and was also on the mantle. I couldn't believe my eyes. He can turn into inanimate objects? This is unreal, I thought to myself. I pushed the half empty bowl of chips aside and leaned over to touch the vase. The smooth porcelain surface was real. I winced at the thought, jerking my hand back.

"Okay, I believe you. I won't doubt you again," I said to the vase. Nothing happened. Narrowing my blue eyes, I kept them locked on the object.

"I said, I BELIEVE YOU!!" I yelled. The moment I raised my voice, he appeared in my sight, smiling with satisfaction. I smiled back and shook my head.

"The charm will be a pair of silver wings, on a pure silver chain. It will be located in your mother's jewelry box on your vanity table. As soon as you go upstairs get it and put it on. Gilad will be here soon. Remember that I'm with you always and that I love you." His voice echoed as he vanished into thin air.

After Angelo left I was alone with my thoughts. I had never had problems with myself esteem until the car accident. For the first time in a long time I didn't feel like myself. I felt like a circus freak who was able to perform tricks at will. My whole essence was beginning to change into something that was unfamiliar to me.

Chapter Seven

Gilad was dressed to impress tonight. He had on a pinstripe black suit with a cream colored tie and shiny loafers. I assumed he drove in straight from work or where ever he came from. Instead of being interested in the handsome creature that walked into my home, I thought about Angelo and the necklace he said would be waiting for me in my jewelry box. Gilad greeted me with a kiss, but I gently pulled away before he could seriously get too passionate. I suggested that he go up and take shower to get comfortable before we had dinner. He didn't hesitate at my suggestion. Gilad placed his briefcase on the floor and went upstairs. He acted like he lived here which was strange, since I realized that he has never once invited me to his place.

After he left, I tip-toed over toward his briefcase, and I glanced in the direction of the stairs leading up to the second level. Scurrying up a few steps, I heard the shower still going so I had to act fast. I maneuvered so quickly that I didn't realize how fast my body reacted to the movement. Feeling like a real gumshoe, I quickly knelt down and opened up the leather bound briefcase and I sifted through the papers. I had no idea what I was looking for as I searched. Then I realized that all of the papers were blank. I wasn't sure what it meant.

I unzipped the side pockets and pulled out a folder and looked inside. The folder was empty. I returned it back to its rightful place and made sure that it didn't appear like it was tampered with. His suit jacket was hung up on the coat rack. I searched all the pockets and pulled out a thick wallet. I opened it and found nothing. I looked in the cracks and crevices of the wallet and did not see a driver's license, registration or insurance paperwork. Not even one credit card. I stood still, extremely perplexed over the bizarre discovery or lack of discovery.

Something inside me wasn't satisfied. Placing the wallet back, I went back to the briefcase. Stunned, I just kept kneeling down in awe. Seconds later I looked over the briefcase again, studying it more intently. This time I noticed a side zipper carefully hidden behind another zipper. I unzipped it slowly, still listening for sounds from upstairs. I reached and yanked out a folder from a hidden pocket. I opened it, and pulled out the contents. My eyes widened as I peered at a collection of photographs. My mouth dropped. The stack had pictures of men and women, each with a small handwritten description underneath the photo: Suzie Andrews, White Witch; Walter O'Dea, Shifter; Parker Marie, Fairy; Christine Harrison, Human; and Sydney London, Powerful Nephilim. I studied my photo and Christine's. On the back of Christine's photo was a note written in pencil: *Christine is the key to Sydney's power and the circle.*

"A nephilim?" I whispered to myself. "What?" I softly murmured, as I continued to investigate the stack trying to make some kind of sense of it. Several things were written on the back of my photo, but I was frightened that Gilad would catch me snooping around, so I neatly put everything back and trotted over to the recliner, plopped down and turned on the television. I ran over lots of possibilities of reasons why he had those photos in his brief case. I grabbed my phone off the table and went online to search for the meaning of what a nephilim was. Seconds later the search came back with a definition. I had heard the term before but this time it meant something specific to me.

A nephilim is a being who is half human and half angel. The nephilim are the offspring of the "sons of God and the "daughters of men." I followed the words with my eyes as I processed the definition.

Gilad gawked at me as he hovered down the stairs dressed in jeans and a t-shirt. I felt his eyes on me. I pressed the red button on my phone so he wouldn't know what I was searching for. Seeing the photos and the information on me confirmed what Angelo had said, and what I had suspected. Who was this creature that stood in my living room? I wanted him to leave, but I didn't want to let him know that I was aware that something was going on with him. He started to sit next to me, but I jumped up before he could touch me. I cracked a fake smile.

"Hey, I'm going make something to eat!" I said with pseudo excitement. "Just sit back and relax. I'll be back; first I need to freshen up before I begin to cook." I jetted upstairs, hiding my fear. I closed the door to my bedroom and locked it. I called Angelo a couple of times, whispering in great panic. Angelo popped in directly in front of my face. His tight chest muscles were clearly visible through his shirt. I gently traced the outline of his muscular body with my eyes. My heart stopped at that moment.

"How did you know how to summon me?" he asked.

"I don't know I just panicked. I'm really scared. I found out some strange information that confirms what you've been trying to tell me about Gilad. I looked in his briefcase and found a folder with a lot of pictures of different people. In the collection was a photo of me and one of Christine. Each picture had a brief description of who we are and what we are." My hands were shaking as I revealed my findings to Angelo. "The others were various creatures like shifters, witches and fairies. The note on Christine's picture read that she was human; she was the only full-blooded human in the collection. My picture said that I'm a nephilim. Does that mean anything to you?" I wanted a quick answer before Gilad came looking for me.

"I didn't want you to find out this way. I'm sorry Sydney. A nephilim is person that is the offspring of a human and an angel. That is who you are. That is where your powers come from."

"Why do you hide things like this from me? Every day there's something new. I am sick of it. I don't even know who or what I am anymore. I feel like I'm wasting my time by entertaining Gilad. He wants me for something. I know that now. How can I get rid of him so we can talk about this further? I'm not going anywhere with Gilad now." I felt the tears form. I felt so hurt. "I want this to be over." I was furious the urge to confront Gilad came over me.

"Keep cool," Angelo warned. "Pretend that you don't know any of this and go back down there and fix dinner as planned."

"How can you tell me to do this? What if he does something to me? He wants me to go with him to save Christine but at this point I think it *is* a trap. I believe he could have killed her.

Why does he have those pictures on him? And what is the Circle? He had a note on my picture about my powers completing a circle?"

"I promise I'll tell you everything you need to know— later." Suddenly Gilad called me from down stairs, and Angelo disappeared. I unlocked the door and the next thing I knew Gilad popped in. I wasn't comfortable with him popping in and out.

"What are you doing?" he asked in a cool tone. He stepped towards me.

"Nothing. I was planning a surprise for you." Putting on a fake smile is not something I am good at. Folding my arms across my chest, I didn't know what to do or say next. I glanced all around the room trying to visualize where Angelo was. Taking a deep breath, I ran my fingers through my hair. It felt a little greasy. Jumping in the shower to freshen up was a good idea, I thought. We stood across from each other, speechless.

"So….should we go to see the Guardian or go to the Pit first?" That wasn't the real question I wanted to ask. I waited for his reply.

"We must go to the Pit and collect a soul and then go to the Guardian. Are you okay? Ever since we started discussing..." His voice tailed off as I interrupted his sentence.

"Let's go now. We can eat later. We don't have much time." I said in a shaky voice. I couldn't believe what I had gotten myself into, especially since just moments before I told Angelo that I wasn't going anywhere with Gilad. Now I was in more trouble. He nodded his head and we stepped over towards my king size bed. I went to the left side and he went to the other. We stretched our bodies across the bed, our heads flat and bodies relaxed. I remembered the necklace that Angelo told me to get. I jumped up and ran over to my vanity table. I opened the pink painted box.

The outside of the box was porcelain and had hand-painted roses all over. My mother had given me the box when I was five, just like her mom had given it to her. It was the "big girl" gift that every little girl wanted, and I was planning on giving it to my daughter when she turned five. I smiled thinking about my mother.

Music plays when the top is lifted up, but I turned it off, so Gilad wouldn't hear it. I pulled open the tiny drawer by the small pear shaped knob, and saw a beautiful silver chain with a diamond charm sparkling against the plush velvet lining of the box. The charm was in the shape of two wings just as Angelo had said. It looked extremely expensive, and out- of- this- world gorgeous. It was very lovely, almost enchanting. I wanted to be alone and enjoy this moment. I quickly slipped it around my neck and hid the charm under my top so that Gilad wouldn't see it. I returned to the bed and got back into my position. My mind was at ease knowing that Angelo was with me.

"Why did you get up?" Gilad asked.

"I got up to check the clock on my vanity," I replied, thinking quickly.

"Don't worry about time. It works differently when you're between worlds and dimensions."

Within a few moments I found myself going through the tunnel of time and space. I sensed Gilad's connection to me but didn't feel confident about it. Distracted by my thoughts I cleared my mind and remembered that Gilad had heard what I was thinking on the trip to the Poconos. I did my best to block him out of my mind before he read it. It was gravely important for me to keep my secrets.

We arrived in a deep cave, dark, rocky and dank. Mountains of rocks and boulders floated through the atmosphere. There was no solid ground. A black abyss rested beneath us, as the sounds of unfamiliar creatures echoed in the darkness. Tiny balls of dim lights danced everywhere, gently illuminating the pitch black pit. There was something in the dark that made me uneasy, and I ran my fingers over the diamond charm to give me peace of mind. My heart pounded at the thought that I was essentially here to retrieve someone's soul. Gilad guided me with his hands. I hovered slightly behind him. A voice entered my mind and pierced into my brain.

"Don't be alarmed, it is me, Angelo. You must capture the soul in the gold bracelet that your father gave you. Once you get the soul in the bracelet, break the connection with Gilad. Just think about your true form lying on the bed and your astral form will automatically return to its place. I will be waiting for you there." The sweet sound of his voice made me anxious. I looked down and noticed that I was indeed wearing the gold bracelet that my dad had given me. I wondered why Gilad didn't tell me how to obtain the soul.

"Do I just reach for any soul?" I asked him, barely opening my mouth.

"If you don't have an object to capture it in, then you can reach for it and it will go into you. You can release it when you want, but don't let it possess you—possession is the risk." He mumbled. I looked at this guy and got sick from the sight of him.

"Do you think that a mere human can hold the soul of someone in their hands? Why would you not tell me the risk in this?" My voice grew louder. It rumbled in the distance. I rolled up my sleeve and held out my right arm in the direction of an oncoming spirit. The spirit entered the bracelet, vanishing as it made direct contact with the gold.

Gilad's eyes bulged. They changed into something ancient and evil. I closed my eyes and visualized my body, my home, my bed. I released my hand, from his and at that very moment I felt my astral form returning back to my body. I drifted further and my mind became lighter, spinning as the space that contained the floating mountains and black abyss faded into the dark. I opened my eyes and found myself on my bed. Rolling off of the bed, I prepared for another encounter with Gilad. I thought about the new impression I had made on him. I called Angelo telepathically.

"I can't show myself now. Gilad will be there. He is coming." Angelo's voice pierced my brain. Gilad appeared, sitting on the bed. This time his presence did not startle me. He had a surprised expression on his face, but there were many more things I read into it.

[64]

"Sydney what happened? Why did you break the connection? And how did you know spirits attract to gold objects?" He stood up lightly, gliding over to me.

"It was just a hunch. I assumed that gold is a natural element the spirit would attach itself to." Although it was a bullshit answer, it may have been correct. "You have a lot of questions for me but I have a few of my own." My voice was steady. "I need you to quit the crap and be honest with me. Why are you really here? And most importantly, why do you have pictures of me and Christine hidden in your briefcase? And what's up with the blank papers? I WANT THE TRUTH!" I yelled.

Gilad stepped back for a moment, surprised that I knew about the briefcase. "Do you really want truth?" he asked.

"That would be nice," I snapped.

"You're one of us—but not completely. You're half human and half angel."

"A nephilim, I know." I rolled my eyes, speaking with an attitude. "What are you *really*?" I asked, narrowing my eyes at him.

"You're a very powerful being, Sydney. That's why you have abilities. It's in your blood. And I'm not what you think. I'm a Fallen Angel," he replied with deep remorse. "I was originally sent to bring you back to where you belong."

"Bring me back to where? How can I go back to somewhere I have never been?"

"All Fallen Angels and the council of the fallen dwell in the dimension of Kalaston, which is on the border of Alshaldon. It is a world where all of your wildest dreams come true, a place where beauty is infinite. It is a land where you don't ever have to hide who or what you are. It is not like the Earthy Realm.   The council members want you to join them. You won't be fully accepted until you come into all of your powers, and you must go through a magical transformation." He stepped closer to me. I sighed deeply, trying to take in the new knowledge. "You just don't understand the great power that lies within you and the awesome things that you could do with your power. There are so many full-blooded humans that would trade anything for the chance you have been given."

"I know what I am now," I said with acceptance. "I can't even describe how I feel anymore. It's just that I wish I had known from the beginning. All the other things that I've gone through would have understood, my abilities, the mysterious events, the paranormal experiences, everything."

"Don't be upset about it. I envy your freedom, your passion for life, your love. It's your humanity that makes you so unique and special, your connection with the humans. There is nothing ordinary about you."

"Why haven't you completed your duty yet?"

[65]

"I must admit that some part of you has influenced me in such a way that I can't explain. When I leave you, I go to Kalaston. I must report back to them every day. They don't know that I have found you yet or that I'm in love with you. They just know that I have a few leads on your location. Your destiny is to save the Fallen." His eyes gleamed, and he realized that he was being a little too honest with me. And in his honesty I discovered his true identity, the identity that exposed the true darkness within him. Gilad was one of the Fallen. That deeply troubled me. He touched the side of my arm gently. I pulled away with anger.

"Save them from what? I know who the Fallen are. "I don't want to be around you or them." I said firmly. "I know the truth. The Fallen are evil beings that have spread darkness and despair to humans."

Without warning Gilad's demeanor and appearance changed. Long, black, silky feathered wings emerged from his back. His handsome young face wrinkled with a wrath I had never seen before. Bones surfaced from his face, turning him into a creature with deadly intentions. I backed up. He rose from his feet.

"Don't call me that, I am not evil," he growled.

"Look at you! You're trying to scare me and it's not going to work. If you love me like you say you do, then you won't hurt me." I desperately wanted to call Angelo, but I remained strong in my efforts to get information out of Gilad. I moved so far from him that my back pressed against the wall near my closet door.

"Let's get down to it. Did you kill Christine?" I wanted him to confess so badly that I could taste it. My anger festered.

"I did not, but her death was for your own good!" he said, with a loud, agonizing bellow. I couldn't believe what he said. I knew his involvement was deeper. I started to cry. "Please understand that it had to happen. Her death is the key to you obtaining your full power. It is the love and the bond you shared that opened you up to receive a part of yourself that has lain dormant within you." I shook my head in disbelief. Everything that Angelo said was true. Gilad did hurt me, he may not have tried to kill me but he had betrayed me in the worst way possible.

"You made a big mistake," I said. "What was the point of you trying to help save her?"

"I did it to redeem myself in your eyes. I wanted to prove to you that no matter what I was assigned to do, it didn't matter because of my love for you." His face softened, his wings folded back and vanished. He descended, placing his feet carefully on the floor. He looked normal again.

"That is the most twisted thing I have heard so far from you!"

"This is deeper than your friend. She was a causality of war, a sacrifice. This is about your power."

[66]

"Fuck the power! I don't want it and I don't want you," I said throwing up my hands. This thing between us is over. Get out!" I screamed as loud as my voice would allow. He disappeared and I threw my body on the bed and cried my eyes out.

I felt the warmth of a tender touch on my back. I lifted my head from the soaking wet pillow to see that Angelo was sitting on the edge of the bed.

"Did you hear the whole thing?"

"Yes. Don't blame yourself. He's a deceiver—that's what he does. I am not a Fallen One." He answered my question before I fixed my lips to ask it again. He adjusted his head to meet mine. Wiping the tears from my face, his hands felt soft and tender.

"I'm so happy that you're here with me. I'd rather be with you than anyone else." The tone of my voice was raspy. I scooted over and patted the comforter to give Angelo the signal for him to join me in the bed. He looked a little reluctant. Angelo carefully positioned his body across the bed. I closed my eyes for a minute and thought about this outrageous situation I was in.

"What am I going to do when Gilad tries to come back here?"

"We'll be ready for him," Angelo said. "I understand that you're in a fragile state but you need to get yourself together. You can't defeat him with your bare hands, or with any kind of weapon on this plane. We must go to retrieve the Dagger of Doshon."

"What about Christine? Is it too late?"

"No—we still have time. It is more important that we get the dagger first. We won't know when or where Gilad is going to attack. He doesn't know that you know about the dagger and its power. You have to be prepared for anything, especially now that you know what you are and what the council wants."

"I couldn't agree with you more." I sat up, regrouping from my encounter with Gilad. "I'll feel better once the dagger is in my possession."

"Are you ready?" he asked.

"Yes," I nodded.

"Okay. Look out for various parasitic creatures like Gnomes and Sprites. This world is filled with many different species of magical creatures. Some are good and others are not. Anything is possible in the dimension of The Neatherwood. The Keepers won't give up the dagger without out a fight. They have the power to torture and kill at will, but they're not very intelligent. We can outsmart them. You have the power to control the emotions of others, humans and nonhumans. You can use that power to enter their minds and change their emotion to benefit you."

"I never knew I could do that! I only thought I could feel the emotions of other humans," I said amazed.

"You can feel their emotions but you can change them as well. It's like over-powering their will, influencing their thoughts and feelings. Don't get nervous. You've done it before but you just didn't realize you were doing it. Don't you remember times when people around you have disagreed with you, or been in a foul mood, and without any warning they changed their mind suddenly?" Angelo's eyes twinkled. I slowly nodded, remembering those incidents.

"I think it's amazing that you know everything about me. I do remember." I played with my hair for a few seconds. "Can I ask you another question?" A modest expression swept across my face.

"Sure. I promised to tell you everything. You have a right to know your past."

"Since I am a nephilim, which one of my parents was human and…" I cut my sentence short. Angelo looked at me intensely, shifting his weight to his side to face me better. His eyes were stunningly beautiful. You could see the sea rushing in them.

"Your mother is an Angel; your father was obviously human."

"I don't understand. If she's an angel then why did she lose her mind and allow herself to be locked up? I know she didn't have an evil bone in her body. How could she be a Fallen One?"

"Your mother was a Guardian Angel of humans at first. She protected your father, but when she learned that an Angel of Destiny was sent on a mission to change his destiny, she grew furious. It was his destiny to die. Pandora did not believe death was his destiny. She spent so much time with him and believed that his destiny was to continue the healing of humans. Your mother fell in love with him and tried to change his fate. She chose to leave her Angelic life and assume a human form to be with him, to better protect him. Your mother was happy, so happy that she and your father married and conceived you. She kept your heritage a secret in order to protect you. After years of hiding, The Circle of Destiny found her; your father's fate—death— was caused by a Dark Angel, who was sent to discover her hiding place. The Circle punished your mother for trying to alter your father's destiny by destroying her sanity." I stormed up with aggravation and anger. I wanted to hit something and hit it hard. I paced back and forth.

"How could this happen? They knew my mother and father were good people and didn't deserve that. *I* didn't deserve that. I'm still paying for what The Circle did. I suffer without my parents every day!" I took a few deep breaths and tried to calm down. "What do the Fallen really want with me? What did they want with my mother?"

"The Council of The Fallen is made up of 12 of the most powerful Fallen Angels in the entire universe. Each member has a special power. They chose your mother to be the 13 member, to complete their circle. Centuries ago Fallen Angels were once worshiped like Gods within many of the Earth's early civilizations. The Fallen exchanged technologies and other useful information with these civilizations so that they could use the planet's resources, but most importantly to harbor humans as slaves. The Fallen glorified the power they had and felt superior."

"This is insane!" I said, interrupting Angelo.

"Their evil intentions and actions continued, but once the Mayans, Egyptians and other ancient civilizations died out, the reign of slavery and domination died out as well. The Circle thought your mother would be the key to regaining the strength and influence they once had. But now that they know about you and your direct connection to your mother, they want you and your power as a nephilim to complete the circle, to give them the strength to execute their plans." I paid close attention as Angelo explained. It all made sense somehow, but it was still hard to swallow.

"Gilad told me that he reports to Kalaston. He also said that he hasn't told them that he found me. Should I believe him?"

"It's possible—who knows when it comes to a Fallen One."

"Tell me how to use the power to influence moods. How can I access it?" I strutted over towards the window. Angelo rolled off of the bed and walked towards me. He placed his hands on my shoulders. I abruptly felt safe and warm as he touched me. He leaned down; his body towered over my frame. Drawing me closer, I closed my eyes and felt his soft lips brush against mine. I deeply wanted him, but a part of me felt weird about kissing Angelo since Gilad and I just broke up. I pulled back slowly enough for Angelo to not feel offended.

"Sydney." He said my name in such a delicate fashion. The heat from his body radiated as he pressed against me. "Just focus on looking through and beyond their eyes, go past their thoughts and center yourself on their emotion or mood. You'll begin to feel what they feel, and then you can alter their feelings by influencing them however you need to. You 'll automatically feel which creatures you can allure." Angelo paused for a second. "It is called the power of allure." He added.

"Ok, I think I'm ready," I said as I took a deep breath.

We repositioned ourselves on my bed, clasped hands, closed our eyes and floated away, traveling through the tunnel of space and time. Our bodies were no longer weighed down by gravity, even though our astral forms appeared to be solid. I could do anything my physical form could have, but also had increased abilities. We traveled past the white fluffy clouds and infinite stars. We entered the atmosphere of several planets along the way, and I saw them like no human had seen them. The magnificence of their beauty was indescribable. We travelled fast, and reached our destination instantaneously. We approached a fast-moving whirlwind of a black hole, and I tightly held onto Angelo's shoulder, making sure I didn't lose my grip.

"How will we know when we've come to the right place?" I looked all around. The brightness of the stars sparkled with greatness. All I could think about was the beauty of the in-between.

"Angels like me who haven't fallen, can feel and sense the power of the dagger. The Fallen cannot sense it. If a Fallen One is stabbed with the dagger it extinguishes their life."

"Do the Fallen know about this kind of dagger?"

"The existence of this dagger and many others are a myth according to the Fallen. No fallen angel has ever died by this dagger. There are several daggers like the Dagger of Doshon. To defeat the Fallen many angelic groups got together to forge special weapons that would have the power to vanquish them. The council of the Fallen is very powerful. They've mated with other creatures including vampires, which has made them almost invincible."

"Vampires?" My voice trembled.

"Shhh, yes Vampires." Angelo whispered "That's why I found it very interesting that you asked me about the existence of Vampires. They're a race of their own but The Council of the Fallen has evolved into something even more dangerous." Angelo spoke with a serious tone.

"How can you be so sure where the dagger is? We have to find it!"

"Just trust me; I can sense the location, and so can you." He spoke into my ear. His warm breath tickled me.

The black hole sucked us in like a vacuum. I had to close my eyes after we entered. Particles of black dust spun around us, and I had no idea what direction we were going. I had no control over my body. Our bodies wavered through the dark portal. After what seemed like a lifetime, we began to slowly descend upon an open area. Scattered trees and grassy lands were beneath our feet but we didn't touch the mossy ground. Gliding over the surface, I stayed close to Angelo.

"I can sense the power of the dagger. Once we get deep enough in this world I will know where it is," Angelo said. Something inside me did not feel secure in my decision in coming here. All I could think about was saving Christine, but after I realized the personal risk, I had second thoughts about it.

"This is a suicide mission, Angelo. Maybe we should turn back," I suggested.

"Doubting yourself isn't going to make this go away. Even if you don't complete your mission to save her, the Council will still seek you out."

"I didn't ask for this."

"What are you talking about?" Angelo said. "Yes you did. You never wanted to be normal. You've always been on the hunt for adventure and purpose. Now that you have it, you don't want it! Your fate and destiny is predesigned. You are what you are and now you must face it." Angelo stared at me sternly. I wanted to ignore what he said but he was right. It was hard to try to hide things from someone who knows you better than you know yourself.

The landscape of this world was quite magnificent. The area we traveled through consisted of many hills and valleys. A small pond nearby shimmered brightly and gave off a light that illuminated the entire territory. I lowered myself down, relieved at the feeling that I was on solid ground. I gazed at the splendor of the sight enjoying, every moment. Angelo insisted that I keep my feet off of the ground, so we continued to hover until we found a more secluded location.

Exhaustion soon settled in and all I wanted to do was rest. The skies darkened as we went through a wooded area filled with hundreds of different species of trees, many of which I had never seen before. The largest trees caught my eye, and I realized they were Sierra redwoods. I had never seen them up close before. The giant trees covered the brightness of the night skies. I could no longer stretch my head up to gaze upon the trees without straining my neck. We stopped so I could get a better look at them.

"Aren't they stunning?" Angelo softly asked me with a smile.

"Yes they are. It's so beautiful here. How do you manage to stay on Earth when there are places like this?"

"Earth is a beauty as well. You make it beautiful. Take my hand." He extended his arm out. I tenderly placed my hand in his, smiling at the compliment. His skin was cool and silky. Butterflies fluttered in my belly as we touched. We ascended up above the redwoods and I was able to see them in all their beauty. Gliding over them, I could not help but compare myself to Lois Lane when Superman flew her to see the cosmos. I smiled at that thought. We strolled above the trees as I looked up at the purple night skies and the silvery twinkling stars. Two moons graced the skies to give off a delicate glow. It was amazing to gaze upon them. We heard the sounds of chatter and witnessed a small blaze. A gathering of creatures stood around a fire. They were almost five feet tall and, wore deep green robes. I noticed that my vision had clarified in such a way that I could see details of their features from far away. They had pale skin and dark brown hair. I saw that they had pointed ears and claw-like hands and feet.

"What are they?" I asked, clinging on to Angelo's arm.

"They're a race of dark elves. They can't be trusted, so let's hope they don't spot us. This is their territory. It should not be a problem since we are just passing through." I nodded and said nothing.

We floated over the immense redwoods as we passed by the dark elves without being noticed. I felt relieved that we were moving away from the mysterious creatures. We settled in an area concealed by the forest. It felt nice to plant my feet on the ground. My body started to give and weaken. I panted, trying to catch my breath; my greatest desire at that moment was to lie in my bed under the covers.

"Angelo," I called as I stopped and stood still for a moment.

"What's wrong?" he replied.

"I'm not feeling well. I need food and rest."

"My apologies," he sincerely said. He held out his right hand and blinked twice and, a small bowl of fruit emerged from the glow of his palm. I smiled at the wondrous sight, and took a seat on a nearby tree stump. Angelo handed me the fruit. I hesitated for a spilt second and looked at him for approval.

"Only fruit from the Great Tree is worthy enough for you, my dear." Showing his white teeth as he smiled, I felt a longing for him. My eyes widened. The fruit gave off a tiny glow. I picked up a vine of neon purple grapes and stuffed several in my mouth. The sweetness of the tender fruit and the moist nectar spewed out, dripping down my chin. The taste was out-of-this-world delicious. I devoured the whole bowl within a few minutes, wanting more. A pitcher and two crystal goblets appeared out of thin air. The pitcher magically poured some liquid into the goblets, filling them to the rim. Angelo inclined his head as he gave me the signal to take a goblet. As I reached for it, the silver liquid sparkled in an enchanting way. He sipped his, and I followed suit, lifting the goblet to my lips and allowing the substance to glide down my throat smoothly. The honeyed relish of the beverage warmed my mouth and coursed through my body.

"What is this?" I asked, staring at Angelo intently, still enjoying the after-taste.

"It is water from the Silver Spring," he replied.

I couldn't take my eyes off of the angel. There was something about him that was extremely sexy. I wanted him. I saw my childhood friend so differently. To take my mind of my lustful thoughts, I reached into my pocket to pull out my cell phone. The second I pushed the display button to reveal the time, the phone disintegrated in the air, leaving a trail of black dust particles behind.

"What just happened?" I asked with my mouth open and hand clutched like the phone was still in it. Angelo stopped drinking and quickly looked up at me.

"What were you doing anyway? Who did you think you were going to call?"

"No one, I only wanted to see what time it was?" My voice sounded so innocent.

"This place has its own time. It works differently here. Each dimension has an individual time frame or zone. It's not like I expect you to understand the way dimension time works yet. You will once you get used to being in this form. Technology such as phones and computers don't exist on this plane."

"Then how do creatures communicate in these other realms?"

"Face-to- face meetings, telepathically and magically. You must remember to block your mind to keep others from invading it, especially if you have information you want to conceal. Remember, you're half human. Don't let anyone in or they'll know everything you're thinking. Keep your emotions at bay. You don't want Gilad or anyone else breaching your mental security." As I listened to Angelo, I rubbed my eyes, forcing them to stay open. Angelo noticed that I was too tired to go on and said, "We'll camp here tonight." Out of the ground came a tent and in front of the tent surfaced a roaring fire. I stood up, stepped closer to the flames and rubbed my hands together. I had to admit I was enjoying every moment of this. After warming my hands I went inside, and surveyed the cozy tent. Two sleeping bags and a small table with a lantern were nestled deep in the shelter. I crawled inside the thick sleeping bag and snuggled in its comfort.

Chapter Eight

Getting to sleep was difficult. I kept thinking about Christine and my mom, then I started thinking about Gilad and what he did to me. I couldn't describe the hurt and pain. Just when I thought that my feelings for him were real, they were only an illusion. Tears streamed down my face. I quickly wiped my eyes when I heard the rustle of Angelo stepping inside the tent. I sighed deeply and pondered over how I was going to kill Gilad.

 I don't like being forced into doing things. All my life, my mother did everything to protect me from being forced into a lifestyle she knew I wouldn't want. She tried to save my father, but the Fallen went after them and caused his death. As I got lost in my thoughts, I felt a brush of cool air disrupt my warmth as Angelo swiftly slid inside my sleeping bag. He threw his head back to get his untamed hair out of his face. He grabbed me from behind and wrapped his strong arms around me.

"I understand what you're going through. You don't have to feel like you're alone. Sydney you have never been alone." He held me tighter and I felt his breath escape from his lips.

"I don't know what to think anymore. What am I supposed to do? I don't believe that I can run away from this," I said.

"Running isn't going to help. I'll keep you away from them for as long and as far as my powers will allow me. The dagger is the first thing we must retrieve. With that you'll have the power to extinguish any Fallen that poses a threat to you. Get some rest; we have a big day tomorrow." He kissed the nape of my neck and I felt a surge of heat vibrate through my body. Angelo waved his hand and the top of the tent became transparent. We huddled up together and observed the stars and the two moons in their magnificence. The skies were filled with activities. Meteor showers exploded within the distance, giving off a major Fourth of July effect.

"This is unbelievable," I uttered softly.

"You are gorgeous," Angelo whispered, speaking into my ear. I slightly turned to meet his handsome, chiseled face. He swiped my long bangs out of my eyes and traced the outline of my countenance with his finger. Angelo's lips touched mine. I did not object to the gesture. Moments later he slipped his moist tongue inside of my mouth. Our tongues massaged around sensually as we kissed deeply. His hands wandered up and down my legs. I felt his excitement when he pressed his hard body against mine. We peeled off our clothes tossing them all over the tent. He cupped my breasts in his hands, as I stroked him. Heartbeats increased and our breathing was in sync. I closed my eyes took a deep breath and, wrapped my legs securely around his body.

"Are you all right?" he asked, listening to my erratic breathing. I nodded my head in response and braced myself. He entered me gently. Feeling so close and connected to him, our thrusts intensified. The erotic encounter lasted for some time and ended on a very pleasurable note.

[74]

I had to be honest with myself, and admit that I did absolutely, positively, definitely and ultimately had fallen in love with Angelo. I realized that I had always loved him. He brought me a happiness that no other could, and that was something I knew I very much desired and deserved. I had no trouble falling asleep in his arms.

The brightness of the morning light peered through the roof of the tent, waking me up. I turned over in the sleeping bag to find that Angelo was no longer next to me. I grabbed my clothes and dressed quickly. I really needed a shower. I peeked outside and saw Angelo suspended in the air. His white wings appeared silver as they shined against the light of the sun. His bare chest glistened with moisture. Angelo appeared to be in a trance of some kind. As I stood there, I thought about what I was going to say, and how was I going act around him, now that we had slept together? Angelo told me before that he loved me and always had. We had kissed a couple times when we were little. He even took me to Prom our senior year, when my boyfriend at the time bailed out on me at the last minute. I knew I loved him, but after years of being friends, how could we suddenly deal with becoming lovers? I just don't want to ruin what we already had. After waiting and watching him for about 20 minutes, I couldn't wait any longer.

"Angelo," I called to him softly so no one else could hear me. We still had no idea what could be lurking in the deep woods. The second he heard my voice he opened his eyes and descended back to the surface.

"Hey. How did you sleep?" he asked, retracting his wings.

"It was the best sleep I've had in months," I said with a smile. "I wish there was somewhere I could take a shower."

"There is a waterfall that leads to a lake not far from here. You can freshen up there."

"Great! What are we waiting for?" I ran to the tent, slipped on my sneakers and came back out. Angelo threw on his shirt and the boots he had worn last night. With one snap of his fingers the camp he had conjured disappeared. I found it extremely sexy that he openly used his powers in my presence. The unstable ground had become stable on our travels to the waterfall. I followed him as he moved swiftly through the woods. We eventually heard the crashing sound of the waters. Angelo and I came to a clearing, and saw the waters flowing freely from a crack within the grassy mountains. Streaming with ferocity the waters shined gold and silver. The pool appeared inviting and the atmosphere was indeed magical.

"May I?" I asked in a demure manner.

"This water is just as pure as the waters from the Silver Spring," Angelo told me. "They have healing properties. Jump in! I'll be there in a second." he said excitedly. I examined the area quickly to see if anyone was watching nearby. The coast was clear, so I pulled off my clothes, feeling a little shy for Angelo to see me nude in the daylight. He observed my body intently. I jumped in the cool water before he could say anything. The water felt so soft against my skin. I laughed at how much fun I was having. I waded around, splashing and enjoying the peaceful serene atmosphere.

[75]

I watched Angelo as he threw off his clothes. He rose above the ground, stretched out his silky wings and dived forcefully into the water. He shook the water out of his hair as he rose to the surface. I wiggled my toes feeling the water sway between them. We waded together towards the falls. I closed my eyes, standing under the flow, allowing my hair to soak up the purity of water. Angelo poked me when he approached me from behind. He started to touch my shoulders, I rolled my neck back, and he kissed it once again. His hands moved to my shoulders and then to my breasts. He held them each with his hands lightly twisting my nipples. The steaminess of the situation intensified as he then began to caress my upper thighs. I let out an erotic sigh and turned to kiss him. We kissed passionately, and in a moments time he shifted his left leg and slipped himself into me. We climaxed at the same time, which calmed me and made me feel more connected to him. For a moment I almost forgot about all of my troubles and my reasons for being here in this magical dimension. The sounds of birds chirping resonated in the expanse, and we soon got out of the water.

Angelo's jeans and boots had vanished and had conjured his angelic garb. He was draped in a long white robe and covered his head with a thick hood. After we both got dressed, we returned on the path of our travels again. We sifted through thick dark green bushes and tall, burly trees. The orange and red leaves hung from the branches in a tired, lazy fashion. The southern breeze picked up a bit, and the branches swayed back and forth. My hair was still damp and the coolness of the air made me a little chilly. I walked with my arms crossed against my chest to secure some body heat. He must have seen me lightly shivering; he stopped and looked at me.

"Sydney? Are you cold?" he asked. I nodded in response to his question. "Oh I see it takes you some time to dry and warm up." He grinned and blew his warm breath on me. It felt like a warm summer breeze. My damp hair and clothes were dry within an instant. A white cloak manifested around my shoulders, and I was warm and cozy. I thanked him with a kiss, and we started walking again.

A part of me wanted to talk about this new thing between us. I knew we only made love, but I needed to know what this was. Before I officially started asking questions, however, I wanted to see how things worked out in the Earthly Realm first. I decided to keep my mouth shut about it. Angelo reached for my hand, and I read on his face that something was wrong. He kept looking at something in the distance behind us. I narrowed my eyes but couldn't see anything. I was afraid that whatever or whomever Angelo saw had been following us from afar.

Before I could part my lips to ask Angelo if everything was all right, I suddenly felt the sensation of pain pierce the right side of my back. I quickly reached my arm around and touched the area, trembling as I felt some kind of arrow stuck in me. The arrow must have had some kind of poison on it, and I could feel it coursing through my veins. My heart throbbed and my body ached. I lost control of my limbs and grew weaker with every moment. Angelo caught me in his arms as he collapsed down with me. Silent tears rolled down my cheeks. I gasped for air.

"Someone followed us. I have to go. They'll come for you. Don't say anything. You won't be able to see me, but I'll be by your side, so don't worry, I'll get you out of this and heal you." He spoke so quickly that I couldn't get a word in. I didn't want him to leave. We had no idea who was after me; it could be the Council for all I knew. I coughed, trying to get some words out but couldn't muster the strength.

"No," I said in the lowest tone possible. Angelo had disappeared.

"*I told you. I am here,*" Angelo's voice whispered in my ear. I gasped for air and tried to turn my head to see if I could spot him. I struggled to fight the force that was taking me over. My body shook uncontrollably and then the poisonous toxin coursing throughout my veins took over me.

Waking up from a deep, agonizing slumber, I opened my eyes and found that my surroundings were not so enchanting anymore. My legs and hands were bound with what felt like bones and flesh, but it was too dark to tell. The moisture of the dangling material made me queasy. My body was fixed in a fetal position and pressed against the cold damp concrete. The sound of my breathing hummed and ricocheted all over the hollow environment. The ground was wet and muddy and the rank odors of feces and urine assaulted my nose. I heaved a bit to get some kind of relief, but it didn't help much.

A ferocious growl startled me. Moving my body, I wiggled against the stone wall and tried to stay quiet. I had no clue what kind of creature was near me. The events of what happened sprang on me and suddenly I had a vision of a small creature looming towards me holding a sword. Afraid of what I had seen, I tried to prepare for the worst.

The pain from the arrow still stung my back, but I was afraid to touch the injury. I silently called for Angelo and began to sob. My clothes were torn and filthy. I felt like I had been dragged or run over by a car. I knew that panicking wouldn't improve my situation, but it was an appropriate reaction at this point. I had to think of a way to get out of here without being noticed. The first thing I had to do was to free my hands and legs. I ran over a few ideas and came up with nothing plausible.

"Angelo, Angelo… Please help me," I whispered aloud. Within a few minutes I heard the scuffing of footsteps walking in the direction of the dank cell. I positioned my body in a way that I could at least defend myself with the bones that bound my hands. The iron door was tall and had three bars positioned vertically. A small trail of light reflected through the bars. I stared at the door, waiting for the creature to enter.

The door made an awful screeching sound as it opened, which told me it was extremely heavy. In came a short creature with dark, wide-set eyes, discolored aged spots on his forehead, sharp claw-like hands and feet and pointed ears that protruded from his small oval shaped head. His stringy blond hair looked nasty, and I curled up my top lip when he came across my sight. I noticed that his skin was pale and appeared leathery in texture. I recognized the creature as being one of the dark elves Angelo had warned me about. Angelo hadn't given me any real information about these creatures except to stay away from them. Since that was no longer an option, I had to come up with a good idea that would get me out of here. I took a deep breath and looked directly at him. His dark green eyes gave off a florescent glow that read death. They looked like two flashlights shining through the darkness.

[77]

"Who are you, girl?" the elf asked in a flimsy but frightening voice. Ignoring his question I decided to ask a couple of my own.

"Where am I? Why am I here?" I asked trying to use a forceful tone.

"You first," he replied. I pondered for a moment over whether to give him my real name. What if the Council had hired these elves to capture me? I sat there quietly for a second.

"My name is Sydney."

"What a lovely name," he said gazing into my eyes. You are in the Realm of the Neatherwood. You and your companion were trespassing on our lands. He vanished before we could contain him. It is forbidden for a creature like you to be within our boundaries. The punishment for your violation is death. You smell like a human but there is something else to you that I cannot quite place." I gulped hard and didn't say anything. "My people and I are called the Elves of Nebulous. I am their principal general, Sable. We live here with the wolves. They do our bidding and do not protest or go against our wishes." The dark element of his voice made me cringe. I needed to find Angelo and fast. I couldn't believe that Sable was willing to give me all this information so easily.

"We didn't know we were trespassing. If we did we wouldn't have done it." I sounded sincere and apologetic.

"It is a rule that I cannot change," he said as he looked at my gravely. What are you doing here on this plane?" he wondered, looking for an answer. I turned away from the elf regretting having spoken to him. After a moment, I turned back and, gazed into his stare intently. I felt my eyes change and something in me felt the sensation of loyalty and determination within the creature. I penetrated his feelings, knowing that he wanted to impress his leader by following through with her instructions. I pushed his emotions aside and created a new one, the feeling of being released; freedom. The glow in his eyes softened and his face grew tender and calm.

"Listen to me carefully; I need you to help me," I said. "I am on a mission to save someone I love. I'm running out of time, so please release me." My voice vibrated with magnificent divinity, something that hadn't surfaced within me before. The elf looked as though he was in a trance. He smiled at me and placed his sword in a corner. "Can you please tell me what keeps growling over there in the dark?"

"Do not be fearful. It is Harbor, one of our were guards. He is locked up, and will not harm you." He pulled out a ring of old keys, bent down and unlocked the bone shackles that bound my hands and feet. I let out a sigh and tried to touch the open wound in my back.

"Thank you," I said, feeling my wrists. "I'm very weak. Is there any water from the Silver Spring that I can drink?"

"Yes, there is. I will return with the water you need."

"Remember to come alone; don't let anyone see you bring me the water."

"As you wish," he said in a tender tone. The elf turned around and was about to step out when I called him back for him to retrieve his sword. He grabbed the weapon in a dazed manner and strolled out. I wobbled and made an effort to stand up.

"Angelo, get your ass here NOW! I am in TROUBLE!" I raised my voice, but not loud enough to be a shout. My tone apparently worked, because Angelo popped up looking dazed and confused.

"Where have you been? I've been trying to track you for hours?" he said, throwing his hands up.

"A group of elves captured me. They were looking for you also. The general told me that we broke some trespassing law and the punishment for trespassing is Death! We have to get out of here," I said nervously. "I used my power to change his mood and to influence him to free me. He went to get me some water. I'm hurt, Angelo." I turned to show him the wound, lifting up my shirt as much as I could. The area throbbed with pain.

"The wound is deep. Just relax, this will sting a little." I felt the softness of Angelo's touch, and peered over my shoulder and saw a bright white glow fill the wounded area. My skin tingled and a cool sensation stunned me. The wound closed and my body was healed. Strength returned to me.

"Thanks," I said, throwing myself into his arms. He looked down at me and kissed me.

"We have to get out of here before Sable gets back," I said.

"I want to see the elf. I want to see how well your power of allure is."

"Is that what it's called?"

"Yes. I've mentioned that before. I'll stand in the shadows and wait for him."

"No, you can't he might smell you."

"He won't be able to," Angelo reassured me. Before he could finish his sentence, I cut him off.

"Don't say too much! There are wolves being held here, and they can hear us," I warned. Angelo nodded, but from his lack of surprise I knew he had already sensed the wolves' presence.

I really didn't think it was that important for him to see the effects of my power. The stench of the cell was becoming unbearable, and I wanted to high-tail it out of there. Angelo understood how I felt even though I said nothing. He took my hand, and poof! We were gone.

Once we were out of the cell I noticed that my body had vanished. I still felt present, but when I held my hand up to my face I saw nothing.

"What happened?"

"We're invisible—I cast a charm over you. It's our best shot of getting out of here without being noticed. Stay close to me. The elves must not find out who we are. They can't know that a nephilim was spotted in this dimension."

Sable knew my name. Maybe I shouldn't have been so quick to leave the cell without Angelo seeing the elf and convincing him that he had never seen me. I hoped my mistake wouldn't catch up to me.

We coasted toward the outskirts of the land. In the distance I heard the angry growls of several wolves. As we exited the dark territory, the brightness of the sun nearly blinded me. Moments later we glided back into another dark area. The trees were gigantic and the forest grew so deep that the sun-light couldn't penetrate it. It appeared as if night had fallen early. We arrived at the entrance to a large rocky cave. Coming to a stop, Angelo's arm felt warmer than usual.

"Are you okay?" I asked him with a concerned tone.

"Yes," he answered, in a shaky voice.

The outside of the cave glistened with what appeared to be crystals. I wasn't sure what I was seeing.

"The Dagger of Doshon is deep within this place. I know that the Keepers of the Deep are near, but I don't know what else might be down there," Angelo softly murmured. I suddenly felt a gravitational pull from the cave.

We carefully climbed up into the cave's entrance. Loose rocks and pebbles descended down the face of the rock as we climbed. I was not intimidated by heights—all of my experiences with rock and mountain climbing came in handy.

We eventually made it inside the dark cave. A swarm of bats flew out as we stumbled in. I had to admit that I was afraid of the unknown, even though Angelo was here with me. We maneuvered our way through the unstable terrain. Centuries-old boulders with sharp edges floated everywhere. We avoided the edges with caution, leaping from one boulder to the next. One by one we took turns. The solid sarsen trembled as our feet landed on the surface. I was good at keeping my balance. At the end of the boulder trail Angelo and I came to a huge door made out of smooth limestone. I thought it was strange that the door was not guarded.

"Angelo!"

"Shhh," he replied back.

"Don't speak aloud. No one must know we are here." His voice throbbed in my brain.

"Okay. Sorry." I replied telepathically.

We were able to pass directly through the door without even opening it. Tall thin creatures dressed in dark robes stood against the stone walls. They wore brown sandals and appeared to be monks of some kind. Clearly not human, they all held large spears in their hands. Small glass lanterns were mounted alongside the walls. Three steps lead up to an altar, where a small golden box rested on a large granite table.

I could sense that the box contained the dagger. *"This seems way too easy,"* I warned Angelo telepathically. *"I know,"* he replied. *"How are we going to get past all these guards?"* I asked. *"I'm going to call for it."*

I told him that I could use my power of allure to influence the mood of the Keepers so they wouldn't object to our retrieval of the dagger and he nodded. Still invisible I made my way around to each and every one of the Monks, staring into their strange gaze. The looks on their faces softened. I then stood in the middle of the altar, focusing my power and energy on all of them. Angelo closed his eyes and called for the dagger to appear before him. The box opened, and the Dagger emerged out of the golden box and floated to Angelo. It stopped in midair and I became entranced by its beauty.

Without breaking my concentration, I walked over to the dagger and gazed upon it. The Dagger of Doshon was stunning. Holding out both hands, I called for the dagger and it drifted into my palms. The hilt was made of wood and metal that was shaped in the form of a thick tree branch. Out of the branch emerged the outline of a fully bloomed rose. The blade was molded out of pure silver and gently sparkled against the dim lanterns in the cave. Remnants of stardust encased the dagger and made the weapon even more magical. I had never seen a weapon of this kind before. Seconds later, the dagger disappeared in my grasp. I looked at Angelo with great alarm.

"It's fine. The dagger is with you," he said telepathically. I smiled at his reply.

The keepers of the dagger didn't suspect a thing. I mesmerized them, keeping them from realizing that anything had change. Still in our invisible forms, we slowly made our way out of the cave, and focused on returning to the Earthly Realm. I took a deep sigh as I soon realized that we were back in my bedroom, safe in my home.

I looked over at Angelo, and gaped at him. I laughed for a moment, thinking about everything I had just experienced. I felt something tightly bound to my leg. I sat up lifting the hem of my pants and saw The Dagger of Doshon resting peacefully, strapped to my ankle.

I lowered my pant leg to cover the dagger, and realized that my clothes were indeed torn and dirty and my hair was a total mess. I couldn't believe how awful I looked when I glanced at my reflection in the mirror. Angelo stilled looked beautiful. We rolled off of the bed, and I unlocked my bedroom door, and stepped out into the hall. I did a quick assessment of the upstairs area to check for disturbances and, then went straight to my bathroom to take a shower.

I was afraid that Gilad would return so I took the fastest shower on record. As I dried off I kept my eyes fixed on the dagger as it rested on the bathroom counter next to my hair dryer. I threw on a pair of blue jeans and a black t-shirt and slipped on some socks. From the bathroom I could hear Angelo turn on my bedroom television, he was getting comfortable. I thought about our time together and those passionate moments. I couldn't even remember my feelings for

Gilad because they really didn't mean anything. I thought he had probably placed me under some type of Angelic spell, and I never want to see him again. If he crossed my path and tried to hurt me, I would be ready for him.

It was almost five o' clock, but the time difference between worlds took a toll on me. Almost 24 hours had gone by in the Neatherwood. I still had so many questions for Angelo, but I knew it was time for me to start discovering my supernatural identity on my own.

Chapter Nine

Being home was nice, but despite the extreme dangers of the Neatherwood I wanted to return to the magical realm. The word in town was that Christine's autopsy was pending because of reasons unknown. Since my cell phone had been destroyed, I ordered a new phone and had to readjust to using the landline for all my calls. I rustled up a couple of turkey and cheese sandwiches and made some sweet tea, a recipe my mother gave me. Angelo and I sat in the kitchen stuffing our faces.

"Is extreme hunger a side effect of traveling to other worlds?" I asked, chomping on my sandwich.

"Yes, but that's only because of your human side. I just felt like eating with you," Angelo said with a grin. "The more you use your angelic gifts, the more your body will adjust to your new life."

"What are we going to do about Gilad?"

"Nothing, we have to wait for him to make the next move." He took a sip of tea. I finished my sandwich, downed the tea and refilled my glass. I sat back in the wooden chair and started to play with my hair. Since I hadn't bothered to take a flat iron to it after my shower, my hair had turned back into its natural curly form. I realized that it had been a while since I'd seen my stylist.

"I need you by my side in every way Angelo," I said as I thought about our current problem. "I can't battle Gilad alone."

"I'll be here for you. But you really underestimate yourself—you have a great power. That's what the Council wants from you. I was quite impressed when you used your power of allure on the elf and the Keepers in the Neatherwood." I smiled as I looked down at the rose-printed table cloth. It was nice to hear that kind of compliment.

"I will always be by your side," he said in a soft romantic tone. I fluttered my eyes at him, giving off a coy attitude.

"I wonder when Gilad is going to try to come back here. Maybe he tried to call me?"

"Who cares? Why do you worry about him so much? How can you care about me, then have those hang-ups about him? That is one thing about you that I don't understand. His magic must have been stronger than I thought."

"Let's not get into this. I am *not* hung up on him. I have to protect myself against him and I have to be prepared. This whole thing scares the shit out me. I don't want him to think that I'm in this house alone and defenseless. I think I should tell him about you."

"Would you tell him, knowing you'd blow my cover?"

"I want to let him know that I'm protected and that he can't just waltz in here and do what he wants." I let out a deep sigh of frustration.

"If we spring this on him to tell him that I am your Guardian, your Protector, he could go back to the Council and report that information. They'll try to capture you and force you to take your mother's place as a member." The intensity in his voice made me distressed.

"I didn't realize that the Council could do that."

"Is there a way I can get out of this? Hide like my mother did?"

"No. You're not going to make the same mistake your mother did. You're going to face this with me and conquer this."

Before I could respond, the doorbell rang and someone pounded on the door. My heart stopped briefly feeling it was Gilad at the door. The relationship we had was over, and I was furious over the fact that he had something to do with Christine's murder. I turned to Angelo as a question occurred to me.

"Is there a possibility that Gilad is an angel vamp?"

"No it's not," Angelo replied. "I would have sensed it on him, besides he walks in daylight."

"Then whoever killed Christine had to be a Council member."

"Not necessarily," he replied. I got up from the table and moved into the living area with Angelo trailing behind.

The moment I touched the door knob, a sudden flash entered my brain. I saw the image of myself lying on a blanket, asleep in a large wooded area. The shape of a dark hooded figure stood over me with his hand extended over my body. I suspected that he was Christine's killer. A dark shadowy vapor swarming with flies came out from the creature's mouth and flew into mine. My body shook for a second and my eyes rolled back, turning white. Angelo interrupted the vision by shaking me profusely. I stumbled back from the door and I blinked twice to get myself together.

"You had another vision? It looks like this one had a strong kick to it. You blanked out."

"I can't let him in," I said with fear.

"He is right there. You have no choice. I am not going to leave."

"I wish that people would stop telling me that I don't have a choice—I do. It is my house, I don't want him here," I whispered.

"Open the door; I won't leave until you give me a chance to explain," Gilad yelled from outside. His voice was deep and direct.

"No! I don't want to see you!" I yelled in return.

"Please. I never meant for any of this to happen. I'm sorry, and I do love you. They made me do it." I wanted to see his spineless face so I could slap it. I let out a deep, frustrated sigh and opened the door. He was more casually dressed than before, in khakis with a white shirt underneath a brown leather jacket. His hair was slicked back smoothly. I rolled my eyes at him, placing my hand on my hip.

"Stay there. Don't come any closer. You really have some fucking nerve coming here," I spat. "You never felt anything for me and I never felt anything for you. I was under the power of your allure. It wasn't real. I know everything now." My voice was stern. My goal was to make it clear to Gilad that I wanted nothing more to do with him.

"Please give me a chance to explain," he said. Just then, Angelo emerged from the shadows to let his presence be known.

"What is *he* doing here?" Gilad snapped.

"I belong here," Angelo snapped in return.

"That is none of your business, Gilad," I retorted. "Nothing I do is any of your business anymore. What you did was unforgivable."

"I thought that one of the most beautiful aspects about humanity was your ability to love and forgive." Gilad seemed to think that his words would make me flinch.

"You really are clueless. You have no idea what it is like to be human."

The coldness of the evening air blew into my warm home. I didn't want to invite Gilad in. I wanted this visit to be over quickly.

"I want to explain myself." His eyes had turned dark and were filled with despair.

"You think that I can just forget this? I'm so mad at myself for falling for your crap. Now leave! Despite what you might think I'm a lot stronger than I look. I don't need you. I have the power to do what I need to do." Reaching for a heavy knit sweater on the coat rack, I threw it over my shoulders and slipped my arms into it. My body immediately responded to the warmth.

"This is a private matter between us," Gilad said, eyeing Angelo with resentment. "I still don't see why he's here. What does he have to do with us?" Gilad asked suspiciously.

"I have everything to do with you," Angelo said, standing with his legs apart and arms folded across his chest.

I put on a fake smile, stepped aside and told Gilad to come in. He took one step towards the open door and clutched his stomach. I shifted my eyes to Angelo and moved away from the entrance of my home. Gilad felt the power of the dagger. It was indeed harmful to him.

[85]

"What's wrong?" I asked in a condescending tone. "This is Angelo, my guardian, and my protector."

Gilad backed away. Still holding his abdomen, his face was unreadable, but I knew what he was thinking.

"I love you! How can you trust him and not me?" He was doubled over in pain. I thought it was one of the dumbest questions I'd ever heard.

"I can trust him because the love *we* have is real! You lied to me about everything, I don't love you. I never did. And I don't want you." I inhaled with force. Looking at Gilad made me sick to my stomach. Speechless, Gilad turned, backed up and slowly strolled down the snowy path. I watched him vanish into the night. I was pleased over his departure. I slammed the front door shut and doubled-bolted the locks.

The house felt instantly relaxed. I went to the kitchen to get something to drink, feeling calmer already. I thought about the vision I had before I let Gilad in, and it really made me worry. Angelo appeared by the kitchen door.

"Do you think he knew that I had the dagger on me?" I asked, pouring some cold milk into a small pot. While it was heating up, I reached for a mug and retrieved a packet of cocoa.

"No. I think he believes that a part of him is becoming human. Sometimes fallen angels will live in the human world so long that they feel like they're slowly obtaining human emotions and characteristics. Once an angel has fell their hearts turn black, and they lose their ability to love and feel. He thought he was feeling pain from hurting you. Maybe he did feel something for you at one time, but you'll never know if it was legitimate or not."

"Well, I would rather him believe he loves me than to realize that I'm planning to kill him." The milk was perfect. I poured the boiling contents into the mug and stirred for a second. I put three teaspoons of sugar in it and gently sipped to see if it was the way I liked it. "The vision I had before I let Gilad in was terrifying. I saw some kind of hooded creature release a black energy into me. Whatever it was, I think it killed me." My hand trembled; I held the mug with both hands as we walked into the living room together.

"You didn't see yourself die: That was the Darkness entering you," Angelo informed me.

I settled on the sofa, carefully trying not to spill my cocoa. I looked at him, deeply disturbed.

"Who was that creature?"

"I'm not really sure. There are several entities that are bringers of Darkness. The Council may have sent a group of dark bounty hunters out to search for you. Once they find you and unleash the darkness into you, it will be easier for you to join the Council of the Fallen."

"Let's get Christine now. I'll deal with this shit later." I placed the mug on the coffee table. Angelo didn't object.

[86]

We sat next to each other and readied ourselves for travel. My body was still drained from our last trip to get the dagger, but I had to ignore what I was feeling. Angelo placed his hand into mine and we closed our eyes. My head started to bother me a little and all I could think about was a getting my medicine and drinking a nice cold glass of water with large ice cubes in it. A warm and fuzzy feeling came over me, and when I opened my eyes seconds later my medicine pouch and a glass of water with ice cubes were floating directly in front of me. My eyes grew with astonishment.

"Angelo look!" I said with amazement. Angelo opened his eyes and scooted a little closer to me. I fixed my eyes on the two objects suspended in the air. I continued to concentrate. They moved closer to me and I reached my hands out and grabbed them. I took my medicine, sipped some water and, placed the pouch on the sofa and the glass on the table. I tried to find the words to describe my amazement. Perplexed over what had just happened, I scratched my head in awe and smiled from ear to ear.

"Telekinetic?" I said, softly questioning Angelo. He nodded and cracked a smile.

"Your powers are returning to you at a rapid rate." I jumped up with excitement and ran over to the fireplace. I stared at the photograph of my parents, focusing intently as the pressure in my head increased and my hands became warm and numb. The picture lifted off the mantle and hovered in the air in front of me as, I kept my focus. Moving my eyes slowly, the photo followed the movement along with my eyes. I moved my eyes and head over in the direction of the end table and the photo followed, landing gently near the lamp. I clapped with enthusiasm.

"Why is all of this happening now?" I asked Angelo, watching him watch me.

"I told you. It's who you are. Being part angel is in your blood. It's happening now because you finally are aware and have accepted who you are." The deepness of his voice rumbled and his face glistened a bit. I smiled at him, thinking about how much I wanted to put a brush to his head to tame his wild hair.

"I hope we don't run into any kind of trouble while saving Christine." I marched over to the sofa and plopped down.

"Try not to worry." Angelo replied as he slowly leaned in and kissed me. My heart melted as he placed his arms around me. We soon went upstairs to get comfortable.

Dressed in floral pajamas that my grandmother gave me, I snuggled under the covers. Even though I had taken my medication a little over an hour ago, it wasn't working. My head pounded and I felt weak. I didn't feel up to the long journey ahead. I wanted to push on but my body just refused to. Angelo sat up in bed wearing only his boxers. I lay my head in his lap as he gently stroked my silky hair.

"How do you really think Gilad took the breakup?" I asked in a flimsy tone.

"There's no telling with him. It is hard if not impossible to read the intentions of the Fallen. They only have one agenda, which always includes them coming out on top." I listened to the sound of his smooth voice as I drifted off to sleep.

The resonance of rain pounding on the window pane woke me up the next morning. I still felt a little weak but not as bad as the night before. I glanced over to see that Angelo was not in bed with me. He was making a habit of sneaking out before I woke up. Realizing that time was not on my side when it came to saving my friend, I scurried out of bed franticly. The rain was pelting down, but I was happy that the snow was almost gone. The roads would still be pretty slick but Milford did a great job by making the streets safe for its residents. Observing my reflection in the bathroom, I noticed my appearance was slightly altered. My eyes had turned into a deep sea blue, and lightly glowed in the dim bathroom. I felt myself changing in a subtle manner. I admired the changes, studying my high cheek bones and broad dark eye brows. Proud of the improvements in my looks, I brushed my teeth and washed my face. The smell of bacon wandered upstairs as I opened my bedroom door and peeked down the hall. I looked at the phone that rested on my night table. There were a couple of messages. Luna had called saying that it was urgent and for me to meet her as soon as I could. The manager at Loving Hills Mental Rehabilitation Center also called. He said that my mother's condition had gotten worse and he needed me to come in.

I abruptly became afraid for her. I didn't have time to meet with Luna but I made a mental note to invite her over for tea so we could talk. I got ready in a flash. After I showered I put on a black sweat suit and suede boots. Leaving my hair curly, I slapped on some makeup and strutted down stairs. Angelo was in the kitchen making breakfast. The table was set and a nice cup of hot cocoa was waiting for me.

"Good morning." I said flatly, giving Angelo a kiss on the lips.

"Hey, what's wrong?" He felt that I was hurting.

"I'm ok. That is so sweet of you to make breakfast," I said, looking at him standing in his boxers. "I got a call from Loving Hills. The manager said that I have to come in. My mom is getting worse. What do you suppose happened?"

"I don't know," he said. "Eat first and then we'll go see her." He placed a plate of bacon, eggs and cheese grits in front of me. I gawked at the steam that emerged from the food. It smelled wonderful.

"The cheese grits are definitely a surprise." I said with a bright smile. When I was a little girl my mom used to make cheese grits all the time. I spooned a little bit of butter, over the grits and dashed some salt on top of them. Stirring them carefully, the creamy grits were perfect for a cold winter's morning. The bacon was nice and crispy, with a hint of maple flavor and the eggs were light and fluffy, just the way I liked them. The meal did put me in a better mood but I was still concerned about my mother. Having Angelo around made me feel like I was not alone. We ate our breakfast and talked about my mom and Christine. Today was the day, we decided. I couldn't wait any longer. If I didn't make it today, it was possible that I could blow my chance to save Christine.

The morning news kept me company while Angelo got ready. I casually sipped on a cup of cocoa and wondered what was going on with my mom. Within 20 minutes Angelo waltzed down the steps wearing a long sleeved white button down shirt and dark jeans. His hair was tamed and freshly washed. Angelo's shirt couldn't hide his attractive physic. I imagined him without it. I placed my mug on the table and turned off the television, we grabbed our coats and left to go see my mother.

The iron gates of the Loving Hills Mental Rehabilitation Center opened as we approached in Angelo's SUV. We found a pretty decent parking spot, but I still had to put up my umbrella so I wouldn't get wet. I felt a little weird about seeing my mom this time. This would be our first meeting since I found out my mother's true identity and the secrets that she tried to keep in order to protect me. I signed in and asked to speak to Dr. Cantori. The security guard led us to an office on the seventh floor. We were greeted by a blond husky man wearing glasses. He shook my hand and then shook Angelo's, offered us a seat then took his own behind his large polished wooden desk. His white coat was so fresh that it almost shone. I could tell he loved using bleach. I observed the décor in his office and did my best to prepare for what the doctor had to say.

"Miss London, how have you been?" He looked up at the ceiling for a second.

"I am ok; a little worried about my mom. What's going on?"

"Well..." he sighed, sounding like he was a bit frustrated. "I called because there are some new developments with your mother's condition." The doctor's eyes were glassy and weak-looking. He may have done a double shift and was working on borrowed time. I thought about my dad and how he would push himself to the limit when he used to work in the E.R.

"Is my mom ok?"

"Your mom is fine *now*. We had to sedate her. I apologize, but your mom has become extremely violent over the past few days. She can no longer participate in daily activities." The doctor had a dismal expression on his face.

"What kind of violence is she demonstrating?" Angelo asked. I was surprised that Angelo had jumped into the conversation. I looked at him, and then back at the doctor.

"Kicking, screaming and spitting at the doctors and nurses, writing strange symbols on the walls with red lipstick. She has the strength of six men." His voice was a little shaky. "I'd never heard anyone scream like her before. It was very haunting, practically terrifying." He said with a deep pause.

We all sat speechless for a moment. I needed some time to think about this. Now I had to consider all of the new information I learned about our past. Exasperated over the news, my mind went all over the place.

"Can I see her?" I asked, rubbing my hand over my chin.

"Yes of course. But I must warn you, she's not like she was the last time you visited."

"I understand," I said softly, nodding.

The doctor escorted us out of the office. We took the elevator down in silence, and within a couple of minutes, we'd arrived on the floor where my mother's room was. Scared to see how my mom's condition had worsened, I felt relieved that Angelo was by my side. He gripped my hand as we strolled down the hall. We stepped into my mom's room together with Doctor Cantori leading the way. Two very large orderlies were keeping watch in the room.

To my surprise, my mother was perched on top of a small chair with her legs crossed. She rocked back and forth, grinding her teeth and pulling strands of her matted hair out. I wanted to scream and cry. I felt so helpless. I saw what the doctor was talking about when I looked up and noticed the strange symbols drawn on the walls. It was too weird. I recognized a few of the symbols but couldn't remember where I had seen them before. Sad and disgusted over everything, I didn't know what to do.

"What is this?" I asked Angelo with my mouth barely open. He looked at me, afraid to reply.

I sluggishly moved closer to my mom. Her eyes were glued on mine, watching my every move. Before I could blink my body was being thrown down on to the floor. She hoisted herself on top me with a force so strong that another entity had to be responsible. Her small hands whaled across my head and face. I held my arms and hands up to block the power of the blows. I tried to throw her off but my effort was meaningless. Her nails were sharp and dug deep into my skin. I cried out, and the orderlies and two doctors ran over to pry her off of me. She struggled to fight against the five strong men. Angelo knelt down to help me up. I huffed and puffed, gasping for air. Angelo placed his arm around my shoulder and surveyed my face for any scars and scratches.

"Baby, are you alright?" he said, as his blue eyes searched mine.

"Yes, I'm fine. I'm more worried about Mom." I held my head down. I could no longer watch the horror of my mother's fit, or whatever it was. She suddenly screamed a deep, loud, angry howl that frightened everyone except Angelo. I looked over at her as she belted out the terrible sound. Her pupils had turned black and her body was slowly lifting off the ground. This was no longer a case for the doctors. This was a supernatural case that involved the creatures that were after me; the same ones that had punished my mother.

"Step Back!" Doctor Cantori yelled. "Get the nurse now! We have to sedate her again!" he yelled, looking at one of the orderlies.

"Wait, NO! NO! I can calm her down but you all need to leave," I begged. My voice trembled with nervousness. The brown-haired orderly ran out of the room.

[90]

"I am sorry Sydney, but I have to." The doctor replied sternly. The next thing I remember was being escorted out the room as the orderly returned with a long syringe. I sat on the bench outside while Angelo observed what they were doing to my mom. I was shocked to see they didn't make him leave, but I assumed he used his power of allure to make them do what he wanted. For a second I had completely forgotten that I was able to influence the mood of others. I felt like the same lost young woman who was just recovering from the accident all over again. I held my head back while a nurse tended to my wounds. My face must have been pretty banged up. She blotted the cuts with cotton balls. Blood melted into the sterile pads. I tried so hard to collect myself.

"Go to the truck Sydney. I'll be there in a few minutes." Angelo's voice stung in my head. A few moments later, the nurse was finished.

"Would you like to talk to the doctor, Miss London?" Her voice was low and sweet. She smiled at me but I knew she was also shocked about what happened.

"No, thank you, ma'am. I appreciate all of your help." I stood up but felt dizzy. I placed my hand on top of my forehead and I balanced my body by gripping on to the shoulder of the nurse. She jumped up. I held on to her tightly.

"Maybe you should stay here for a while," she said with a worried tone.

"No. I'll be okay. I'm going to go to outside to wait for my boyfriend."

"Please don't get behind the wheel. Let him drive." She escorted me down the hall.

"I won't. I'm in no condition to drive; besides its still raining. I won't take that chance." I thanked the nurse again and took my time getting to the front entrance. I told the security guard that Angelo would sign us out. He nodded with a slight grin.

Fishing Angelo's keys out of my purse took me a couple of seconds. I opened the umbrella as I stepped out in the pouring rain. I got to the truck, and climbed in slamming the door. I sat in silence and tried to fight against the tears. All it was going to do was make my headache worse but my emotions once again got the best of me. I buried my hands in my face and cried as loudly as I could. Getting out the pain was therapeutic for me.

A bright white light beamed down and settled into the driver's side. I lifted my head, turned and saw Angelo appear before me.

ngelo was magnificent in the light. The light diminished the second he was back in his physical form. He held out his hand and looked at the bandages that covered my face. He gently placed both hands on me and turned my head from side to side.

"What is going on with my mother?" I asked in a raspy tone.

"Someone has released the darkness into your mother. You're under attack. Tell me how you're feeling." I kept my mouth closed tightly. I couldn't find any words to describe how I felt at the moment.

"Maybe you should really consider calling this thing off," Angelo said. "You need take care of yourself. I don't think you're well enough to make the trip over to save Christine. Your strength is failing."

"I have to do this. I'll be fine," I insisted. I sat up in the seat to show him that I was okay. I rested my head on the head rest. I forgot to schedule a meeting with Luna so I sent her a text message from Angelo's phone inviting her over for tea, so we could have a chance to chat. We arrived at my house within 20 minutes. Luna must have already been on the road when I sent her the message because her small red Volvo was parked in front of my house. I was still shaken up over the events of the morning but I didn't want Luna to read how I really felt. I was not in the mood to talk supernatural business, but I knew there was no way around it.

I wiped my face with a towel that I had in my purse. My makeup was not holding up well, but I fixed what I could before hopping out of the truck. My hood covered up my face as I jetted through the rain, ran up the front steps and opened door as quickly as I could while Angelo parked the car. I motioned for Luna to come in. She hung up her damp rain coat and trailed in after me into the kitchen. I threw my purse down and hustled over to the sink to fill the tea kettle up with water. Tossing my coat over the chair near the back door, I turned on the burner and placed the kettle over the fire avoiding eye contact with Luna. Angelo popped his head in and I wished he hadn't. I didn't feel like introducing them. She rose up when she spotted him and smiled a gracious smile, inclining her head to show respect. She knew Angelo was powerful.

"You're Grace," she said softly. He stepped fully into the kitchen, and bowing in return he acknowledged Luna. I couldn't believe all it took was a second for her to identify him. Angelo sat at the table. I kept my back turned away from Luna, glancing over my shoulder to see what she was doing.

"My dear, I wonder why you are always trying to hide things from me, when you know that I know." Luna sat back down. I quickly rustled up some tea and fixed a tray full of tea cups, milk and sugar. Luna almost sounded like a witch, speaking in a slow, high voice. I turned to face Luna as the tears streamed down my cheeks. Licking my lips, I tasted the salty flavor. Luna reached for a napkin, as I sat next to her, almost missing the edge of the chair. I fixed my body and dabbed my eyes with the napkin. I felt the overwhelming influence of the situation I was in.

"I'll leave you ladies alone. Sydney I'll be right outside if you need me." Angelo went through the swinging kitchen door.

"Let's get down to this," Luna said. "What's going on? I haven't seen you in this much emotional turmoil since you lost your father. Who did this to you?"

"My mother did it earlier today. She attacked me when I went to see her. I got a call from one of her doctors and he asked me to come in. Her condition has gotten worse." Luna filled both cups with tea. I gazed at the steam that rose from my cup.

"I'm so sorry about Pamela. If there's anything I can do please let me know. What are the doctors doing for her?"

"Well... They are pumping her full of drugs until they figure out how to handle her, and they don't even realize that it's not working." I poured a little milk in my tea.

"The reason I wanted to meet with you is because I had a terrible vision about you," Luna said.

"What was the vision?" I asked, eyeing Luna's wildly tousled hair.

"You were lying down in a forest asleep, when all of a sudden a dark figure appeared standing before you. He let out a black shadowy substance from his mouth and it went into yours. Your eyes turned white and you vanished along with the dark figure." Luna took a sip of her tea. My cup was half empty. I felt the alarm within me grow. My eyes widened when Luna told me her vision.

"Luna, I had the same vision but didn't see the ending. When the creature released the dark substance I woke up at the shock of it." Luna listened to me carefully. I had a true respect for Luna's gift. I needed to tell her everything so she could better understand what was going on with me.

"Do you remember the conversation we had the last time we met?" I asked.

"Yes. I've been meaning to ask you about your new beau. I get a different vibe from him. I knew he was not the one I had my vision about. This one, he really loves you and is truly divine." She kept her voice low, remembering that Angelo was in the room next to us.

I filled Luna's tea cup for the second time. I starred at the designs on the cups as we continued our conversation. They are made of French porcelain and have hand painted Roses and Calla lilies decorated all over them. I took a deep breath, and told her all the details about my story, my mother and our newly-revealed past. I heard her gulp hard after she processed the information. She seemed like she believed me but, sill appeared to be shocked at learning the truth. Her mouth dropped once I confessed to her that I was part human and part angel. She insisted that she had always known there was something deeper in me. I think that my

[93]

supernatural connection brought us closer together in many ways. She said it was more than my ability to astral project. I wanted to show off my powers, so I closed my eyes and went to that place deep inside of me. My newly discovered power had me very excited, and I beamed at the thought of showing it to Luna. I felt the energy building in my body while my left hand tingled and grew numb. I opened my eyes and saw a platter of cookies floating to the table. I guided the platter to the table with my gaze.

"I am very impressed, Sydney. You are a gem. I haven't seen too many with active powers, and you are the first nephilim I have ever met. You do seem very different, more beautiful and charming than ever." I felt bashful listening to her compliment me.

"Thank you for accepting me Luna. It has meant a lot to me, for you to be in my life guiding me all these years. Angelo is my guardian angel but you are as well." I saw the happiness in Luna's face. She grinned with delight, and I had a happy moment.

"Even though I came here only to tell you about the vision I also want to offer my services and help you two, now that I know what's going on."

"That's not a good idea Luna. I don't want you to get hurt. The fewer people involved the better."

She did not argue with me like she usually would have. She smiled and nodded at me.

"Okay, but please be careful, darling. The worlds beyond ours are highly dangerous. They are full of temptations that can suck you in. Be on your guard at all times. The dark entities are trying to use your mother as a vessel to lure you to them. Continue to be resilient, and you will find the power to defeat them."

"I will," I replied, smiling at Luna. She stood ready to leave, and I didn't blame her. The weather was getting worse; we were supposed to get more rain all day and night, and some areas were expecting flooding. It was afternoon but the skies were so dark that it looked like it was almost five in the evening. I gave Luna one of my umbrellas, hugged her tightly and escorted her to the door. I watched Angelo walk her to her red Volvo. I was sad when I saw her drive away and prayed that she would make it home safely.

Angelo ran back to the house, wiped his feet and then shook the water off. His clothes were dry in seconds. I closed the door behind him and appreciated being home once again.

"Take my hand," he commanded directly extending his out. I automatically obeyed. A woozy feeling entered my head, and I stumbled as we suddenly materialized in a deep cavern somewhere within the cosmos. The space was dark, but illuminated by thousands of small crystal vials filled with a silver, glistening substance. The vials were embedded within the carved rock walls. The sight was very spellbinding.

"Where are we?" My voice echoed throughout the deep.

[94]

"We're in The Cavern of Healing," Angelo replied, tenderly grabbing a vial from its secured place. When he removed the cap, a small trail of white mist escaped from it. I followed the mist with my eyes. He held the vial out toward me.

"Drink it," he told me, barely parting his lips. Angelo placed the vial up to my mouth. I trusted him with everything, so holding my head back, I consumed the elixir. It went down smoothly, like a shot of caramel, coating the inside of my throat. The vial vanished in Angelo's grasp. My body began to tingle and all my aches and pains were gone. I touched my face, removing the bandages. Feeling my skin with some caution, I felt the wounds close and the swelling dissipate. I felt stronger and rejuvenated.

"This is wonderful! It's so enchanting," I exclaimed. The texture of my voice was light and airy.

"This place is for good magical creatures, like the white elves and glimmer pixies. Creatures like you. The healing power went deeper than your outside wounds. This will help you better handle your situation and prepare you to defend yourself. It will also bring you closer to our world." I wrapped my arms around him, embracing him tightly, then planted a nice kiss on his sexy mouth. Looking at him with great desire, I said the first thing that came to my mind.

"When are you going to take me out on an official date?" I blurted out without thinking. His face lit up with exhilaration.

"I've been waiting for you to ask me that question. I promise that as soon as we get things straightened out, I'll take you on a dream date."

"Really?" I asked, jumping up like a giddy school girl. He nodded trying to hold back a laugh.

I noticed tiny sparkles rising up in the air, drawing my attention away from Angelo. Refocusing my energy, I released my grip from Angelo's neck.

"Look over there," I told him, pointing west. He turned around to face the direction to which I pointed. We were both facing the same direction. Tiny sparkles like bright little lights were flying all around. It seemed like they were coming from an opening in the cavern that I couldn't see.

"Are those pixies?" I asked, as one of them flew by my head.

"They're harmless and are called nixies. They're cousins to the pixie and have similar abilities."

"This doesn't feel like another dimension."

"It isn't. We are on Earth, near the Amazon."

"So there *are* mystical creatures on Earth?" I followed the motion of the nixie. She fancied me a lot. She flew up to my face and I cupped her in my hands, carefully not trying to harm her delicate body. The nixie had long bronze hair that almost touched her feet. Her wings were silvery and almost transparent and her legs and feet moved against the air. She gave off a peaceful demeanor and when she waved her tiny hand I felt a positive surge flow through me. I turned to gape at Angelo.

"Nixies have the power to inspire and bring good fortune to others, kind of like the way a muse does."

This time I was ready. Licking my lips, I wanted to tell Angelo that I love him but a part of me knew that Angelo knew how I felt.

"Do you feel it?" His eyes glowed.

"Yes," I replied, taking his extended hand once again.

The tunnel of space and time was becoming too familiar in the in-between places we ventured off to. We arrived in the marsh lands of a dimension that sent shivers up and down my spine. I was aware that we were in the Borderline of Souls; the place was dirty, dank and desolate. My feet were already damp the moment we stepped onto the soggy grass. Plowing and pushing through rough, unknown territory made me realize that despite my small frame, I was indeed not in shape for this strenuous activity. As I looked down I saw dark muddy arms and hands planted in the ground.

"Avoid the hands at all costs," Angelo warned with a sound of vigilance deep in his throat.

"I will. They look evil," I said like an idiot.

"They're the demons of this world. If they suck you in, they'll possess you and take you as their prisoner to the Underworld."

"You don't have to tell me twice," I said, gripping his arm tightly. I felt the strength in his body the second I touched him. "Can we just hover?" I pleaded.

"No, we can't. Using our abilities is too risky here. If there are any bounty hunters out there they may sense our magic, and it can make us an easy target in getting captured."

That whole idea of us not using our powers sucked. I pouted like a little girl.

"Don't do that, we don't have time," Angelo said, looking over his shoulder. I trotted behind him, mimicking his every move.

The putrid smell of the marshlands stung my nose. It was the aroma of rotting corpses and blood. The odor was so strong that I let out a cough. I covered my mouth to avoid puking. This world had a frightening element to it. There were no stars, or moons. The flat, gray light of this world created the sensation of a cloudy day. As I became lost in the dismal atmosphere, I felt something suddenly seize my ankle. I yelled at the shock of it, yanking and pulling my leg as hard as I could.

"Shit, Angelo!" I called out to him. The fingers wouldn't relinquish their hold. Angelo jerked around and saw the grimy hand clutching on to me. He carefully avoided the hands that surrounded us. Out of nowhere he pulled out a long silver sword; the handle glistened and was in the shape of a dragon's head. The blade was ready to do some damage. Angelo's eyes glowed silver, as he held up the weapon with a great strength and the sword glided down on to the arm of the deadly creature cutting the arm off at the base. The fingers of the demon stiffened, sliding off of my ankle and into the gloomy, thick muddy abyss. I placed my hands on my hips, looking very impressed and feeling aroused.

"Nice. I didn't know you could wield a sword," I said flirtatiously. Angelo's sexiness had increased by a thousand percent.

"Yes, guardian angels are warriors too," he said. "Considering our situation," Angelo said, "We can't travel this way. It's too dangerous for you. I'll cloak my scent, so we can use our powers without being detected. It's still a risk but it's worth it." He gripped my hand and my body instantly transformed before me. I felt completely void from the inside out. I got closer to him and knew that our angelic essence had been cloaked from the outside world. Distracted by Angelo's warm brawny body, I melted in his comfort. We continued our journey and eventually ended up in a wooded area.

Thick, damaged and dead trees were all around us. Some were burned and even ripped down. Branches and large twigs were strewn around on the ground. I studied the environment carefully, taking in every element of it. With our magic still cloaked, Angelo picked up a large branch and made a torch out of it. The bright light guided us along our way. The path we traveled on was not much of a path. The rubble concrete was severely cracked and covered with dead brown leaves and pebbles.

After traveling for an hour or so we made it to a rock wall that had two seven-foot doors carved into its side. The doors were covered with long vines of ivy, so much that you hardly realized that they were there.

"These doors look like they haven't been opened in centuries," I murmured.

"Not too many people go searching for the soul of a loved one," he said with a grin. I didn't think it was funny so I didn't give him the satisfaction of a reply. I shut my eyes and thought about the door opening. Breathing deeply, I concentrated intently. The ground beneath us shook like a force from an earthquake. The doors slowly opened, and out came a breeze that extinguished the fire of our torch. As we stepped in, the darkness made me fearful. I could sense that something was in here with us. As we walked, things wiggled underneath my feet, making me squirm. I didn't want to know what was under each step I took. I grabbed on to Angelo's hand and we walked into the blackness. Guided by our angelic vision, it allowed us to see through the darkness. As we continued to make our way deeper into this place, I felt the presence of a large animal towering over us from behind. An eerie feeling crept up my legs and back, and the hair on the nape of neck stood up on end.

"Something is following us," I stuttered, speaking telepathically.

"*Move fast*," my guardian responded.

"*How, we don't even know where we are going?*"

"*Stop talking, and let me think*," Angelo snapped. Oh shut up, I thought.

The huge monster trailed our every step, breathing down on our necks and growling lightly. Its breath was foul and its body smelled. Without turning around I sensed that it was a werewolf. Angelo felt that I was growing afraid of the creature. With his free hand a blue and white light radiated from it. He held up his palm and the trail of light guided our path into the dark.

As we continued on, hairy fingers touched my shoulder and I shrieked, trying to remain calm. I whispered Angelo's name and he whipped around. Holding his hand up, he allowed the beam of light to pulsate. The force of the beam knocked the werewolf down and he grunted with pain. As the creature went down, he let out a howl and his claws grazed my neck.

"He scratched me!" I yelled, feeling the open cuts. Reaching for my dagger I was ready to plant it deep in the side of his temple. I was getting sick of being hurt. I rolled my eyes and clutched on to the wound. I was bleeding and afraid that I could be turned into a werewolf.

"Keep still for a second." Angelo pointed the light that emerged from his hand on to my neck. "You drank from the Cavern of Healing, give it a minute," he instructed.

The scratches tingled and in a flash they closed up. When I felt my neck for claw marks, nothing was there. Smiling in the dark, I took Angelo's arm and we proceeded to move out away from the injured werewolf.

"WHO DISTURBS THE RESTING PLACE OF THE SPIRITS?" a strong female voice roared. The echo vibrated throughout the cave. We stopped dead in our tracks and Angelo made the light from his hand diminish. We were standing in the dark once again.

Flashes of lighting sparked from all corners of the cave, making the darkness slightly dissipate. A ball of brightness appeared in the short distance and we were able to see where the voice came from. Standing on top of an elevated mound was an extremely tall and beautiful woman. She had curly yellow hair that reached her waist. Her skin was pale and eyes glowed yellow-green. They were the eyes of an exotic cat. She wore a bright red strapless sequin gown. The Guardian looked too lovely to be down in this dank place. What a waste of a good dress, I thought to myself. I didn't know exactly what she was and what she was capable of, but I was prepared to fight if I had to.

"It's the Guardian," Angelo whispered from the corner of his mouth. He must have thought that I hadn't been paying attention or that I couldn't put two and two together.

I stood tall to face the Guardian. She lifted her bare feet off of the ground and floated toward me, landing on a large platform of broken stone. She was a few feet away from me. Her beauty was transcending.

"It is I and my companion that have come to you on this night." I chuckled inside after I heard the words come from my lips. My voice had a robust pitch to it.

"What do they call you?" she asked.

"I am Sydney. Sydney London." Angelo and I were still holding hands.

"I humbly ask you to please release one of your spirits. It was not her time; she was ripped from the human world."

"What spirit are you asking for?" Her tone was flat and she had a dead facial expression.

"Christine Harrison," I replied quickly. Tears spilled down my face. I wanted to hold them back—showing any kind of weakness in front of the Guardian would not bring me favor.

"Come closer, my child," the woman ordered. I released my grip from Angelo's hand and looked at him for approval. He nodded and I stepped up on one of the huge stones. I wondered where they came from, because when we first entered the room the ground was flat and pretty stable. Stepping in front of the unique beauty, I gazed upon her face. I heard a grunting sound behind Angelo and looked back, seeing the beast that Angelo had knocked down with his power. Feeling unthreatened, the wolf snarled and retreaded within the shadows. I stood stiff as a board, almost paralyzed.

"I am Hope, The Guardian of the Spirits," she whispered as her words came out slowly. Hope gracefully reached out and touched the edge of my chin with her slinky fingers. They were as cold as ice, and I flinched when her flesh made contact with mine. "You are no mere human," she said. "Humans do not have the power to enter here." I realized that her voice was accented. I felt a strange force flow in me when she touched me. "What are you offering in exchange?" She gave me a piercing stare.

I lifted up my sleeve to show her the charm bracelet.

"I offer you a lost soul. Something that I know you want," I said. Her yellow-green eyes sparkled. I knew she was willing to bargain, but despite the circumstances I didn't feel comfortable giving her someone else's soul. It was not my place. It was wrong, but I was in way too deep to turn back.

"So what is your case? Why should I let your friend return to the living?" My gaze was set on to hers as I took a deep breath, preparing to state my case to the Guardian.

"Everyone that I have ever loved has been taken away from me. My life is filled with loss, death and tragedy. I'm not just asking on my behalf, but on hers as well. Christine was torn away from her life before she had the chance to really live, it was not her fault. She deserves to live a life filled with promise and love and have a chance to make her dreams come true. She was my best friend, my sister, and I truly love her. Please give her back to me." Keeping silent I gave Hope a chance to think about what I said. Hope touched my head with her cool hand and I saw a flash of what my life was like before and after my family disaster. The flash startled me, but I tried not to show any reaction.

[99]

"Isn't that what everyone would say if they had the opportunity to bring a loved one back from the dead?" She looked at me for a response but I acted like I did not hear her. Her question was cold. I held my head down. The area was too quiet. My thoughts were so loud that I wasn't sure if they were private anymore. "Very well," she replied, parting her lips slightly breaking the silence. "You may have her. I am sure that your angel made you aware of the process."

"Yes My Lady. I'm aware." I replied. The bracelet glowed the second I touched it, and a dim white light emerged from it and floated towards her. She opened her hand and captured the soul in her palm, then closed it, extinguishing the light. Seconds later Hope shivered. She had consumed the soul.

A small glow emerged from behind her radiating from two large stone doors. She turned to look over her shoulder and the door opened, making a loud sound as the stone pushed against the rocky ground. The grinding almost made me cringe. The light was extremely bright, but it didn't hurt to look at it. Hope raised her hand and out of the light surfaced a transparent orb. I extended my arm and the Guardian narrowed her cat eyes. The orb headed in my direction and went straight into my charm bracelet.

"Thank you," I whispered with a smile. "May I ask you a question My Lady?" She nodded and permitted me to speak. "Is there a way we can leave without bumping into the werewolf?" My voice sounded sincere.

"My apologies child, Uran is my protector. He will not harm you or your guardian angel. I have full control over the beast." I had a feeling that the werewolves were also slaves in this world. I felt his oppression. And how come he was not able to transform into his human form? I guess that was a question best saved for later. I thanked Hope, kissed her hand and jumped down from the stone platform into Angelo's arms. An odd feeling fluttered in me after I kissed her, and sensing this, Angelo looked at her suspiciously. We stepped away but Hope rushed up to me from behind, touching the back of my neck. I shuddered the moment her hand made contact with my skin again. She was so creepy that her touch sent shivers up and down my spine. We left as quickly as we could.

Exhausted from our travels, we decided to make a camp in the forest and go back home at first light. I collapsed on to the sleeping bag next to Angelo, and he held me close. I placed my arms on top of his.

"How do you feel about all of this?" he whispered with worry.

"I'm proud of myself. I can't believe I was strong enough to accomplish this. I've been thinking. Have you ever met the Guardian before? And what is she?"

"She's an angel just like I am, but—no I've never seen her before. I just know of her and her power." There are so many different types of angels that it would be impossible to cross paths with everyone in several life times." I didn't say anything else to him about Hope. But there were so many thoughts on my mind about her. I wanted to know what other magical powers she had and what kind of angel she was. My body needed to rest. I threw my leg on top of Angelo's and we dozed off. As I drifted off I felt the softness of Angelo's lips kiss my forehead a few times. Halfway asleep I realized that when Hope did touch me, she did not have the warmth in her that Angelo did. I wondered if she was a dark angel, then thought that I'd ask Angelo about it, but I decided not to because I needed to clear my head.

The thumping sound of heavy feet alarmed me, and I felt the presence of a dark entity lurking around our tent. I decided to investigate. I made sure that the dagger was still securely strapped to my ankle, then slipped out of my cozy position and got into my boots with no effort. I was as quiet as a mouse as I listened carefully at the entrance of our tent. My hearing was on point tonight. Whatever was out there was trying to keep their breathing shallow. I pulled the dagger out of its holder and wrapped my fingers around it tightly, holding it behind me. Despite my love of horror movies, I ignored the risk and slowly stepped out of the tent. A glow emerged from my eyes allowing me to see through the blackness. The fire had burned out and the night air was cold. My back was almost against the tent. I carefully maneuvered my body, watching, ready to face the creature of the dark.

There he was, standing against a large tree, leather jacket open, arms folded and hair its usual ebony hue. It was the son of a bitch who tricked me into a false love. It was Gilad.

Chapter Eleven

There was something different about Gilad tonight—I sensed his true nature. Angelo had told me that he had the power to mask his scent, and I think that Gilad had that kind of power as well which, was why I couldn't detect his darkness before.

"Sydney," he said trying to control the fierceness in his voice.

"What do you want? Are you here to collect your bounty?" I narrowed my eyes, and my glow faded. My face met his.

"I'm not a bounty hunter," he said with a sarcastic tone.

"Whatever," I said rolling my eyes.

"So, are you following us?"

"I wanted to make sure that you were safe. I was worried about you," he said. I rolled my eyes for the second time.

"You really need to stop pretending. It doesn't suit you. I know what you are and what you want, and you're not going to get it." My words were clipped and vengeful. Suddenly his eyes turned black, and his wings dark as tar forcefully erupted from his back and flapped with ferocity. Gilad grew with such anger. I stepped back and gazed upon the monster I knew he was. His jeans and jacket had transformed into the dark bronze armor I saw in my vision. Standing a few feet away from me, he hoisted me up with his wings. I hadn't realized before that angel wings could be used as a weapon. My legs were suspended in the air. I pulled against his strength, squealing, trying my best to keep the dagger concealed from him. It must have brushed against his left wing, because he trembled and winced in pain. He threw me on to the ground with great force and the dagger was released from my clutch. The impact of the ground pierced into me. I rolled over and scanned the ground for the dagger. I had no idea where it was.

Just then Angelo stormed out of the tent sensing my pain the moment I hit the ground. He whipped around and appeared in his full angelic form, dressed in gold armor, his silvery white, soft wings protruding from his back, standing at attention. His white cape was trimmed with gold and shimmered with brightness. Angelo's skin was luminous. He appeared so magnificent and extremely sexy as he sported his modern Roman Gladiator attire.

"This is not your fight, Guardian!" Gilad spoke with his teeth clinched spewing saliva from his mouth. He snarled at us. I got up and stood in front of my guardian angel. Angelo had drawn his sword. Gilad rose, moving toward me. Using his wings again he picked me up, and pressed my body up against a nearby tree. His hot breath steamed like a dragon, but I wasn't afraid of him. Our faces met once again and I felt something change in me. I began to tremble all over.

"BRING ME THE DAGGER!" I said with a deep voice. The Dagger of DOSHON appeared in my hand the very moment I called for it. The white glow was intense. Gilad's eyes widened as he saw the dagger in front of him.

Without a word I drove the dagger deep into the side of his neck. He wrapped both of his hands around my throat, as his wings slowly became limp, then he let out a howl. I felt the vibration of his pain as he held me, my back pressed against the bark of the tree. The skin on his face was slowly withering away. His lifeless body fell to ground and Angelo caught me before my body made contact with the ground again. He held me there for a moment, and then I kissed him deeply and stood up. We stood over the disintegrating corpse. The wings had flattened out and his whole body withered to ash. The only thing left of Gilad was his bronze armor and a steel mace. I glanced over my shoulder at Angelo, still in his true form, and pointed at the weapon.

"I didn't know he carried a weapon," I mused.

"We all wield weapons that are specifically made for us as individuals."

"Do you mean that this dagger belongs to me?"

"Yes, it's yours," Angelo said.

"So that's why I'm able to call for it."

"Of course, the symbols carved into the handle are your name."

"Then why did I have to go through the hell of obtaining it, if it belonged to me all along?" I asked.

"It's part of the journey. We all must embark upon a journey to find our true weapon." His eyes sparkled. I was confused over the experience I had with the Keepers of the dagger. I thought it was my power of allure that had influenced them. I didn't even feel like asking Angelo about that.

An unexpected blue mist materialized from the ground and settled above me, entering my body. The impact of it forced me down on one knee, and I struggled momentarily for spiritual and physical control. With a couple of deep breaths, I began to feel strong and courageous. I closed my eyes and the dagger returned to its rightful place on my ankle.

"What just happened?" I asked, a little shaken.

"That is what happens when one of the fallen is vanquished. You've assumed his abilities, but I am afraid you can't wield his weapon. No angel is able to wield the weapons of other angels."

"Isn't that what makes me so special? I'm not a pure blood. I'm a mixed breed," I said smiling. Angelo smiled and knew what I was thinking. He nodded his head in assent, and I bent over to pick up the mace.

A light surfaced from both of my hands. The weapon trembled on the ground as my fingers touched the angel's true weapon. This new discovery could make or break me. I held Gilad's weapon in my hand, observing its craftsmanship as it became mine.

"Let's go. We're wasting time here." Angelo took a couple of steps towards me. His sexy body sang a song to my secret place. His silky wings displayed a beauty in their own right. They had a life of their own as they swayed back and forth. For a moment I envied him and his true form.

"I'll never be beautiful like you. I'll never know what it is like to fly with you among the heavens," I said.

"You are very beautiful, unimaginably, stunningly, undeniably beautiful. We all have our own destinies. You are my destiny. You were meant to be who you are now and your true destiny is shaping itself as we speak." Angelo's voice was light and meaningful. Placing my hands on top of his shoulders I, kissed him passionately, he wrapped his wings around me and we became one within the light.

An intense hunger came over me as I settled quickly in my home. It was day four since Christine's death and rain was still sweeping the area. We hadn't been gone long. Just after midnight on the Earthy Realm, I jumped into the shower to wash all of the grimy dirt off of me. I lathered my body with a nice Almond Rose body wash. The warm water felt so calming on my flesh. I relished in the experience of bathing my body. Halfway into the shower, the curtain pulled back and Angelo stepped in. A light draft of air crept up my spine. I moved over so that Angelo could comfortably fit into the shower and he stood under the running water with me. His dark hair was now soaking wet with water and shampoo as the dirt from our bodies dripped away. Angelo touched the nape of my neck. His hands wandered to my waist, but he avoided my breasts and other parts. I wanted him to touch me. I had my hands all over him. I poured some body wash, rubbed both hands together to get a good lather, and massaged his firm bottom and penis. He started to kiss me all over, and dropped his head to suck on my erect nipple. His teeth lightly bit it and then he swirled his tongue around it. In a passionate frenzy he lifted me up and I wrapped my legs around his body, and we proceeded to make love.

I was stretched out across my bed with the towel still draped around me. Totally relaxed, I felt like I couldn't move a muscle. My stomach started to growl but eating wasn't on my mind. I closed my eyes for a moment, thinking about the man that I had truly fallen in love with. As I thought about Angelo new worries settled within me. I was in a lot of hot water even though I did not want to admit it. I had escaped from being the victim of a werewolf; I killed a Fallen One, assumed his power and took his weapon. I knew that I would eventually have to face the conseguences.

I didn't want anything to happen to Angelo. Although he was my protector, I had to protect him as well. I rolled out of bed and went straight to my underwear drawer. I slipped on some cotton

[104]

white panties and a white Victoria's secret bra, pulled on some cozy white socks and went to my closet. I grabbed a pair of thick jean leggings and a black long sleeved t-shirt. Slipping into a pair of boots, I went down stairs and retrieved my black sweater that was hanging on the living room coat rack. Angelo came through the swinging kitchen door with a mug of hot cocoa. I took the mug and smiled at him. He looked so cute in his jeans. I stared at him while sipping the cocoa.

"Do you want me to rustle up something for you to eat?" Angelo asked peering at me.

"No. I can't eat now. I think we should leave for the coroner. We're less likely to get caught if we go now."

"Babe, the weather is bad, roads are dangerous. We should wait."

"I am so sick of waiting. That's all I've been doing. We can use our powers. We don't need a vehicle." I knew that using our powers was risky, especially if the Council didn't know that Gilad was dead. They were the ones that sent him to follow us and I knew that they were aware of my location. I was just way too impatient, but despite the risk we had to act. It was almost one in the morning and time was something we didn't have. Running over to the coat rack, I slipped on my rain coat, grabbed my keys and purse and was ready to go.

"What are you doing?" he asked folding his arms across his chest. My eyes shifted to his feet. He looked funny puttering around the house barefoot.

"I'm going to take my car and go." I waited for his response. He looked up at the ceiling and walked over to the coat rack. He pulled on his boots and threw on his jacket. The car keys dangled from my hand. Angelo seized them and opened the front door. The rain poured. The second I saw the dark, soaked street I wanted to revert back inside and slide under the warm covers with Angelo.

"We could just go upstairs," he said. His grin was totally sexy as he raised his right eyebrow. I thought about it. I felt like I was denying him if I told him no, but he knew the reality of the circumstances. I parted my lips to reply, but he interrupted me. "I'll go around back and pull up the car." He slammed the door shut and went through the kitchen.

Within a few minutes he pulled up in front of the house. The brake lights appeared lonely on the empty street. I threw my hood up, slammed the door shut and ran straight for Angelo's SUV. We sat there for a few minutes to let the vehicle warm up. We eventually pulled off into the night.

"Can you do something with the cameras if there are cameras up?" I asked.

"Sure, I'll take care of it."

Within an hour we arrived at the Crimson County Medical Examiner's Office. We drove around the block twice to survey the deserted parking lot. I thought that was a good idea. If we pulled up directly we knew that cameras would catch the image of the vehicle. We didn't want the cops or anyone else catching a glimpse of us on video.

The rain had let up a little, so we decided to park a block away. Our plan was to tamper with their security system so that the cameras wouldn't catch any images of us, and then astral project inside. We stood outside, the rain soaking our clothes. I took Angelo's hand and we vanished into thin air.

So far our plan was working. We glided down the long dark halls silently. We had to be prepared for anybody that could still be in the building. The rain pounded hard on the windows creating a haunting sound, as it echoed throughout the empty halls.

I tried to stay calm, but I was excited to see Christine being raised from the dead. I came here to do a job and I was going to accomplish it. We followed the signs that led to the examination room, and we entered through the double doors. The sound of conversation startled me. I turned to see through the window of the door, as the hall light popped on.

Our first instinct was to hide. Two women were walking in our direction. With the threat of possibly being caught, my body automatically went into its invisible form. I hid in a nearby corner, trying not to think about where I was. Angelo retreated to an area near the large freezers in his invisible form. This was the first time I was able to tap into that power without channeling it through Angelo's.

"So, do you think this is a good idea to be doing this at this hour?" a high pitched voice whispered.

"Sure Ann, you worry too much. If we're going to get anywhere in our training we have to do this," the lower-pitched voice said. They pushed through the double doors dressed in white lab coats and carrying clip boards.

I looked at the two women. They must have been forensic students. If my plan was going to work we had to get those two out of here, and fast. I thought about what my next move was going to be. I stood still, going over some ideas in my head. I saw Angelo peering at me. I telepathically told him my idea to scare the shit of out them.

Still in my invisible form I walked over to a slab that held a body covered by a sheet. Near the slab was a tray full of medical instruments. Slowly picking up one, I coughed to get the women's attention. To them the shears looked suspended in the air without any support. Their eyes budged when they saw it, and one woman froze, not moving a muscle. They were thinking about whether they should run. I took two steps with the shears in my hand, then placed my other hand under the sheet making it look as though the body was about to rise. Suddenly the two women ran out screaming. I chuckled as I began to reappear unable hold back my laughter. Angelo appeared in front of me with a smile on his face.

"I must admit, that was hilarious," he said, flicking off the overhead lights to avoid attention, and turning on a small lamp to give us some kind of light. With the joke aside, the examination room gave off a dark feeling. The smell of death made me sick to my stomach. I gulped hard and tried not to think.

Several gurneys were around the room. Angelo stood next to one them, and touched the top of the sheet to see who it was. The deceased person wasn't Christine. It would be devastating to have to search all of the freezers and look at the bodies of the dead, so I closed my eyes and tried to focus on Christine's body. Suddenly my body became numb. I felt a surge of energy and slowly followed it toward a freezer.

"She's in here," I said to Angelo, patting the freezer door. It was hard for me to really believe that I was doing this.

"Step back. Close your eyes if you need to. I'll open it," Angelo directed firmly. Though I knew it would be hard, I'd come this far. Closing my eyes wasn't going to make it any easier. I wasn't even sure what I was feeling.

With one hand Angelo pulled open the freezer door with ease. A mist of cold air spewed out, releasing a large smoky trail into the atmosphere. I looked down at the body of my friend with deep sorrow and pain. The skin of her naked body was pale. Her blonde hair was dull and lifeless, and her eyes appeared sunken in her head. Her arms rested by her sides, her hands were discolored and the wound on her neck looked just as angry as it did the day the coroner rolled her away.

I felt sick and wanted to run out of there, but I had to finish what I started. I saw a white tag on her right toe with her name written on it in permanent marker. I pulled up the sleeve of my coat to expose the charm bracelet which was now shimmering majestically. I held my arm up toward her body, aimed my wrist, and the blue orb emerged out of the bracelet. It hovered over her body and danced around a few seconds.

"Go on, Christine," I said to the orb glaring up at it. I closely watched as the orb entered her body with a piercing force. My eyes stayed focused on the body, waiting for Christine to open her eyes. I waited, and waited and absolutely nothing happened. Angelo had both hands on his hips and had a perplexed expression written on his face. I continued to stare at the corpse.

"Why didn't it work?" I asked, looking directly at Angelo. Shaking his head, he couldn't speak.

A movement caught my eye from the corner of the room. I turned to face it just as Angelo saw it too. A small bit of light flickered on a figure dressed in extremely long, black velvet robes. He was ghostly in appearance and had horrific scars settled deep into the crevices of his face. His eyes were deep with a black emptiness. The sight of him made me weary.

"It did not work because life and death does not work that way," the figure said. "Reincarnation is forbidden. Your guardian should know that." his voice was flat and had a grave tone to it. To hear him speak frightened me.

"Who are you?" I snapped. Angelo reached over the body to touch my hand and he gave me a look that said "shut up."

"You know who I am, Gaia."

[107]

He was right—I knew exactly who he was. Still pretending otherwise, I said,

"Why don't you refresh my memory?"

"I am Demas, the Angel of Death," he said, with a creepy grin.

"What do you want?" I asked with a sturdy voice. He chuckled, and his evil laugh pissed me off. I stepped away from the body and was ready to reach for my dagger. "Why won't you give her to me? I was given permission."

"You got permission from the wrong source. I have my orders. Your friend lying on a slab is the least of your problems. Come with me now," he replied with authority.

I had been backed into a corner into a trap just like I was warned. They made me believe that bringing her back was going to work. I turned to look at Angelo but could not read his expression.

"I know who you are Sydney, and what you are," Demas said. "I do not want to force you to come with me. And please do not try anything with your guardian angel. I know all the tricks."

"Do you really think I'm going to let her go without a fight?" Angelo mumbled through clenched teeth. He moved, standing in front of me, blocking my view of the Dark Angel.

"They warned me about you, Angelo. You like to stick your nose in where it does not belong."

I saw that Angelo was about to draw his sword. I chimed into Angelo's head, preparing to speak to him telepathically.

"*Listen, I don't want anything bad happening to you. I will go with him, follow me there in your invisible form. He doesn't know what kind of connection we have; He doesn't know all of our tricks. Besides, you can track my location. They won't hurt me. These bastards need me more then they even realize. ….…. I love you.*"

"*I am so sorry darling. It wasn't meant to be this way. I tried to warn you of the risk. I tried telling you.… I love you and I trust your judgment.*"

I gave Angelo a look, stepped closer to the Dark Angel, placed my hand inside his and off we went to an unknown world.

Chapter Twelve

T he moment I opened my eyes, I remembered what had happened at the morgue, and was filled with disgust. I sat up, examining my surroundings. I was lying on a purple bed with lilac silk sheets and fluffy matching pillows. I looked around the room and saw that the place was absolutely stunning. The walls and ceilings were made out of pure gold that shined softly against the radiance of the candle flames. The curtains were white and appeared to be satin, draping onto the floor and gently touching the marble, golden tiles. Small green pots were in every corner of the room, each containing a beautiful blooming rosebush. Their sweet aroma opened my nostrils.

Maneuvering off of the large canopy bed, I walked over to an armoire, opened the door and saw a full length mirror on the inside of the panel. My reflection was quite impressive. I was wearing a long black renaissance-style gown with a modern element to it. The bodice had white and silver sequins and beading scattered around. The sleeves were long and thin, split in various areas to reveal a red underlay. My hair was styled in a half up do, a tight bouffant with some curls cascading down my back. A small tiara with a jewel in the center rested on the crown of my head. Someone had retouched my makeup and added a pink hue of blush and lip color. The dark eyeliner and mascara brought out my deep blue eyes and gave me a romantic yet gothic look. How did they dress me like this while I was unconscious?

I couldn't remember the last time I ate a solid meal. I was starving and worried about Angelo. These creatures had no right to hold me here against my will. I shut the door to the armoire and went straight to the door. I turned the knob and pulled gently. At least it wasn't locked. I peeked down the hall and realized that I was in a large medieval castle. Dark stained glass windows were lined up and down the beautifully designed arched hall. I was so enchanted by my surroundings that I barely noticed the guard standing in all black with a sword strapped to his side. He turned and looked at me. I was startled by his initial stare, but it was too late to revert back inside the room.

"Welcome My Lady. Please follow me," he said in a deep accented voice. I closed the door and walked behind the guard. The high ceilings, marble floors and exotic stained glass windows captivated me. As I trailed behind the guard I remembered my dagger. I stopped without him noticing, bent down and patted my ankle. The dagger was missing.

Oh Shit, I thought to myself. I had no form of defense, except for my powers, which were all too new to me. I still didn't know where I was and who was holding me here. My thoughts were interrupted when we came to a well-guarded entrance. We went through iron double doors. The symbols and designs engraved on the doors were impressively crafted. Some looked very familiar. I studied the two guards for a moment and slowly walked past them into a grand dining room decorated in warm golden hues. Bronze and copper statues of griffins and dragons stood all around the space. A raised platform that looked like a decent-sized stage was in the front, draped with black and red velvet curtains and carpeting. In the center of the stage was a podium with a bronze base shaped like the dragon Drac. The top of the podium was flat and forged out of crystal. It was a beautiful piece. A large rectangular table in the middle of the room held platters of fruit and meat and other tasty looking foods. Shiny glass plates and silverware, along with white lace, decorated the table, and clear crystal goblets sat at each place setting. There were thirteen elaborate upholstered chairs made out of an enchanting Goldenrod fabric surrounding the table. I was in awe over the vision that graced me.

"Please sit," a familiar voice instructed me. Coming down the carpeted steps from the stage area was the Guardian of Spirits, Hope. I was shocked to see her again and bewildered over her presence. She was dressed in a long blue gown, similar in style to mine but more elaborately detailed. Her long yellow hair was gracefully pulled back off of her face. Hope's yellow-green eyes stung me. Standing tall, I looked back at her with the same intensity she bestowed on me.

"I'd rather stand, if you don't mind," I said with a formidable tone. "What are you doing here?"

"This is the dimension of Kalaston, the world of the Fallen. I do not want to make things difficult for you. You belong here. This is your home. Sydney, your place is by my side, sitting in a seat on my Council." She sounded soft and sweet, yet powerful and direct.

"You lied to me. How can you be both the Guardian of Spirits and Leader of the Council?"

"I never lied. I have always been the leader of the Council." She came closer to me, stirring all kinds of emotions. This, then was the woman responsible for destroying my family. I hated her with such fervor, but there was no way I could let her know how and what I really felt. I wanted her to tell me everything so I decided to play along. I switched my demeanor to make her believe I was interested in the knowledge of The Fallen.

"May I speak freely My Lady?"

"Yes go ahead," she replied.

"Why did you give me Christine's spirit when you knew that Demas would not let me take her?"

She motioned for me to sit. I sat down and she sat next to me.

"I must apologize for that. It was not my doing. Despite what you might think I do not have dominion over all angels. Every angel has a duty, a purpose. I have two, to guard the spirits of the dead and to lead the Fallen to our destiny to triumph over the Earth." She let out a sigh after she spoke. I had a strong sense that she was lying to me again that she wasn't in fact the original Guardian, but had seized the position—doing God knows what to get it—and was consuming the souls of the dead to fuel her power.

"I am not a Fallen One."

"No, but you are destined to be one of us." She paused. "The others will join us shortly."

As we continued our dialog, two elves dressed in black tuxedos came in holding pitchers filled with a thick red substance. They stood quietly on opposite sides of the table, holding pitchers on trays in a sophisticated fashion. Someone brought in a beautifully decorated cart with platters of braised short ribs on it and parked it next to me. I was so hungry, I thought about diving on top of the cart and devouring the ribs. Then I thought about not ruining the lovely dress I had on.

I was afraid of being here without Angelo and wanted to desperately to call for him. I had to find out who had taken my dagger and where it might be. I had to get it back as soon as possible. There was no way I could be defenseless on this plane.

I was uncertain about this dinner party, and knew it was leading me nowhere good. Moments later a group of extremely attractive men and women strolled into the dining room in a single file dressed in long crimson robes with hoods attached. The women took their seats on the same side of the table where Hope and I were sitting. Before they sat, they removed their robes to reveal stunning beaded gowns in the same style as ours. The men sat on the other side of the table, keeping their robes on. There were six women including Hope and me and seven men. Dinner had officially begun.

After examining the features of the council members, I realized that there was something very different about them. Besides their extremely pale, almost translucent skin, their eyes had a hunger in them that Angelo's didn't possess. Even Gilad hadn't looked like these Fallen. Could they be something different altogether?

The elves proceeded to fill everyone's goblet with the red beverage. The goblet next to my place setting was filled but I didn't pick it up at first. When the members all held up their goblets in a toast, I decided not to arouse suspicion, and picked it up out of respect.

"Here's to Sydney," Hope said in a smooth voice. The council members unexpectedly hissed in unison, and their canine teeth altered into sharp fangs. I realized the danger of my situation immediately: my half human butt was sitting in a room filled with angel vampire hybrids!

I timidly smelled the contents of the goblet, and detected instantly that the beverage was warm blood. The smell of it made me throw up in my mouth. I placed it back on the table, completely having lost my appetite. One of the elves walked over holding a bottle of white merlot and poured it into an empty glass that was next to my plate.

"Is there something wrong Lady?" one of the female members asked.

"No, not at all. It's just that I really don't drink," I said nicely. The female council member was sporting a short edgy haircut.

"I would like to take this opportunity to officially welcome our sister home," Hope said. "Let's toast to the home-coming of Sydney as we look toward a new age where, all our worlds will merge to grasp the power over humanity." Hope said in a meaningful accented voice. I had noticed that every magical creature I came into contact with from these other planes spoke with an unidentifiable accent. I held up the glass of wine after she finished her sentence.

"To Sydney... To Sydney! Hear! Hear!" The mixture of voices from the council members called out. Once again I realized that I was in deep shit, and there was nothing I could do at the moment. I needed to come up with a plan but didn't know where to start, so I took a large gulp of wine and savored the moment of feeling like a real princess. It was not going to last long.

As the dinner proceeded Hope began to introduce each of the members of the Council starting with the men. Their fangs had turned back into normal teeth, which was a good thing for me.

"Sydney, may I present to you Dionysus, Apollo, Ares, Cronus, Poseidon, Hades and Zeus." Each of the members nodded their heads to receive me. Hope then gestured her arm gracefully towards the female council members. "This is Demeter, Hestia, Aphrodite, and Athena. I my dear am better known as Hera," she uttered daintily. I didn't want to seem shocked so I inclined my head just as elegantly as Hope or Hera did. Were these people really the Greek gods of myth?

"My pleasure. It is an honor to be in your presence," I said to everyone at the table. I couldn't believe this was real. I served myself some of the meat and fruit and started to eat. The flavors were outstanding. The council members were served raw, bloody meat but I was so hungry I really didn't pay any attention to them. I was simply happy they ate with style and grace. Conversations started up around the table, and as the evening progressed the members didn't seem as bad as I originally thought they were.

One by one each angel showed me one of the powers they possessed. I knew that they didn't know what powers I had, so I showed them only my basic telekinetic ability. I moved the crystal goblet across the table away from me. They appeared to be satisfied and I was quite impressed with all of them.

The next thing I knew the bottle of white merlot was half gone. It had been years since I'd almost polished off a bottle of wine, a time before the accident. So many things crossed my mind about these creatures sitting before me. I then started to think about my past and what my direct connection was to them. I had a feeling that they knew almost everything about me. I wanted to speak to Hope alone soon, but feeling a little woozy after all the wine I drank, I thought I should go to my room and retire for the evening.

After dinner the council members invited me to join them in the gardens. They strolled out of the grand ballroom and I followed behind. Two guards dressed in black armor with red cloaks opened glass doors that were covered by thick, black drapes. Millions and millions of stars glowed in the blackness of the night. The sky resembled the Earth except for the three moons that made the horizon appear alien. I realized that I had been to this world before.

I took a seat on the first lounge chair I saw, adjusting the gown, I crossed my legs and leaned back against the soft silk pillows. All around the gardens were small balls of lights that floated in the atmosphere. I looked closely, narrowing my eyes to see what was inside the balls, and saw tiny rotating machines inside. Wheels within wheels, I thought, as described in the Bible. I'd never seen anything so beautiful before.

Flowers of every kind surrounded the area: Purple Orchids, Lilies, Roses, Tulips, and then I noticed unusual flowers that you might find in different parts of the Earthly Realm, like the Fuchsia Prince of Orange, and the Rosa Flora Pendula. The brick wall off to the right of the castle was covered with the Dwarf Creeping Fig. I chuckled inside when I thought about the Dwarfs that were inside the castle. Did they find it offensive? The flowers were so alive that they lightly shimmered. I heard them breathe and felt connected to them on a whole new level. For a moment I felt happy and enchanted.

Still pretty buzzed from the wine my vision was slightly off. The waiter that served me the wine earlier came out with a platter of fruit and cheeses. I gladly accepted the snack and enjoyed the attention I was receiving. Everyone was just lounging around comfortably. Some were standing and talking; others were sitting on nearby benches or resting on top of lavish blankets on the ground. They each had goblets filled with blood. I wondered if they wanted mine.

One of the balls of light wandered near my face. Gazing at the bright golden wheels, I lost myself in thought, rehashing what I had known—and what I was learning—about these creatures.

All of the council members are not just angels, and not just vampires but they're the deities that were known from Greek Mythology. They were once pureblooded angels that were in the service of the True Being of Light, but they grew jealous and greedy and wanted more than anything to be worshiped and exalted by the humans they believed were inferior to them. So they rebelled against the Light. The Light saw their treacherous ways and cast them out of the Heavenly Plane. They came to Earth with knowledge, technologies, and supernatural abilities making the humans believe they were gods. It actually makes sense. So how do I complete the puzzle? I continued to stare into the little lights, allowing my mind to take me to my past. *Our names; my mother's name is Pamela Pandora London. Pandora is Zeus' daughter. My name is Sydney LaGaia London. Gaia is the goddess of Mother Earth. This is weird. I didn't think of this before. My mother hid our true identities in plain sight.* My thoughts were interrupted by a voice ringing in my head. I looked up to see a tall figure standing before me.

"My Lady. Can you hear me?" A cool voice wavered at me. I nodded, slowly coming back from my thoughts.

A very pale, yet extremely handsome angel approached me. He took my hand and knelt down on my right touching his full lips to my skin. His body gave off a golden light and his aura was pure in goodness. I wondered why he was on this plane.

I am Lothos," he said introducing himself. I immediately heard an accent surface from his lips. He was dressed in a black leather Renaissance doublet and matching pants that fit him like a glove. His style was elegant and modern. I studied his features: he was tall, nicely built, with baby blue eyes and wavy dirty blond shoulder-length hair. There was innocence to his face and demeanor. His nose was perfectly pointed but it was hard not to notice his nice voluptuous lips. It was a pleasure to look upon his face. Accepting his kiss with a smile, I motioned for him to take a seat next to me. He moved his body in a regal manner.

"Do you remember me?" he asked.

"No forgive me. Should I?" I asked in a matter-of-fact tone. He kept his eyes on mine, and didn't answer me, which made me uneasy.

"How are you enjoying your stay with us?" he asked. Looking up toward the sky I didn't know if I should tell him the truth or lie about this whole experience. I had been deceived by these people once again and I felt resentful and angry, emotions which I had to hide.

I gave the waiter back the platter, even though I was not finished snacking on the fruit. He stood there quietly.

"This place is magical," I said smiling. I concentrated on the platter of fruit next to me, focusing my energy near the area. An apple rolled off of the platter and floated in the air in my direction. I felt the numbness in my palm. It moved closer and hovered in midair right in front of my face. I picked it up and took a big bite. The juice exploded upon my tongue. My taste buds screamed with excitement. It didn't taste like a typical apple. Smiling with pleasure, I chomped on the luscious fruit.

"I see that you're getting used to your abilities. Well done. Don't fear them."

"I must confess that I do feel stronger here more than I have ever felt in the Earthly Realm. Why do I seem to grow weaker in the Earthly Realm?" He turned to look at me more closely as he prepared to answer my question.

"Sydney, you are not weaker on the Earthly Realm. It is your connection to your angelic existence that gives you strength. You feel the influence more on other planes because of your divine essence. You are both a celestial creature and a human," He paused. "Sydney you are more angelic than you know, and that is why your strength lies within the dimensions that are beyond the Earth."

"I understand. Thank you Lothos," I said. I no longer wanted to speak freely in the presence of the elf that stood near us hanging on to our every word. There was something about Lothos that made me trust him. Somehow I felt that he knew me from another time.

"*Lothos, if you can hear me, just smile, don't say anything.*" He smiled brightly. "*I believe that I can trust you. Did you know my mother?*" I blurted out telepathically.

"*Yes I knew her very well. What the Council is doing to you and to her is wrong. I keep my true intentions concealed to save my life, but you can trust me. The angel vamps are a ruthless group and will stop at nothing to get what they want from you.*"

[114]

"They want my power. My power is the key that they believe will entice humans to worship them again like the civilizations of old."

"You are exactly right. I believe that someone has removed your weapon. Is that true?"

"Yes. I am planning to search for it when the sun comes up and the angel vamps go down for the day."

"You are not one of The Fallen." I asked him.

"No. I pretend to pledge an allegiance to them. I made a vow to help your mother, a secret vow. The angel vamps have other species of angels and various magical beings working for them. Many of the angels that are enslaved to them are trying to gain information. While the angel vamps are making arrangements to inspire your recruitment they're also in the process of building an army to wage war on all those angels that are not fallen." Lothos had a clear tone that massaged throughout my head.

"When they captured me, I was separated from my guardian. Can you help me find him and my weapon?" I asked.

Lothos told me he would help, but first we needed to leave the gardens. I rose to my feet, thinking of a reason to tell Hope why I was leaving for the night. Before I could make a step in her direction, the ambiance of the gardens changed. I noticed a sudden dark feeling. The structure of the council members' faces altered near their cheeks and foreheads. Their canine teeth extended with ferocity. I kept my face level and eased back down into the lounge chair. Their eyes were glued on me. They pierced bright yellow.

"Will they hurt me?" I asked Lothos.

"No. They need you," he whispered.

An assembly line of topless men and women strutted into the gardens, standing side by side. The only clothing they had on was underwear bottoms. The noise of a gong sounded, which alarmed me. I sensed that they were human and in pain. They did not want to be in this predicament. Each council member picked their human of choice, sinking their fangs into their human's flesh. Blood oozed all over the clean bodies of the donors. Some were bitten on the traditional spot on the neck, some on the arms and legs; others were on the ground wallowing in the grass being bitten on the upper thighs near their private areas. I had not anticipated being the witness to a vampire feeding. It was not the sensual erotic thing I'd read about in books. I was disgusted and felt so sorry for the humans. I saw that some of them had healed bite marks all over them and guessed that the angel vamps were holding them captive somewhere in the castle and keeping them as their food supply. I wondered if there were others held here against their will.

"What's the story? How does an angel become a vampire?"

"I realize that seeing this is uncomfortable for you. Push through it and look beyond this," Lothos said.

I couldn't believe he was telling me to ignore the fact that these angels were vampires and vicious killers. I'm getting really pissed that every guy I meet keeps asking me to push away my emotions.

"Once the angels became Fallen Ones and were being worshiped as gods, the humans started to incorporate them into ceremonies and bloodletting rituals. That eventually developed into them consuming the blood of willing humans such as tribal leaders. It was said that drinking the blood of humans or consuming the flesh of humans extended the life of the Fallen. That continued for centuries and the Fallen grew into a much darker entity and eventually fled being swept into the darkness. They soon started to plan a revolt against the angels that still held Grace, and made a major attempt to resurface in the sun but it was too late. The blood had transformed them into deadly, powerful, beautiful, immortal beings. To sum it up in one word it was evolution."

Stunned over this new information and having seen way too much blood for one night, I jumped up and went back into the castle. The guard allowed me to pass with no problem. I telepathically told Lothos to meet me back in my chambers when he felt it was safe enough.

Did I just say chambers? I've been here too long.

I strutted back to my room like I owned the place. The moment I looked back to see if someone was behind me, a flash hit me in an instant. I saw Hope approaching. She stood erect, towering over me. Blood slowly dripped from her mouth. Her menacing golden poppy eyes deeply studied me with hunger. It felt like she was really seeing me, but that was impossible. This was my vision. Not sure of what it meant, I shook it off.

I threw myself down on the bed and thought about how I was going to get my dagger back. As I was thinking, my worry for Angelo increased. Where was he? I got up and started to investigate the room. I moved the curtains to reveal that there were no windows. No type of fresh air could get in and there was no escape. The place was beginning to feel like a prison. My searching stopped when I heard a knock on the door. I quickly ran and opened the door to find Lothos there. Peering down the hall, I saw that the guard wasn't there anymore. I pulled Lothos in by the arm and quietly closed the door behind him.

"What took you so long? I thought maybe you became the meal," I said jokingly.

"I had to be sure it was safe. They are still feeding, so you don't have to worry about them for a while. That was just a show, that whole thing back there." He turned toward the door.

"I know. They were trying to intimidate me. I have to admit, it scared me a little but that's all."

"So the last time you saw your guardian was when you were being led here?"

"Yes. Wait." I cut Lothos off. "I thought I heard a rustling sound." We stood still for a few seconds. Everything seemed to be fine so we continued our conversation with our voices low. "After I took the hand of Demas that was it, that was the last time I saw him. Angelo promised that he would find me." My voice trembled, and I almost started to cry. Being separated from him hurt my heart. I loved him so much. If anything happened to him I didn't think I could ever forgive myself. He had done so much for me and I owed him everything.

"They sent Demas to bring you here?"

"Yeah, and I think he took my weapon."

"You don't have to worry about that. Didn't Angelo tell you about the weapons of Angels?"

"Yes, he said that it's mine. It was forged just for my hands, for my destiny."

"You know what that means don't you?" I looked up at the ceiling searching for an answer. Then it struck me.

"What's wrong with me? Of course! I can call for the dagger!" I said to Lothos excitedly.

"Thank you Lothos, that will be all. I won't let you risk your life for me. It's not right."

"Please. I want to help, and you need all the help you can get. It is my pleasure. I owe you and your mother."

"I can't tell you how much this means to me."

"Say no more," he said, looking at me sincerely. "I really cannot say what happened to Angelo. Guardians have a deep connection with their charges. Try channeling your powers, connect, let them flow above yourself and beyond. Focus on him and what you share with him. Your astral form should feel the presence and location of your guardian. I will give you some time alone. Just call my name out loud and I will come." Before I said another word, he disappeared.

"Thank you," I murmured tenderly.

I sighed deeply and thought about what Lothos said. I laid flat across the bed. Closing my eyes, I inhaled and exhaled, and focused intently on Angelo, picturing his face in my mind. My body vibrated, over-taking me, with great the force. I felt myself levitating off of the bed. I opened my eyes. Bright blue and white orbs circulated near the area by the armoire, and Angelo materialized from the orbs.

I lost my focus the second I saw him and down I went. Before I hit the bed I was in Angelo's arms. I loved greeting him in that way. Gripping on to his neck and smiling from ear to ear, I held his head and planted my lips on top of his. We embraced each other tightly. Words were not exchanged. For at least five minutes our lips were locked in a passionate kiss.

"You are the most beautiful woman I have ever seen," he whispered, and I shuddered in pleasure at his words.

"I thought I'd lost you," I whispered.

"For some reason, I couldn't enter the boundaries of the castle by my own powers. They have an enchantment on the area. Their magic is very powerful. We must be careful; the angel vamps can also tap into other creatures' magic," he informed me as we both sat up. I hoped that didn't include my magic.

"I figured that. You were right about everything—I saw them feeding. They keep humans here as food. It's disgusting, and we have to save them. I sensed fear in all of them. The humans are under a spell but I could detect traces of their emotions."

"We'll save them, but first I have to look out for you and get you out of this." Angelo brushed his hand against my back.

It felt like I had spent several days at the castle, but the truth was I hadn't been there long at all. I had managed to keep my cool even though I was led into a trap. Christine was about to officially join the afterlife and I had no power to reverse it. Gilad was dead and my mother was still locked up, in more trouble than ever. A week before I would have been crying my eyes out, but now I realized that drowning in sorrow wasn't the way to handle everything. I was stronger now. I would conquer this and set things right. I told Angelo everything about Lothos and my experience in the castle. I also expressed concern over my missing dagger. Whoever took it from me knew it belonged to me and knew I could get it back.

"I'm going to stay the night with you. Our best bet is to retrieve the dagger and find the humans after the sun rises. They'll go down for the day and won't sense the use of our powers. You'll have the opportunity to call for it then." Angelo held me closer as he spoke into my ear.

Chapter Thirteen

I t was very boring waiting for the council members to go down for the day. I couldn't get comfortable enough to be with Angelo in the way that I wanted to. It was nearly dawn, and my body was tired but I couldn't think about resting. We had to make sure that we didn't make a sound while on our search for the human captives.

When daylight came, I peeked out of the door to my room as I assessed the area. Sunlight beamed through the stained glass windows. There were no guards in sight, so I thought they had to be vampires too. The coast was clear.

I thought about my dagger long and hard. The energy in my palm increased and my hand became numb. A cool blue light emerged from my left palm, and the Dagger of Doshon appeared in my grasp once again. I felt relieved as, if somehow the dagger completed me. I grew stronger when it touched my skin. I strapped it back on to my ankle ready to face anything.

We cloaked ourselves with the power of invisibility and glided down the hall, suspiciously peering all around. I could tell by Angelo's attitude that he just wanted to get me out of there, and not worry about the captives. I knew that saving the others would be risky, but at least I'd be doing something good for someone else. I'd traveled to other worlds across the galaxies, and beyond the state of the living to bring my friend back from the dead and it didn't work. Despite what I am I couldn't save her, but these people weren't dead not yet, anyway. It was my duty to keep them alive and bring them to safety. I held on tightly to Angelo's belt, following his lead. We both thought it was extremely bizarre that not one guard was around. I was pleased over the fact that no one would stand in our way but something told me that it wasn't a good thing either. A part of me hoped that Lothos would surface and join in the rescue efforts.

"We need to leave here, Sydney. I know you don't want to hear it, but you're in danger. We can come back for these people," Angelo whispered softly as we came to a large steel door at the end of the hall. I looked over my shoulder, annoyed over what Angelo had said. I felt that this was something that I had to do. This time I was not going to fail anyone.

"We have to, Angelo. I wish you could understand."

"I do, but what you don't get is that these creatures want you desperately," Angelo shot back. "You believe that you failed at saving Christine, and that have to make up for that by saving these other people. I get that. But you're being so stubborn about this. Not once did you think of a real plan. What are we supposed to do once we get them all? How are we going to get them out of the castle without being noticed? We have no idea what state they're in. I'm sorry but you're being way too impulsive." Angelo quietly opened the door which led to an area that was different from parts of the castle I had seen. A winding steel staircase led downwards and, red walls, chipped paint and exposed pipes lined the narrow pathway down. The stairs didn't appear to be very stable, which worried me. I pushed the door closed gently and realized that there was no knob on the other side.

"Shit," I said, alarmed. Angelo whipped around to see what I meant. Tilting his head to the side he was extremely aggravated.

"We have no idea what's down there," he said.

"Well, we can't go back now. Let's check it out. The second we see the first sign of trouble we're out of here." I held both arms around Angelo's fit body. Maneuvering single file down the steel steps, it was hard to keep the noise to a decent level. The stairs creaked with every step we made.

As we reached the bottom of stairway I peered around from behind Angelo. We were in a large, dank room that looked like a dungeon. Puddles of blood were everywhere, and I had to shift my footing to avoid stepping in it. I lifted up my gown carefully to watch my steps. The most shocking sight of all was when we looked up and saw several bodies hanging upside down from the ceiling with wads of torn flesh and muscle exposed. Their skin had been pulled back as if they were bananas, and their veins and viscera were exposed. Their bodies were dismantled, but their faces were intact. The corpses were in various stages of decomposition, so they had been there for a while.

I covered my mouth, afraid to let out some kind of sound. Feeling fear and deep remorse for these victims, the tears streamed down my face. I had seen so much blood and gore recently, but it was still something I couldn't get used to. I buried my face in Angelo's back to avoid the sight.

I had to find the men and women I had seen last night before they ended up skinned alive. I jumped from behind Angelo to get a closer look at the scene. Gradually making my way around the dark room, I saw that there were large cages at the ends of four narrow corridors that branched out from the room. Inside each of the cages were three sad, dirty and injured people. I ran back and forth down the corridors hoping that the captives wouldn't hear a sound. They were on top of each other, naked and in great pain. My angel followed me quietly, waiting for me to act. It was a good thing that they couldn't see us, because if they did they would have panicked.

"We have to move fast. First we have to heal them," I told Angelo as we stood in the middle of the blood soaked dungeon. Adrenaline coursed through my body. This was my chance to make things right. Angelo shook his head.

"Once the Council finds out, they are going to suspect us."

"You think it's okay to just leave these people here to die?" I asked parting my lips subtly.

"No, but you must listen to me. I want to save them just as much as you do, but we can't right now. We need backup. These captives are way too fresh. The angel vamps are nowhere near through with feeding off of them. We have time. We need to try to at least weaken the Council before we risk in getting caught or killed." He grabbed my hand and spoke earnestly.

[120]

"Fine. We'll do it your way." Relaxing my arms, I shrugged my shoulders. My eyes glowed in the dark.

I hated leaving the captives. All I wanted to do was turn back and get them out, but I suppressed the impulse. I remembered being held against my will, and no human should have to experience that. I really felt disappointed with Angelo for wanting to leave. I understood the risk but, a part of me still felt like he didn't understand why I needed to save them.

We managed to get back to my room without anyone noticing us. I made sure the door was locked and began to summon Lothos.

"What are you doing?" Angelo asked. It was kind of awkward but I didn't care.

"I'm calling for backup." I replied. Lothos popped in, emerging from a brilliant light. The entrance impressed me, and Angelo noticed that I noticed.

"Hello my darling," he said as he greeted me, and then kissed my hand. Lothos was very charming. Looking over at Angelo he said, "I see you took my advice and were able to find that connection between the two of you. You are a fast learner." Lothos said with a smile and I smiled proudly.

"Lothos, this is my guardian angel, Angelo. Angelo, this is my friend Lothos." They nodded at each other, extended and clasped their arms.

"We need your help. What do you know about the humans from last night?" Angelo questioned Lothos.

"Not much, I know that they are the current feed."

"Is that what they call them?" Angelo appeared astonished.

"Yes."

"How long does the current feed last?" My Guardian wanted to know just as much as I did about these creatures. Lothos looked at us, then at the golden ceiling. He thought for a moment.

"They usually feed on them for about a week, unless they die before the week is over. Then new ones are brought in. It is a never-ending process."

"That's insane," I blurted. "How can they do that to people? That must be torture, to be ripped from their families and lives and brought to a strange world. I wonder if they can sense the difference between the worlds."

"Most likely they do not. The angel vamps usually alter their minds to such an extent that by the time they reach the boundaries of this world, they are practically zombies."

"That's awful. We have to stop them. They have no right to be doing this!" My voice swelled with anger. Both angels shushed me simultaneously.

[121]

"Another thing," I added. "When we went searching for the humans, we realized that there were no guards around. Why is that?"

"The guards are vampires. The Council has wards to protect the castle but they also have day time protectors that are wolves. They highly regard their privacy and discretion."

"They call feeding from human's right in front of my face discretion? I'm really starting to hate these fucking creatures." The guys' eyes widened, but saying that word made me feel a little better —just a little. Looking down, I saw that the bottom of my dress had blood stains on it. I wanted to get out of it.

Our conversation was cut short when someone knocked at the door, and nervous flutter hit my stomach. I hadn't had time to change my gown and the guys had nowhere to hide in the room. I gestured for them to pop out. They vanished into thin air, traveling to the in-between places of the dimension. Adjusting my gown so that my guest couldn't see the blood, I relaxed and carefully unlocked the door, to reveal who it was.

"I am sorry to bother you My Lady, but I am Galveston. I was sent here to accommodate you for the day." A humanoid creature stood before me with white skin and ears shaped like the letter V. He appeared to be very young—no more than seventeen or eighteen years old— but I knew that he was magical and older than he looked. His white long hair was slicked back in a neat, low pony tail, and his light gray eyes brightly stared into me.

"I thought everyone was down for the day," I said with a smile.

"My condition is not as unique as the council members." His voice bore an accent I hadn't heard before. I smirked flirtatiously.

"Do you mind if I freshen up a bit before we go out?"

"No not at all. Please go ahead," he said elegantly. I closed the door, went to the armoire and pulled out another dress, and ran straight to the bathroom. I freshened up as quickly as I could. The blue frock was not as elaborate as the black gown, but it was still nice. I pulled the tiara out of my hair and fluffed my dark, loose locks, and then I jetted out of bathroom. On the way out both angels startled me by popping in suddenly. I guess there's no way you can warn a girl when you have powers like that.

"You're really going out with him?" Angelo was upset, a side of him I rarely got to see.

"Yes," I replied. "It's not like I want to. I have to. Someone sent him. If I don't go he may report it."

"We have no clue what he is or what his intentions are. We don't know who sent him and why. Accommodate you for the day?" What a line!" Angelo said hotly.

"Look, jealously doesn't suit you. Stay here, the both of you. This gives me an opportunity to snoop around in a non-obvious way." Lothos just stood there, looking back from me to Angelo. "Lothos, who is he?" I asked quickly.

[122]

"I am not sure. I have never seen him before. If you must go, please be careful."

"I can't get a read on his essence. I need to get closer," Angelo said to Lothos.

"We can't follow them because we do not know what kind of powers he has. He may be able to detect us," Lothos stated.

"Then she'll be left on her own." Angelo looked at me after he spoke.

"I'm still here, you know. I'll be fine. I'm well protected." I touched the door knob to let the guys know I was ready to step out of the room. They went behind the door to see me off.

"You look very lovely," Galveston said as I stepped out of the room.

"Thank you," I replied in a low tone, pulling the door closed. I studied him intently but I couldn't see his aura. I could not keep my eyes off of him. I kept wondering what type of creature he was. We turned left and went in another direction down the main hall.

"I thought that giving you a proper tour would be appropriate, but first I wanted to take care of you." I ran my fingers through my hair. What did he mean by that? I thought. We came to a door that was draped in rose vines. When he opened it my eyes shifted around. Short female dwarfs were dressed in cream-colored smocks. They all had similar body types and straight brown hair pulled into tight buns. Their ears were extremely pointed and appeared wrinkled. There were tables positioned in every corner of the room, and in the center was a large pool with steam coming from it. Standing to the left of me was a tall female elf holding a tray of croissants with butter and jam. My mouth watered. I was hungry and hadn't eaten since the night before.

"Go enjoy yourself at the spa. I will be back for you later to take you out riding."

"Oh thank you, Sir. This is so nice. I'm sure I'll have a good time." He turned around and walked out. The women greeted me elegantly, and I ate up the charm. I remembered when mom and I would spend time together at the local spa in our town. I rarely went alone. Christine and I used to go sometimes too. Saddened over my loss I thought about the reasons why Hope and the others wanted me to come here. What were they going to gain from it? I took a croissant and ate it with gusto. I savored the flavor of the homemade jam. After I finished, I was instructed to undress in the vanity area near the steam room in the back. I came out in a long white robe.

My spa experience was all a girl could dream for. They gave me a full body massage and wrapped me in exotic herbs. I sipped on some kind of wine the dwarves made from their own vineyard as they bathed me in a pool filled with magical elements. It was the most wonderful spa experience I'd ever had. They even washed and styled my hair with cascading curls, the look I usually did with my curling iron at home. It was beautiful, and my tresses shimmered and bounced.

The ladies dressed me in a sleek spaghetti-strap teal gown with a deep neckline and scattered beading. They sure had a great fashion sense, and were gifted in finding a gown that fit my body type. I learned that they were the ones who picked out all of my clothing. I was dressed too fancy to go riding, so I decided to tell Galveston that we could go another time.

Feeling like a million bucks, I sashayed out of the spa and into the care of Galveston who was waiting for me out in the hall. He led me back to the gardens, which held such bad memories since the incident I witnessed last night. The territory was different during the day. The landscape was thick with green trees and shrubs. The flowers whispered to me. Galveston turned to face me as we stood admiring the landscape.

I suddenly became engulfed by so many emotions, but one was so potent that it was hard to ignore. Lustful desire emanated from Galveston's gaze, penetrating throughout my body. I wanted him too, but sensed that it was wrong. My heart belonged to another, I thought.

I spotted two white unicorns galloping in the distance. I shifted my eyes to look at them for a split second and started to drift off somewhere. I tried to shake it off, but my vision gradually diminished and my heart rate accelerated with a growing fear. The animals hummed from afar. I tried to not panic and struggled to maintain my composure. Galveston moved in closer, standing much closer than I was comfortable with. Gasping to catch my breath, I said something to the creature that I didn't understand. My motor functions in my body diminished, and I seemed to be moving in slow motion. Everything in my sight faded away as time came to a halt, and a large ball of light encircled me, swallowing my entire essence.

Chapter Fourteen

I blinked my eyes, stunned over my latest new found ability, and looked all around me. Lothos and Angelo were there, looking at me with a blank stare. I was just as curious as they were. I sat on the bed with my legs crossed as more questions surged in my brain.

"How did I get back here?" I asked.

"Your power… You felt threatened," Angelo answered quickly.

"That guy that I was with, he's an Incubus. He tried to use his magic to seduce me into doing something. I'm not sure what. At any rate, it didn't work, and now I'm here."

I thought for a moment. "If we're not going to save those people this very second, then I want to go home. This is our chance. It's daytime and the angel vamps will be asleep for a while. There's nothing else here holding me. I won't let them keep me here any longer. I have a life on the Earthly Realm, a mother that needs me, and a business to run."

Anxious to leave, I stood up. "Galveston will be searching for me. I hate being here and despise Hope and what she did to my family. One of the fallen have already met their death by my hand, and one day they all will." The skin on my forehead wrinkled as the words uttered from my parted lips. "They want me to stay and have made every effort to convince me that this is where I belong, but it's not true. I refuse to be victimized by this! I want my life back!" The lump that rose in my throat almost made me choke. I made a silent vow that I would return to this place to save those people from Hope and stop the Council members. I grabbed the hands of both angels, as we channeled all of our magic. The sound of our connection boomed with a rumble, and we reappeared in the living room of my house.

Lothos jerked his hand and away from me. I could tell by the frown on his face that he was not pleased to be in my home. I had trouble catching my breath, and I felt weak with sickness as I coughed and coughed. Going down on one knee, and holding on to the edge of the sofa, I threw up the contents that rested in my stomach. Angelo helped me up and I managed to get to my feet, staggering a little. Wiping my mouth, I ran to the bathroom, and rinsed my mouth out with warm water and Listerine.

Slowly strutting back out to meet my guests, I noticed that the floor was clean. I smiled at Angelo, and silently thanked him for cleaning up the mess. With all the time traveling, I hadn't been consistent with taking my birth control pills, which made me nervous. Brushing my hair out of my face I looked at the angels.

The look on Lothos' face told me that something was wrong. "What?" I snapped at him.

"I never told you that I would be coming here. You have jeopardized my whole plan. How could you? You didn't even ask me if wanted to be here!" He threw up his hands, making an attempt to control his anger at me.

"What plan? What are you talking about?" I asked, placing my hands on my hips.

"I already told you that the angel vamps believe that I work for them. If they ever learn that I am here with you, helping you, they will kill me for sure."

"Don't be such a coward. I can protect you," I said without thinking. Angelo didn't seem too happy about the situation either, and I felt offended. Looking at both of them with disgust, I paced back and forth on the soft carpet. Lothos shook his head at me.

"I can't believe you. I told you that I am here you for and your mother. I can't help you like this. I'm going back. I will check in with you later." Furious over what I had done, Lothos faded away into a ball of white light. Standing in the middle of the dim room, I felt bewildered.

"What was that all about?"

"You let your emotions get the best of you," Angelo replied. "Lothos is working from the inside; you really could have fucked things up." Angelo sounded funny saying a curse word. I smiled inside.

"Unbelievable!" Still not understanding what just went down, I stormed up the stairs sulking like a five-year old. I slammed the door to my bed room, unable to enjoy being home for the moment. Sitting on the edge of my bed, I pulled out the top drawer of my night table and grabbed the small pouch of birth control pills and opening it. I was right—I had missed a couple of days. Angelo stepped into room the moment I popped a pill from the pack, startling me.

"Hey. What are you doing?" He asked.

"Nothing, I'm taking my pill," I said, annoyed. He towered over me, looking down into my eyes. "I've missed a few days, and getting sick downstairs kind of made me nervous. I know I've never asked you this before, but can you…?" My voice diminished before I could finish my sentence.

"Yes, I can father children, and I want to. And no I don't have any yet. Do you think you may be pregnant?" Angelo's voice elevated. Sitting next to me he gently rubbed the center of my back.

"I don't know. I'm scared. We have been very active lately." I held my head down, avoiding his eyes.

"Whether it happens now or later, it doesn't matter. I want a future with you. I want a child with you," he softly uttered, and my head rose, meeting his tender gaze.

"You do? We haven't been out on our first date officially, but I know that I want that life with you too," I sighed. He planted his lips on mine delicately. He did everything to help ease my mind, and I told him the truth about how I really felt for him. I felt that our relationship was still way too new for us to even consider having a baby, and raising a child was the furthest thing on my mind. I wasn't even sure if I should take the pill—what if I was already pregnant? I popped it back in the pouch and thought about taking a pregnancy test. On the other hand maybe

[126]

I got sick because I used a power I'd never accessed before. I had transported two other beings in addition to myself so that was a big possibility. I buried my head in Angelo's chest, and closed my eyes, relaxing for a moment.

"Sydney, how would you really feel if you were pregnant?" Oh my God, the question I did not want him to ask me.

"Happy, and sad," I replied.

"Why?"

"Well, because I want you and I want to be a mother someday. But I'd always wanted my dad here to be Grandpa, and I won't have my mother for support. She won't understand." Taking a deep breath I continued, "I wouldn't be married." I swallowed hard and left it at that. He wrapped both arms around me and squeezed. We ended that conversation in silence.

"You need more protection than I can give you," he said changing the subject. I have a friend I can trust, and when you were up here alone, I made a couple of calls. I might need to leave for a short while to take care of something else I'm working on, and I want someone with you. I hate to leave, but I have to do this before the members of the Council come knocking."

"Who did you have in mind?" I questioned, moving over to the window. I carefully pulled the curtain back, and peeked outside. It was almost dark, but I didn't know what day or time it was. I started to feel pissed off about what happened with Christine all over again, and I realized I didn't really want to know what day it was.

"Tristan is his name," Angelo informed me. He's a good guy. We've known each other for a few centuries. We were once travel companions."

"Centuries? He's an old-timer, I guess." I wondered what kind of creature would be coming into my home. I figured that it would be rude to ask who this guy really was—I didn't want Angelo to feel that I didn't trust him, so I decided not to ask at all.

"He'll be here soon," Angelo replied.

"Why do you think that your power isn't good enough to provide appropriate protection for me?"

"Because the Council members are very powerful as individuals, and as a collective entity their power greatly surpasses mine. If they want you right this second they can get you. I'll go down fighting for you, but will eventually be over-powered."

"That's not necessarily true. If you combine powers with me and Lothos and we can find more angels to help us, then we can fight against them and defeat them." I made a valid point.

"The war hasn't begun yet, but you're right. We have to obtain the aid of others to increase our strength." The doorbell rang, interrupting Angelo's speech. We both raced down stairs. Relieved that our previous conversation was temporarily over, I ran my fingers through my hair and adjusted my gown when I got to the bottom of the stairs. It had gotten dark quickly, so I turned on a few lights.

Standing near the door next to Angelo I opened it, seeing my visitor in plain view. He had pale skin, short blond hair, clear intense eyes, and a neatly trimmed, thin beard. His hair was a little damp from the drizzle, and he looked intimidating in jeans and a dark jacket. The attractive vampire mounted on top of the porch was waiting for my invitation to enter. I studied him intently and noticed that he didn't have an aura. Because vampires were actually dead, and can't have auras, he was literally a dead man walking. Shuttered by his presence I think a light smile swept across my face. This was my first pureblood vampire encounter, I thought to myself.

"Hey, I'm Sydney, and you know Angelo," I said, nodding in Angelo's direction. They nodded at each other as I opened the door wider for him to enter. Tristan looked me up and down, wondering why I was wearing such a fancy gown. I gave him permission to come into my home, hoping that doing so wouldn't stand as an open invitation for other vampires to enter against my will. His stride was light and effortless, as the vampire crossed the threshold into my house. My eyes captured a transparent force field that wavered the moment Tristan entered. After I closed the door and flicked on the front porch light, Tristan shook my hand and embraced Angelo fondly. Inviting the two into the living room, I took the damp jacket from my guest and hung it up on the coat rack near the door.

How do an angel and a vampire become friends? I wondered as I sat on my dad's recliner. Both guys sat on the sofa. I turned on the TV for some background noise.

"So when did you two first meet?" I sat back, placing my arm on the cushioned arm rest.

"It's actually an interesting story," Tristan said. "During the early 1500's I lived in England. The world was so different at that time. I was a newly-made vampire, and I had chosen to remain with my family, concealing my nature from them. I was business partners with Demetrius, the one who made me. He was always obsessed with my family and blood-thirsty. I had done some travelling to promote the business and when I returned, my wife and children were dead and buried. I was told that they died by the plague, but I wasn't satisfied with that, so I did some investigating, and discovered that he killed them." Tristan took a deep breath and continued, "He envied the life I had and hated my decision to stay with my family after I became vampire. When I learned that it was he who had killed them, I confronted him about what I discovered. Demetrius denied it completely, and later exposed my supernatural identity, making the townspeople believe that I was the one who killed my family. I was sentenced to death, but Angelo was passing through and found me rotting in a dank cell. He recognized that I was supernatural and sensed that I was honest. He was the first non-vampire supernatural creature I had met. Rescuing me from my date with the sun I left the life I had in England behind me." Tristan's eyes flickered; I saw the pain in him.

"Wow, that really happened to you?" I asked. "I'm so sorry to hear that you lost your family." Tristan nodded in response. I looked down, playing with my nails.

[128]

"That's why when Angelo told me you were in trouble; I dropped everything to come here. I know what it's like to lose family and be left in the world alone. I'm an ally of the Angelic Clan. I will do right by you, by protecting you with my life."

"Thank you, Tristan," I said, reaching over and affectionately touching his knee. In an instant I felt what Angelo once read from him. The vampire was a, genuine caring being. Although I shivered from his coldness when I touched him, he did have a soul. He did have humanity inside of him. Tristan was not the coldblooded killer that vampires usually get credit for. This was a new revelation.

I got up and went into the kitchen, calling from behind the swinging door of the kitchen, to offer Tristan and Angelo something to eat. I got the serving tray out of the cupboard and filled a couple of bowls with chips and pretzels. I had gone shopping a couple days before but had rarely been home, so my fridge was nicely stocked. I retrieved a package of steak, opened it and placed it on a nice plate with floral designs around it. I didn't have time to cook it, so it was nice that my vampire visitor could enjoy it. Curling my lips over the sight of the bloody meat, I snatched a fork and a steak knife out of a drawer adjacent to the stove. I carried the tray into the living room, moved some magazines out of the way, and placed the tray on the coffee table. I smiled as I stood up. Tristan sat up on the sofa inhaling the aroma of blood. Angelo got up, walked over to the bar and got three glasses and a bottle of red wine from the wine cooler under the bar.

I needed to eat some real food instead of chips so I decided to order a pizza for Angelo and me. Angelo gave me a glass of red wine. I was reluctant to drink it because it was possible that I was pregnant, but I took a sip. Placing the glass on the table, I chomped on the chips and pretzels while we waited for the pizza.

Tristan asked me if it was okay if he ate the steak in the living room, normally my mother wouldn't tolerate anyone eating anything in this room, but there were things that I needed to change and that was one of them. I wanted my home to be warm and inviting and to make people feel that this is a place they could be comfortable in. I gave him permission.

As Tristan munched on the meat, I carefully studied him. He didn't look a day over the age of 25. His skin was smooth and wrinkle free and his beard gave him personality and a sense of mysteriousness. Youth and immortality are two things that humans long for. I wondered if I would ever grow old. Growing old frightens me. Would being half angel protect me from it?

We didn't have to wait long for our food. I consumed three sausage and pepper slices along with six spicy wings, not realizing how hungry I was. Entertaining my guests gave me an appreciation of spending time in my home. Tristan devoured the steak long before our food arrived. Angelo kept his eyes fixed on me as I ate, and I could tell what he was thinking. I even thought it myself, but didn't want to jump to conclusions too soon.

Tristan was very nice. He even helped us clear the dishes and put things away. I quickly washed our plates, placing them in the dish strainer to dry. I refilled our wine glasses as we continued to get to know each other. I was surprised that Tristan was able to drink red wine, so I handed him the glass with questions on my lips keeping them tucked away.

As I approached the swinging doors to leave the kitchen, a sudden sense of danger spiraled through me. I clutched the edge of the counter to support myself, my head jerked back in a reflex reaction. I was exhausted and overwhelmed from the influence my flashes had on me. I slid down on to the floor, folded my legs and looked up in confusion. Angelo and Tristan tried to help me up, but I resisted them.

"Someone is coming for me," I said with a shaky tone.

"That's why we are here," Tristan stated. Kneeling down, Angelo caressed my shoulder. Embarrassed by my vulnerability, I just wanted to be alone. I needed to pay my mother and Luna a long overdue visit. I thought about them for a moment. Angelo lifted my wilted body off of the kitchen floor, and carried me into the living room, placing me on the sofa. Tristan looked extremely worried when he gazed into my eyes. It was hard to see a sympathetic vampire.

"Did you see who was coming for you in your vision?" Angelo asked.

"No baby, I didn't. I just saw the shape of two dark male creatures and felt their hostile presence towards me."

"Okay, relax here," Tristan said. "I'm going to do a quick scan of the house and property." He zoomed off with his vampire speed. Angelo and I sat quietly for a few seconds. Breaking the silence, I told him that I wanted to freshen up in the shower and get comfortable, but he insisted that I stay on the sofa for a little while longer.

Seconds later Tristan came back in a whoosh. The drapes fluttered in the breeze his speed created. Tristan calmly told us that the house was clear, but that he had gotten a whiff of a wolf. I knew exactly what he meant and thought about the werewolves that were held captive by the Elves of The Neatherwood. Recovered from my flash, I reassured the guys that I would be fine and left Tristan in front of the TV to go upstairs with Angelo. Feeling terribly fatigued, I found I couldn't even make it to the shower. Before I realized it I had slid between the sheets and covered myself with the thick warm bedspread.

I woke up around 2:00 in the morning feeling refreshed. Sitting up in the dark, I switched on the lamp on my night table. Angelo was so cute, cuddled with the pillow tucked under his arm. Crawling out of bed, I realized that I was in my bra and panties. I assumed that Angelo had removed the gown after I dozed off. I tip-toed to the bathroom and gently closed the door. I turned on the water in the shower, stripped off my underwear and glided beneath the warm flow of water. Lathering up all the important areas, the heat of the steam gave me much pleasure. I was finished in no time, and combed out my damp hair. I decided to let it air-dry. I didn't want to wake Angelo with the noise of the dryer. I pulled on a pair of thick sweat pants and a tank top, threw on my warm sweater and slipper boots, and slithered down the steps on my way to the kitchen.

The entire downstairs area was engulfed in darkness. Wondering where my vampire guest had gone, I noticed the television was out and the lights were not working. I managed to get to the kitchen without bumping into anything. Maybe a fuse blew, I thought. I stopped dead in my tracks when I felt a cold rush of wind brush against me. The back door swung open flapping in the wind, creaking, as it set my nerves on edge. Even the back porch lights were out, which made me apprehensive that something was not right, since I knew I'd turned them on earlier. My eyes were sharp and steady as I scanned the area for any kind of movement. The atmosphere was dark, and I could feel the presence of danger. I knew that calling for Angelo and Tristan aloud was not a good idea, so I pulled my dagger out of the scabbard and tightly gripped on to the hilt, preparing to defend my home. I slowly walked towards the back door, feeling the cold gusts of wind. I had lived on this property for most of my life but the darkness of the night felt unfamiliar.

It had started snowing again and there were about four inches on the ground. Still moving, holding the dagger out with one hand, I was almost to the door. Suddenly strong arms grabbed me from behind. I shrieked as long, sleek fingers covered my mouth. I struggled to break free; the sensation of cool breath grazed my ear and neck.

"Shhh... Don't move, it's me..." a voice murmured. I relaxed a bit, recognizing the voice of Tristan. Still cautious, I let out a sigh and allowed the dagger to gradually go down to my side.

He motioned for me to go hide inside the pantry. There was some kind of intruder on my property but I had no clue where. I backed up, feeling the wall, and moving slowly, eventually feeling the border of the pantry with my flat palms. I opened the door with caution and backed up into the kitchen storage room with ease. Pushing some of the canned goods back on the shelves without making a sound, I adjusted my body and closed the door, leaving it ajar so I could hear what was going on. I thought about Angelo and wanted to see him and Tristan in action.

My back pressed against the cans and cereal boxes. I shut my eyes tightly and contacted my guardian telepathically, telling him where I was hiding. He made me aware that he knew what was happening, and told me to stay put. I didn't like the concept of hiding in my own home. I wanted to come out and fight the bastards that were hunting me down. I felt I owed it to myself, my mother, my father and to Christine.

Angelo and Tristan had an unspoken plan. I heard loud thumps and bangs as a result of them protecting me. Those noises were followed by grunts and the rustling sound of struggling, deep breathing and heavy blows. They were fighting on my back porch. I worried that the neighbors would hear and call the police. We certainly didn't need the police to be involved. The noise continued for a few more minutes, and then everything went quiet.

I was unsure of whether it was safe to come out so, I decided to stay in the pantry a little longer. The door opened, and it was Tristan standing before me, completely calm and collected. The wildness of his blond hair and blood oozing from his mouth were the only indications that he had been in some kind of battle. I think he fed on the intruders.

[131]

Emerging from the pantry, I looked around to see where Angelo was. I stepped a few feet toward the open door, and saw two extremely large, naked male bodies lying dead, as the white snow trickled down on top of them. I was gazing upon the corpses, when I saw Angelo come from the wooded area on the side of my house. His clothes were torn and there was blood was all over his jeans and shirt. He walked in my direction, holding his bloody sword, and stepped into my embrace, as he gently pushed me back inside. He tried to block the ghastly sight from me, but I was curious to gaze upon the bodies again. I slowly released from Angelo's grasp and maneuvered toward the open door.

"Who were they?" I asked my voice shaky and my teeth chattering. The kitchen was freezing and still dark.

"They were wolves, hired by Hope and the council members to take you back their world." Clutching my sweater tightly to me, I looked more closely at the figures on the ground. These wolves were different from the ones in the Neatherwood.

"How do you know that the Council hired them to find me?"

"Because they're marked with the crest of the Fallen," Angelo stated.

"What does the crest look like?" I asked avoiding the sight of Angelo's bloody sword.

"It's a brand in the shape of black angel wings, with drips of blood."

The wolves had some kind of tattoo on their bodies that represented the angel vampire Council.

Angelo lifted the side of my face to see if I was hurt. There wasn't a scratch on me.

"We have to move fast and get those bodies off of my property," I said as I pushed the door back, leaving it ajar so the guys knew it had to be done now. Tristan nodded in agreement.

"Too bad they weren't vampires," Angelo said. If they were, the moment we staked them they would have disintegrated. No offense, man." Angelo said apologetically to Tristan. Shrugging his shoulders, Tristan didn't seem to mind the remark.

"Sydney, do you have plastic bags around here?" Angelo asked.

"Yeah, I have some in the garage. Let me go to put the lights on first. I think a fuse

blew—either that or they tampered with my line."

"Tristan, stay up here while I go down in the basement with Sydney." Nodding at Angelo's instructions, Tristan stood by door in a stance that showed he was ready for just about anything. Feeling my way around the kitchen, I got a big flashlight that was in a miscellaneous drawer under the sink. I also have a few extra candles, lighters and batteries in that drawer. I held on to Angelo's hand, and the light guided us, as we slowly went down the steps leading deep into the basement. It was still neat and orderly in the basement. I hadn't been there in weeks and even though I wasn't alone, it still felt eerie.

[132]

I shined the light on the large gray fuse box mounted on the wall near the hot water heater. Opening the box, I saw that the lights were out only on the first floor. I flicked each switch on and the light from the first floor spilled out creating a trail on the basement steps. Angelo and I quickly went back upstairs.

Back in the kitchen Tristan made sure that the back porch light was still off. It was better to move the bodies in the dark. I grabbed my keys, ran out the back door avoiding the bodies on the ground, and went to the garage to gather the things we needed. My mother's and father's cars looked lonely and somber in the spacious garage. Yearning for my parents, I sadly looked at the vehicles. I then went to my father's storage bins. Tools and other materials that belonged to him were carefully arranged in the bins, and I grabbed two large thick plastic bags out of one of them. It was strange that I remembered exactly where my dad kept his things.

Holding the bags in my right hand and the keys in my left, I stood in front of the shelves and peered at the stacks of bins. Not sure if I could handle seeing anymore death, I thought I was going to be sick, as I visualized the image of my father in the accident, Christine's dead corpse lying in the morgue, and then the sight of the skinned dead bodies hanging in that dungeon.

I wasn't sure if I could handle the disposal of two dead werewolves, as I watched Angelo and Tristan wrap up the bodies in the oversized black plastic. The two wolves, now in human form were stuffed tightly in garbage bags like tortillas filled with too much meat and cheese. Swiftly hauling the bodies in the back of Angelo's SUV, their angel and vampire strength did them a great justice. Angelo said he could handle the rest on his own. I watched him drive off into the darkness, worried about his murderous cargo.

Chapter Fifteen

I sat on the sofa on edge, twirling my thumbs waiting for my lover to return. The vampire was next to me, with some distance between us. His muscular arm was thrown on top of the sofa. I didn't bother to offer him any more blood since he had fed off of the werewolves. Uneasy about the events of the night, we remained quiet, keeping our thoughts to ourselves.

The television was on some kind of infomercial. Not interested in it, I retrieved the remote and started to flip through channels. Even though I was dealing with my transition of being a nephilim, there were so many other things on my mind. There was my mother and father, Christine, Luna, and this new thing between Angelo and me, plus my phone still hadn't arrived yet. I felt that my life in this world had been put on hold. Feeling cut off from it completely, I didn't know how to pick up the pieces of a life that, so far, had been rattled with interruptions, changes and unordinary circumstances.

It was almost four in the morning. Tristan was such a trooper for waiting up with me. The sun would be coming up soon, and I knew he had to go down for the day. My eyes grew heavy, and I was about to doze off when I heard the sound of a key in the door. I perked up and waited with anticipation for Angelo to enter.

He was dirty from his own mysterious adventures, but I hopped off of the sofa and gave him a big hug and kiss. I closed and locked the door behind him as he greeted me with a dismal smirk. Without asking any questions, I prompted him to go up to my bathroom to take a shower. I also offered Tristan the chance to freshen up in the downstairs bathroom. Showing him the way down the hall, I flicked on the light to reveal a pale blue floral wallpapered bathroom. My father kept some extra clothes in a drawer in his study. I told Tristan where to find them and that he was welcome to anything he thought was suitable to fit him. I gave him access to the things necessary for a proper wash up, and left him at it.

While the guys were preparing to get nice and clean, I scurried to the kitchen and filled a pot of steaming hot water. Racing out the back door, I went to the area where the two wolves were taken down. It was not hard to find. There was a medium size band with blood faded deep into the snow. I felt a shudder of anxiety in my abdomen when I saw it. The cops would take me down to the station for sure if they saw this.

Pouring the pot of hot water over the whole area, I watched as the snow and blood melted into the dirt disappearing from sight. Using my impeccable hybrid vision I doubled checked to make sure there was no trace of blood left. Thinking about the bloodstained shirts the guys had on, I decided I needed to get them and dispose of them properly. Reassured that there was no evidence left outside, I trotted back into the house with the empty pot. I placed the pot in the sink, then turned, and was quickly startled over Tristan's sudden appearance. I was still not used to supernatural creatures and their unexpected pop-ins. He fit my father's clothes well.

"Sydney, thanks for letting me clean up," he said in a soft tone. Standing barefoot in my kitchen, he wore a pair of jeans and a dark cashmere sweater.

"Anytime. What did you do with your clothes?"

"They're still in the bathroom," he replied.

"Ok, could you bring them to me?" He zoomed out of the kitchen, the door still swinging when he returned with the bundle in his hands. I removed the jeans from his grasp and looked them over intently. They were OK as far as I could see. I gave him back the jeans and took the shirt. A few splats of blood were barely noticeable, but that was enough for me.

I put the jeans in a plastic bag, making a mental note to put them in the washing machine. We walked back into the living room, and I telepathically told Angelo to let me inspect his clothes when he came down. Moments later he glided down the stairs holding a bundle of clothes. This time he had on sweat pants and a tank top. The tank clung closely to the ripples of his chest, and I blushed when I looked at him. His clothes had much more blood on them, so I threw both of their shirts in the fire. Angelo protested a bit, but I had to get rid of the evidence.

"You act like you're going on trial for murder," he said nonchalantly.

"I could be. We have no idea what kind of lives those wolves lived," I said, bending down to tend to the fire, and keep the flames in control. Staring deeply into the flames, I asked, "Now what am I going to do with your jeans? I guess, I should burn them too," I said thinking aloud. "Tristan's didn't have blood on his, so I'm just going to wash them," I said aloud.

"Relax! You can't put them in the fire here. Let me have them and I'll dispose of them properly," Angelo said.

"Where did you dump the bodies?" I probed.

"It's better that you don't know. That way if it does ever come up—which it won't — you honestly won't have any idea about it."

Shrugging my shoulders, I couldn't object to that. I stood up and wiped the soot off my hands.

"Are you staying here today?" I asked Tristan.

"Yes, it will be dawn soon and I must go down for the day," he said, as he looked around.

"I know. You can crash in the basement. There are no windows down there. There's a small room off to the side that has an air mattress all made up. It's pretty comfortable and you'll be able to get your full day's rest."

"I didn't realize you had an extra room," Angelo interjected.

"Yeah, my dad added it before he died. I really don't know why it's there," I replied holding my head down.

[135]

"It's been too long," Angelo said softly. I gazed into his eyes. A silence came over the three of us. Tristan felt a little awkward being involved in our moment.

"Listen guys. I have to go down or I will get sick the closer it is to day break." I stepped over to Tristan, threw my arms around his neck and thanked him for helping to protect me. Even though I had just met him, I felt that I had made a new friend and was comfortable with him being in my home. He was happy to receive my embrace. Saying good night—or in his case, good morning—he zipped out of our sight and into the room in the basement.

"It's been a long night," Angelo said as he held his hand over my face, closing my eyes I felt the influence of his power.

"I know," I replied.

Holding hands we went up to my bedroom. Dawn approached and we fell asleep without any other disturbances.

February had settled in and Connecticut was lucky enough to be snow-free for a while. Christine's murder investigation was over according to the police officials, but the case wasn't officially closed. They went around again and questioned a few leads that basically led them nowhere. New questions surfaced when Gilad and Robert went missing, and I thought Robert's disappearance was strange.

Christine's was buried by the end of the week. I delivered her eulogy even though I wasn't really into public speaking. I owed at least that to her. Angelo went with me to pay his respects and show support. I was surprised that I was able to hold it together throughout the service. I was disappointed because I couldn't save her from death, and I wallowed in sorrow for a short time.

Tristan and Angelo had practically moved in with me, without me even realizing it. It was nice to have the house alive with people despite the fact that my guests weren't human. I hadn't heard anything from Lothos, which worried me, but I didn't want to get sucked back into the world I so abruptly left behind almost two and half weeks ago. I also found out that I wasn't pregnant, which was a relief. I finally sent in my official notice to the school, leaving my teaching assistant job and made time to go into my mom's office to check on Amy and help out. I wanted to ease into working at my mom's publishing company. The business was doing well even in my mom's absence.

Angelo was spending a lot of time at work, after having taken off so much time to help me in my attempt to save Christine. Now that she was gone, he was not only the manager of Resurrection, but also was running the whole business. In addition, work was important because he needed to keep up his human disguise. While Angelo was at work my vampire guest slumbered in the extra room in the basement. I was a bit apprehensive to be alone in the house during the day while Angelo was gone, afraid that Hope might send out a band of familiars to retrieve me and bring me back to their world. Familiars are non-vampires hired by the Council to do vampire business while they sleep.

Over the last few weeks at home I'd worked on perfecting my powers and dagger wielding abilities. Angelo is a master swordsmen and warrior, so he was training me to properly fight. He told me that all nephilims of good belong to an order led by the Hierarchy of the Angelic Clan, called the Celestial Circle. I'm not an official member of yet. Because my mother hid my existence, I missed years of training to prepare me for the Ultimate Battle. This coming battle is why the Council was trying to recruit me and gain control over my power. I'd learned a lot about myself since this adventure had begun. Even more confident than before, my fighting skills had increased, and so had my stress. I knew there was something more about me that the Council wanted and it was imperative that I find out what it was.

My new cell phone finally arrived on Tuesday afternoon. I awoke from a nap with thoughts of my mother. I hadn't seen her in a while, so I made plans to go see her sometime this week. I just wanted to make sure it was safe for me to go. I was worried about the darkness that settled within her, and didn't know how to handle it. And even though things had been quiet for a while, I was not stupid, I knew that I was still in danger and didn't want to risk any more harm to my mother. I decided to delay my visits a little longer.

I spent most of the afternoon reprograming my cell phone with all of my contacts. I had to do it manually because my old phone was instantly destroyed, including its SIM card. I sent Amy and her sister Luna a text message giving them my new number. I went to the market and bought a few things to tide us over for a few days. As the evening was drawing near, I started to think about what I was going to prepare for dinner. Providing all the meals had started to get expensive, and buying a bunch of fresh bloody steaks added up. I felt strange asking Tristan for grocery money. I pushed that idea out of my head, and focused on other things. I decided that I was going to cook meatloaf for dinner.

While the meat loaf was baking, I showered and dressed in my favorite designer jeans. I slid into a purple sheer scoop necked Diane Von Furstenberg blouse, and I carefully put on my makeup, providing special attention to doing a smoky eye with purple eye shadow. Curling my flat tresses, I fluffed it out, giving my hair some extra volume. It bounced when I moved. I pranced barefoot down the steps into the kitchen, holding a pair of royal purple pumps. I placed them on the floor so I could slip into them quickly.

The aroma of the meatloaf made my stomach growl. Angelo would be home soon and Tristan would be awake shortly. I started making the veggies and rice. I didn't have to do anything to Tristan's steak, but open the package and slide it on a plate. Using my powers I summoned some of the spices I needed to season the food.

While the rice and veggies were cooking, I decided to set the table in the large, formal dining room. I walked through the living room past my father's study and went up the three steps that led to the wooden double doors of the dining room. I switched on the chandelier lights. The room was decked out in warm hues and natural wood, and my mother's large 12 seated wooden table shone against the light. I couldn't believe it was still shiny; no one had been in this room in over a year. I decided to polish the table off anyway making sure I got all every inch of the grand table. As I wiggled my toes in the lush, off-white carpet, I thought that my mom shouldn't have chosen white for the carpet color. I promised myself that I would replace it one of these days. If my mom came home tomorrow, she wouldn't mind the subtle changes I had made, since she always trusted my judgment when it came to decorating and fashion.

I had the table set in no time, and even managed to get hold of some beef blood and I had it bottled in the fridge so that Tristan could enjoy his steak with a drink at dinner. I had enough time to throw together a chocolate cake before I expected the guys. It was 4:50 and darkness approached quickly. I thumbed through a Home décor magazine while I babysat my cake in the oven, as I waited for my guests.

A sudden whoosh of wind lifted my hair off of my shoulders. I whipped around and saw the vampire standing behind me. The pages of my magazine flipped closed.

"Hi Tristan!" I said, moving the magazine closer to me.

"Something smells wonderful, and..." His voice trailed off unexpectedly. Standing up, I greeted him happily.

"Yea, I am making dinner for us," I said.

"Angelo won't be joining us?" His mouth twisted a little. He was dressed in clothes I didn't recognize, all black, that complimented his style. I didn't ask him where he got the clothes from. I just assumed he bought them from somewhere local.

"Did you think I was making all this just for the two of us?" I answered. "No, Angelo will be here soon."

"Why the big fuss?"

"Well, it's been a few weeks and things have been quiet around here. I wanted to celebrate our new friendship and the fact that things have been slowly getting back to normal." Tristan made a face, and I turned away from him, slipping two potholders on my hands, I opened the stove. A rush of heat hit my face, and I pulled out the cake carefully, and placed it on the counter. I inhaled the sweetness, as the steam wavered in the air.

"You like to fool yourself into believing that things are getting back to normal," Tristan said. "Why is that? If everything was back to normal, do you think I would still be here?" Tristan was standing so close, that his breath lightly grazed my inner ear, tickling me.

"That's not true— I don't think that everything is back to normal." I said to him with a stutter. I felt his hand touch my shoulder and something about it made me tense. "What's wrong with me wanting some kind of a normal life?" I actually didn't want him to answer that.

He looked and me and abruptly said, "You look beautiful tonight." He touched my hand, and the coldness of his skin alarmed me for a second.

[138]

"Thank you." I grabbed a knife that was on the counter and stuck it down into the cake. Pulling it out gently, I saw that my chocolate cake was done. "You can turn on the television or go into the dining room," I instructed with a crooked smile.

"You know I'd rather stay here with you," he replied softly. I took a few steps to put some distance between us. I expected Angelo to be home any minute and I didn't want him to see me that close to Tristan and think anything was going on. I ignored Tristan's remark, and trying to keep as busy as possible, I got a large plate and flipped the cake.

What was this all about? I asked myself. I heard my phone ring from the living room, and I raced out of the kitchen to retrieve it. I didn't excuse myself and I didn't care, but by the time I got there it had stopped ringing. I was hoping that it was Angelo, but the number was one I didn't recognize. Tristan was standing right where I left him moments before. Feeling a little uncomfortable, I sent Angelo a text message asking him when he would be home. I remembered him telling me that he had to check on his place after he left the shop. I really wanted him to hurry over.

"Would you like something to drink while you wait?" I asked Tristan in a chipper tone.

"Like what, you?" he replied flirtatiously. I started to laugh out loud, as I went to get a wine glass. I retrieved the bottle from the refrigerator, and poured the blood into the glass. I handed him the full glass, and his eyes lit up with amazement and thirst.

"Thank you. I can't believe you did this for me," he said with a smile, gently moving the glass in a circular motion and holding it up to his nose. It was funny to see Tristan acting like he was holding a glass of fine wine. Thank God I hadn't experienced any kind of headaches or pain recently, so I wasn't taking any of my medication. It was nice to enjoy a glass of wine. I opened a bottle and Tristan poured the merlot into the glass for me.

Tristan and I were sitting at the table in my kitchen laughing and talking for over half an hour. I didn't realize what a great sense of humor he had, and in the mist of me letting out a huge chuckle Angelo walked in through the back door.

"It looks like you two are enjoying yourselves," he said, stepping in and closing the door behind him.

"Hi, Baby!" I said, jumping up and planting a big kiss on his lips. "What took you so long?"

"An unexpected meeting, I'm sorry I am late," he said as he walked in. I got another glass and poured Angelo some wine. He greeted Tristan with a hand shake and accepted the alcoholic beverage.

We found ourselves eating and talking in the dining room. Angelo kept raving about how good my meatloaf was and Tristan was overjoyed to be chomping on a huge piece of blood soaked steak. A little bored over the small talk, I was dying to find out what was going on at this so called unexpected meeting that Angelo was called to.

[139]

"What was your meeting was about?" I asked, taking a sip of wine and peering at Angelo.

"Well, I was trying to wait to tell you at the perfect time, but I guess there's no time like the present." I narrowed my eyes in suspicion. I straightened my face, and then made a gesture for him to continue. "I've been called to meet with the Arcs. Apparently an attack has been planned for the near future, but the Council must recapture you first."

How did Angelo think that was something that could wait? That should have been the first thing that came out of his mouth when he walked into my home. I felt like I was going to burst, but I held my tongue.

"The Arcs?" I repeated trying to read Tristan's body language, which suggested that he was concerned. My heart pounded as Angelo continued.

"They're The Great Seven, the leaders of the Angelic Clan. They know what has been going on and have called all Watcher Warriors to meet. They've summoned me to report to them before the next night fall, but they also want me to present you to them. I believe that they're going to offer you direct protection," Angelo said, and I was speechless for a moment.

"The Great Seven," I murmured. "Michael is the most powerful, but as a collective entity they're magically magnificent."

"Exactly, how did you know?" Angelo asked.

"I know of their power," I replied. I didn't want to be rude by excluding Tristan from our conversation, but our discussion was important, and I was glad that I had some time to read through a few chapters of the book I got a few weeks ago about angels.

"Once you're protected by the Arcs, the angel vamps can't touch you."

The second Angelo said that he hit a nerve in me, and I was a bit annoyed.

"You must be crazy if you think that I'm going to leave here, and leave my mother unguarded. Someone infected her with the darkness, and I'm still trying to think of ways to rid her of it. If they want to meet with me then they're more than welcome to come here!" I jumped up from the table and walked out of the dining room, leaving Angelo and Tristan looking stunned over my outburst.

Chapter Sixteen

I wasn't a smoker at all, but I stood outside on the back porch with a cigarette in my mouth. Long before Christine died I convinced her to stop, and took her carton of Marlboro's. I don't know why I didn't throw them away. She stopped for about two weeks then resumed her habit. My efforts to keep her smoke free didn't work. Although it was dark out, I wasn't concerned about having any kind of company other than my angel and the vampire. I was upset that the Angelic Clan wanted me to leave my mother. Angelo hadn't noticed my outfit or my hair, which also angered me. I knew I was being a big baby about it, but I didn't care.

"Please forgive me if I upset you," Angelo's voice echoed from a white mist that began to formulate behind me. "You look lovely tonight," he said as he fully appeared in front of me. "I never meant to be inconsiderate toward you or your feelings." I didn't say anything. "I want your mother to be safe too, and that's why I've arranged for another guardian to watch over her." I felt his hand softly clasp mine. I put the cigarette out and flicked it into the darkness.

"Where will you go?" I asked him flatly.

"There's a gateway open near here that leads to a realm called the Woodland plane. The gateway only appears when it senses angelic magic. That's where I must meet the Angelic Clan. It's more beautiful than you can imagine."

I sighed in frustration. "Angelo, you can't expect me to drop everything and go just because the land is beautiful! I don't know why you can't understand that. I just don't feel comfortable going."

"Listen, I understand your fear, but honestly I'm more afraid to leave you here. Let me see what I can do. Even if you don't go with me, your mother will be protected."

"Thank you." I turned around and embraced Angelo. We shared a gentle kiss and my anger melted away. His arms gripped my waist and my body became warm.

Back inside the house I apologized to Tristan for running out during dinner. He accepted without any hard feelings. When I went into the dining room to start cleaning up I saw that everything was put away and clean. I smiled, and thanked the guys for cleaning, poured a glass of wine and got settled on the sofa in front of the fire. Angelo was in my father's study making a phone call.

"I've never seen you lose your cool before. It was pretty refreshing," Tristan said with a smirk.

"Why is that refreshing?" I mumbled as I kicked off my pumps. I stretched across the sofa and picked up a book.

"I don't know. There's something about you. You're not the type that just loses it. You can't get enough control." I rolled my eyes at Tristan, his flirtatious behavior was getting on my nerves. It was unfortunate that Angelo didn't have the chance to see this side of his friend.

[141]

Tristan was being shady. Something told me that from now on any talk dealing with the involvement of the Fallen or the Great Seven should be in private, without the presence of Tristan.

I excused myself and went into the study to check on Angelo. Closing the doors behind me, I sat in dad's chair waiting patiently for Angelo to get off of the phone. As soon as he slapped his phone shut, I jumped up and started talking to Angelo telepathically.

"Who was that?" I asked.

"Why do you want to communicate like this?"

"It's safe this way. Are you really going to leave me?"

"Darling, I have to. I have no choice. Two white elves are coming to help Tristan look after you. I shouldn't be gone long, but the Angelic Clan wants me to leave as soon as I can."

"What is the pressing issue all of a sudden? What is it that you don't want me to know?" I threw up my hands, aggravated at Angelo. Obviously something big was about to happen. *"You can't protect me all the time. How can I protect myself, if I don't know everything?"* I shook my head, and sighed deeply. I just gave up, and thought maybe I didn't want to know anymore.

"Are you sure you can really trust Tristan?"

Angelo looked at me surprised. *"Yes. Why do you doubt him?"* I ignored his question, as I thought about my suspicions. If Tristan couldn't be trusted, I could handle him if he made the decision to cross me. Maybe I was thinking too much about it, and maybe I was reading the whole thing wrong. I didn't want to damage the friendship between Angelo and Tristan, so I left it alone and didn't bring up the subject again. I didn't like struggling with doubts.

I changed the subject and asked Angelo about the two elves that were coming to my home. He told me that white elves, were part of the alliance, like many of the vampires. There were so many different races of creatures on the side of the Angelic Clan. The angel vamps must have been more of a threat than I realized. Walking up to me, Angelo stood behind me, holding on to my waist.

"I hate leaving you. This hurts me deeply," he said, breathing on my neck.

"We have to consider that this could be a trap. The Arcs must know that the angel vamps want me and have made attempts to take me back to their world. Why would they call you now? It doesn't make any sense to me. It doesn't matter how many magical creatures you have to protect me, none of them can protect me better than you. Their powers combined cannot match yours." Angelo was fully aware of what I was saying was true. I could read in his face that he was under explicit orders and couldn't change the rules to accommodate me.

We went back into the living room hand-in-hand. I sat down as Angelo filled Tristan in on what was happening. I guess if Angelo trusted him, there was no reason for me not to. Angelo

[142]

promised to stay long enough so that he could introduce me to the elves that would lend a hand in my protection.

I was tired from having to deal with so many exhausting issues, and I felt a bit overwhelmed. The thought of Tristan being here in the house with me along with the elves comforted me in an odd way. I took a deep breath and listened to the guys go back and forth in conversation. Angelo received a text message and told me that someone was on their way to look after my mom. The angel was a watcher. His existence would be concealed from the outside world.

The night was progressing with much boredom, and I felt a little stir-crazy. Reading didn't seem to satisfy me, which was strange, so I fumbled through a clothing catalog for a while, circling the clothes I put on my wish list. When I was done with that I pulled out a furniture catalog, but I wasn't interested in that either. I thought about trying to read through a couple of chapters of the angel book and nixed that. I hadn't checked my personal email in such a long time, so I got out my laptop and started playing on it.

I sat comfortably on the sofa, and carefully went through my email. Amy had sent me a couple of messages about a writer looking for someone to publish her novel. She also wanted me to read a promising manuscript. I replied to her email saying that I would read it. Working for my mother's company was already starting to get demanding and I hadn't even got into the swing of things yet. Tristan and Angelo were watching a basketball game.

After I finished checking my emails, I typed Greek gods and goddesses into the search engine to see what would come of it. Within seconds I got my results. When I clicked the first site, a list of the gods and goddesses came up along with their profile, and historical information. Every member of the Council was listed. As I scrolled down, I saw information about me, and then I saw my mom's angelic name, Pandora. A light bulb went off in my head, as I read her profile. How could I have forgotten about this? Pandora had a box. That was what my mother was running away from—the box. Now everything was coming together, and I understood more clearly what was happening. I was angry that Angelo hadn't shared this important information with me.

I read all the information I could about the mythology of the gods and goddesses. From time to time I shot Angelo a few dirty looks from the sofa. He caught me the last time and I was forced to express my anger. Since he didn't mind sharing our business with Tristan, I didn't storm out and request to speak to him privately. After all, Tristan was there to protect me and had a right to know everything about me.

"What?" he asked in a clueless tone.

"Look. I get that you're my Guardian, my protector, but you can't keep secrets from me. You're doing more harm than good when you do that. I thought we discussed this," I said with a frown.

"What are you talking about?" he asked.

[143]

"I guess I have to spell it out for you. Why didn't you tell me that my mother had the box? I never realized it before until now. I totally believed that the box was a myth, just like they were. This is the major element of my past that ties everything together. That is the main reason why the Angel Vampire Council wants me. Their plan is to have me join them, unleash the evil from the box, then lead the humans back to the lives of slavery and oppression. It will be easy for me to lead the humans because the entity within me is rooted in the nature of the Earth. Out of the oppression, the humans would lose their faith in the True God and go crawling back to worship the Fallen." I smirked as I swallowed my words. Angelo blinked once, and then sighed. Tristan was momentarily speechless.

"Pandora's Box," Tristan said as his eyes bulging in surprise.

"Yes—the box that belongs to my mother," I said narrowing my eyes at Angelo.

"I wanted to protect you." Angelo said, then he paused. There was nothing he could say to get out of this one. After I had said what I needed to, a relief came over me.

"It's OK. I'm learning. I'm getting used to your methods." I said with a smirk. "There's one more thing, though. Who has the box now?" I said, continuing to search through the web site.

"Your mother is the only one who knows where it is. The myth is that she hid the box deep in a vault in one of the outer dimensions."

"Why do they think I can get it?"

"Has anyone mentioned you retrieving the box yet?" Angelo asked.

"No, but now I see that the subject will come up soon." I thought about the situation further.

"If my mother were dead, then maybe the box would automatically come to me, but that's not the case. They already killed my dad, so please make sure the angel who is protecting my mother is competent."

"No need to worry. Your mother is in good hands. Her protector was appointed by the Great Seven."

"Good. That makes me feel a little better." I was happy that we had this conversation and wondered if it was possible that I had lived a past life? Maybe it really was true, if not then why was there information about me on the internet?

The door bell rang and I quickly logged off the internet. I carefully placed the laptop on the coffee table and went to open the door. Tristan ran his fingers through his blond mane and readjusted his body in the recliner. Angelo hopped up, tugged his shirt and came to the door with me. I figured these were my new guests. Since everyone was primping for the arrival of our guests, I fluffed out my long curly hair simultaneously with both hands.

[144]

I invited the two magical creatures into the house. Brothers, they shared the same silvery locks, gray eyes and pointed ears. They looked similar to Galveston, but were more enchanting. One of them had his hair swept back in a neat ponytail. You could see the exaggerated shape of his silky thin ears, and I tried not to stare at them. The other brother's tresses draped past his elbows. His hair was long and beautiful, and all I wanted to do was run my fingers through it. There was no doubt in my mind that these were extremely lovely creatures. Their names were Elwyn and Elin. I kindly invited them in. Thankfully they had already been schooled regarding the situation. Angelo told me that when they touched their magical power was great. I was hoping to see how powerful they really were.

Sadly, it was time to see the man I love depart on his journey. We spent a few moments alone in my father's study quietly, holding each other. Tears trickled down my face as I buried my head on Angelo's chest, and sobbed into his shirt. Angelo caressed my back tenderly and held me tighter. I gazed upon his deep blue eyes and fell into a trance of warmth and ardor. He lightly blew his sweet breath on my face, and my tears dried up within a second. He placed both hands on my face, cupping my cheeks and looked down at me.

"I have traveled to many worlds, and have lived through the ages of this world and yet I was never truly alive until I met you," he said. "I loved you when we were children and I love you more now than I can express. I'm always with you. Remember to embrace your angelic power. It's strong and will not fail or falter." He smiled, and kissed me, and before I could tell him that I deeply loved him a bright white light consumed him and he vanished within it. I stood alone in the study, as emptiness gobbled me up and once again I felt disconnected from my world. The chatter outside the double doors broke the silence. It was time for me to entertain my house guests. When I opened the doors to go back into the living room, Tristan was standing against the wall with his arms folded across his chest. Deep down I sensed he was glad Angelo was gone.

"Are you all right?" he asked with heavy concern.

"Yeah, I'll be fine. Do you know anything about these elves?"

"I'm not personally their friends, but you can trust them. What about your power? Do you sense them as threatening? Or me?" He stepped a little closer. I sighed and moved back a few inches.

"No, I didn't get anything from them. But you're extremely difficult to read."

"Why is that? You know that I'm not a threat to you, but you still have mixed feelings about me, even after I helped to save your life when the werewolves tried to attack you."

"You're just different, that's all. Forgive me if I ever made you feel awkward."

"You've never made me feel awkward—you make me feel human."

"You're a good man. Tristan, I appreciate you being here to protect me. I also appreciate your friendship. I see the humanity in you. It's there."

"I didn't choose this you know, this way of life. I was made vampire against my will."

"Please, you don't need to explain. I admire you." I smiled blinking my eyes, and shifting my footing in a subtle manner. This conversation was wearing me out, and I didn't want it to go any further. I felt that Tristan was being disrespectful to his friend by coming on to me. I was flattered by his compliments but that was all. I ended the conversation, patted him on the shoulder with gentle affection, and trotted into the living room to meet with my new guests. Tristan swiftly trailed behind me.

Not really sure what elves eat or drink, I offered my guests some tea, and Tristan the rest of the blood I had saved from the beef. The brothers weren't too keen on being so close to the vampire. It was written all over their faces. I kind of wanted to know if there was some kind of back story involved, but something told me to just leave that alone. Tristan and the brothers hadn't met each other before, so whatever hostility they shared had to be a thing of races. Maybe the white elves at one time were not allies with the vampire tribe.

We sat down talking and familiarized ourselves with each other. I thought that I was going explode after a while. What were these people supposed to do—lay down their lives for a stranger? I was a stranger to them, after all. I had known Tristan for three weeks and the elves only for three minutes. Why should they care about me?

The weather was bad, but I had to do something other than stare at them. I had to get out of my house.

"Hey guys, do you want to go out for a drink?" I proposed, gazing at everyone.

"Sure, I know a place we can go to have a good time," Tristan jumped in as he stood next to me.

"Where can we go where the elves won't be too obvious? No offense guys, but you are way too beautiful. The humans will suspect something."

"We understand. That's why we're not going to a place where humans are," Elwyn paused. "You're half human; I think it's funny how you refer to the humans when you are one yourself." Elwyn stated curling his lip into a smile.

"I don't know why I do that," I said with a smile. "It's become a habit lately." Throwing my left hand on my, hip I continued, as I shifted my body. "Now, what did you mean when you said we aren't going where humans are?"

"There are places where the enchanted can go be around their own kind, places set all over the world. I'm surprised you haven't sensed the magic of these places. I guess that will come in time," Elin said with a toothy smile.

"Really?" I replied in disbelief.

"Sure. There are bars, clubs and all kinds of underground businesses owned and operated by the enchanted," Tristan answered.

"Well, what are we waiting for?" I perked, up excited to get out of the house. It's been a while, but it's only a drink, which couldn't hurt.

The guys wanted to get out just as much as I wanted to. I freshened up my makeup, sprayed on more perfume, grabbed a cute designer clutch and slipped into my purple pumps. I made sure that my dagger was secured in its sheath around my ankle. I was used to wearing it now and almost felt naked when it wasn't clinging to me. It was cold out, but I decided to throw on my leather jacket to add a little edginess to my look. I gave Tristan the keys to my dad's Escalade because it was more spacious than my Focus. I never really take it out, but I wanted the elves to be comfortable. We piled in the vehicle and headed out. The fresh air in my lungs rejuvenated my spirit.

The club was on the border of another town but still in Milford. This part of town was very industrialized, but still had elements of its original historical design. Tristan found parking on a side street lined with other cars. I stepped out of the SUV and Tristan slammed the door behind me. Something about being out with this crew made me feel excited and dangerous.

We walked down the brick sidewalk shoulder to shoulder as the magical energy in the air lingered, pulling me in. I wobbled on the brick as I tried not to trip or scuff my shoes, and Tristan slipped his arm around me. It was a slick move, but I didn't pull away to avoid him. The elves stepped in front, of us leading the way to the entrance of a large brick building on a side street that appeared to be abandoned. As we approached the building I noticed a small window on the side that slid up to reveal the face of little person.

The wrinkled dark skinned dwarf was very intimidating as he examined me with deep glowing orange eyes.

"Identify," he said in a harsh, raspy voice. Tristan moved to stand in my way. My heart pounded. This was not the nervous feeling you get when you're trying to get in a club and you're not 21. This was something else.

"My party consists of vampire, elves and a nephilim," he said strongly, gesturing to each one of us. It was weird to hear the list of our supernatural identities in a public place in this world. Tristan knew I was about to laugh, he waved his hand behind him, so only I could see. I held back a huge chuckle, and made an attempt to straighten my face, hiding the snicker under my tucked lips.

"That will be $80," the little man said. Elwyn reached in the pocket of his dark slacks and pulled out a large roll of bills. He handed the creature the money and the door swung open with heaviness.

We all trailed in to meet a large bouncer who was decked out in leather from head to toe. Tall with a bald head that glistened with moisture, he told us they had a no weapon policy. We nodded our heads in agreement. Luckily the bouncer didn't even bother to search us. I knew I was violating the policy, but there was no way I was going anywhere without my dagger. I walked down the long dark hall, peering over my shoulder when I realized that Tristan was still talking to the bouncer back at the door. We stopped to see what was going on. Three elves dressed in black outfits came rushing through the two swinging doors. They wore aprons around their waists and looked like bartenders.

Tristan soon joined us and we all went through the doors. The loud music pulsated through me and vibrated throughout the walls and ceilings, and the multi-colored laser lights flashed all over. The place was huge! The bar was in the front of the room, it was a large solid structure shaped like a crescent. All around were neatly placed stainless steel stools that completed the upscale appearance of the bar area. Several creatures were standing around the bar waiting for their drinks. The sides of the room were enclosed cabanas decorated with white drapes. It was very private and exclusive. In the center of the room was a traditional black and white tiled dance floor, which was crowded with so many different races of supernatural creatures, dancing and having a good time. I smiled as I looked around.

I was pleased that I looked sexy enough to be at this trendy place. I could feel that many eyes were on me. Moments later we were approached by a vampire who was the host. He led us to a private area off to the side of the club. I strutted in my pumps pristinely, keeping my head up elegantly. The vampire held the white drape open and we went in. The area behind the curtain was large enough for 15 people, with four white curved plush sofas placed neatly around the space, and red fluffy pillows tossed on top to add a chic touch to the decor. A big glass coffee table sat in the middle of a deep cherry colored carpet made of fur. We each sat on a sofa facing each other.

"Welcome to Spell Bound. I will be your server for this evening," uttered a handsome dark vampire with a pad and pen in his hand. His eyes were deep green and his skin as white as snow. His red hair flamed with unnatural intensity. He was dressed in a black fitted suit that accentuated his body. I gaped at him as I started to think about what I wanted to drink. "Here in the VIP suite the menu is limitless," he continued. Being at Spell Bound made me think of the old days when Christine and my girlfriends would spend a night on the town.

I ordered an Apple martini, the elves ordered a couple glasses of something I'd never heard of and Tristan ordered a glass of blood with a hint of vodka in it. All kinds of questions popped into my head when I heard him order. The DJ was pumping to the sounds of Paul Oakenfold and I crossed my legs stylishly, bobbing my head to the rhythm of the pulsating beats. The waiter brought our drinks quickly, and I picked up my glass. Tristan held up his goblet of warm blood infused with vodka.

"Let's toast to new friendships, new opportunities and a great time!" Tristan said excitedly, glaring at me from the corner of his eye. I gave him a light smile and took a sip of my drink. The sweet-sour apple taste was refreshing to my palate. Tristan moved closer to me on the other sofa. I took two more sips of my martini. Holding his goblet he eased on the sofa next to me. I lifted my glass, and he glared at me and the glass.

"You're going through that at an alarming speed. Be careful, young beauty." He smiled, showing the edges of his fangs. I held the glass up to my lip. Tristan thought that I wasn't able to handle the drink.

"It's been a long time since I'd been to place like this. When you haven't done something in a while you really don't miss it until you experience it again. I'm sorry—I hope I didn't offend you in any way. I understand that you're probably more used to a proper girl that…" He interrupted me, and I was annoyed that I could not get my words out.

"Please. I hope you don't mind me interrupting you but I must. Don't ever think that you're not proper, or not beautiful, or meaningless." The elves hopped up from their seats and excused themselves from the VIP suite. Alone in the large space with Tristan, I didn't know what to think. "You're an extraordinary woman, Sydney," he continued. "It's an honor to be in your presence." Inclining his head, Tristan was handsomely gentle when his cool hand touched mine.

"I appreciate your admiration. What you're doing is very noble." This time we took sips of our drinks at the same time. "I've been meaning to ask you, if you don't mind. How it is possible for you to drink blood with vodka? And what was up with the wine you had at my house?" I asked.

"I can drink vodka as long as it has a blood base. It is something about the processing method of making the liquor. I'm not sure what they do, but it's one of those things that we as vampires can enjoy. As far as the wine is concerned, I can consume it if there's blood in it."

"But I didn't put any blood in your drink," I said, confused.

"I know. I keep a flask with me at all times that's filled with blood just in case I can't get to a supply." He cleared his throat, opened his jacket and revealed to me a medium-sized black flask tucked in an upper pocket.

"I understand," I replied. We smiled at each other as the noise from the crowd intensified and the bass of the music rumbled through the building.

"Would you like to dance?" Tristan asked me.

"Sure. I didn't think you were the type to dance to this sort of thing," I said.

"Well, I do. I love this place." We stood up holding hands and we slithered through the patrons of the club to the dance floor. It didn't take us long to get into the swing with the rhythm of the music. Tristan did a great job keeping up with me. He was a great dancer. I love dancing. I took ballet from the time I was little all the way into high school before my interest changed to contemporary theater.

Song after song came on and we were into the music—and each other—for some time. I was doing something that any other normal woman in her early twenties would be doing on a Friday night any—other single woman, I corrected myself. Tristan got closer and closer as we moved in unison. I was happy that this was upbeat trance music. If a slow song were playing, Tristan would have come on to me even more. He slowly leaned into me, as if to kiss me. Our lips lightly grazed, and I took a step back holding my head down. Tristan moved away coyly.

[149]

After dancing for a while, I grew tired and wanted to sit down. Elwyn and Elin were spotted across the room dancing with two lovely blonde girls. I couldn't tell what type of creatures they were because they were too far away from me. We headed back to our VIP suite, and found fresh drinks already on the table. Neither the crowd nor the volume of the music had diminished. I sipped on my second drink, then my third. Half-way through my fourth I was definitely drunk. I slumped over in Tristan's lap, ashamed at the state I was in. His cool hand rubbed the side of my face.

"Sydney, are you feeling all right? You look like you've had too much."

"Are you saying that I can't handle my liquor?"

"No—you were doing well after two. I think the third one sent you over the edge," Tristan said, as he looked at me with a smile.

"I hope I didn't ruin your night," I said.

"Of course you didn't ruin the night," Tristan said chuckling.

"I think it is adorable that you believe you know so much about me," I said looking up at him.

"You fancy me?" he asked smiling.

"A part of me does," I replied with regret. I couldn't believe that I just said that in front of the vampire. Was I going mad by being so open with him?

"Why do you think you can't trust me?" he asked.

"Do you want the truth?"

"Yes. I do. I know you look at me with one eye open," he spoke softly. I couldn't believe that I put myself in this situation. I didn't feel comfortable answering his question. Being honest with Tristan in my current non-sober state wasn't a good idea. I needed a diversion, just when I thought all hope was lost, Elwyn and Elin came in from the dance floor and announced that they were ready to leave. I was beyond my limit with liquor. My arm was thrown over Tristan's waist as he helped support me up. Being the only plastered one there was not fun.

Someone tenderly placed me on the sofa in the living room. I felt better when I realized I was home. Tristan stayed on the floor, kneeling next me. I felt guilty about sharing closeness with him. I felt like I'd betrayed Angelo. How could I hurt the man I love? I asked myself. My heart pounded hard, to the point where thinking made it hurt more. I did my best to clear my head and slowly sipped on a glass of iced cold water that Tristan handed me.

It was really late, so when the phone rang I instantly became nervous. I told one the brothers to get it while the other was doing a safety scan of the house. I heard light steps and felt a presence step into the room. They were silent, and I knew something was wrong. I raised my

[150]

head up and asked who was on the phone. Tristan and Elwyn exchanged glances, but didn't say a word.

"You know I hate secrecy!" I said to the vampire. "Who was that on the phone?" I asked.

"You're not going to be pleased, and I think you're not ready for this," The elf said. I sat up and started breathing deeply in anticipation of what I was going to hear. It was bad news for sure.

"Your friend Luna was found dead in her car," Elwyn exhaled. "That was her sister. She wanted to talk to you, but I thought you couldn't handle anything that heavy right now. I told her you were ill and she said she'd call you back." Trying to regroup, the news instantly made me sober. Sadness took over me as I tried to catch my breath.

"Sydney, you must calm down. There's nothing you can do," Elwyn said softly. "Her car ran off Highway 19 and crashed into a tree. Her sister didn't tell me anything else." Elin reappeared suddenly and the two brothers held hands. They started panting, and chanting in a language I couldn't decipher. Gradually I calmed down and was able to think clearly again.

I knew that the Council was doing everything they could to terrorize me. They killed my father first, then Christine, and now Luna. The angel vampires were desperate to kill everyone in this world that I loved. I had to make sure that Angelo wouldn't become their next target. For a second I thought I was strong enough to astral project over to Amy's house, but I couldn't, because of the lingering effects of the alcohol. When the bothers stopped chanting, I told them to take me to see her.

"We don't recommend that you use your powers right now. You are not strong enough. This news has altered your angelic energy."

"What do you mean, Elwyn? I need to go to Amy's to see what's going on," I said. "I can't believe this shit. This is utterly, insanely ridiculous!" I said with terrible anger. Tristan reached over and grabbed my neck in a hug. The tears streamed down my face and then I completely lost it.

After I cried for a while I convinced the brothers to go with me to see Amy, Luna's sister. She lived a couple miles outside of Milford. When we got to her house I told the elves to wait for me in the car. I knew the elves couldn't pass for human and I didn't want Amy to ask questions. Although she knew about her sister's powers she wasn't as intuitive as Luna.

As I stood at the front door I thought about how I was going to comfort Amy. I wasn't really good at this sort of thing. Bringing the dead back to life wasn't an option anymore, so that wasn't even an idea I could propose to Amy.

As soon as I pressed the doorbell the door flew open. I jumped when I saw the distraught Amy standing at the entrance in an all-black dress. She really favored Luna. Even her long dark hair was a wild mess. Her skin was pale and she had dark circles under her eyes, and she seemed twice as old as her 33 years. This was not the women who helped to run my mother's publishing company.

She invited me in. As I entered the house I turned to look at the car and saw the silhouettes of Elin and Elwyn. I had the strange feeling that something or someone was watching me, and I was concerned about leaving them out there alone. I went into the home. It felt different in the absence of Luna. I think that all homes give off a feeling of emptiness after someone dies.

"Hurry in, someone is watching," Amy said in a trembled whisper as she pulled me in by the arm. She closed the door and double-bolted it. "Please sit down," she said. I sat down and I took a deep breath.

"I'm so sorry Amy. What happened to Luna?" I asked, feeling my eyes well up with tears.

"She was on her way to see you," Amy said. My heart sank. I gulped, preparing to hear what else she was going to tell me.

"Luna dozed off in the den and woke up in a great panic. She said she had a dream about you and needed to see you right away to warn you and bring you." She stopped in mid-sentence as a loud crashing noise came from the back of the house. We both turned in the direction of the alarming sound.

"Bring me what?" I asked impatiently.

"I'm not sure. The strange thing about it was that when the cops found her they said that something had clawed her chest so deeply that the bone was showing—and her organs had been taken. Also, her tongue was taken out". She choked on her words. Amy was about to cry so I grabbed her and hugged her tightly. I had to be strong for her; I had to be her support system. I prayed that the Arc's would send Angelo back to me. I had to find out whom or what had murdered Luna. This had gotten way too personal. Amy whimpered and I fought my way through the tears.

"What could do something like that?" she asked, and I didn't know. I was unsure if Luna had really exposed her sister to the magical world of the unknown. Amy and Luna were like family to me, but Luna and I had a deep connection, and she shared everything with me when it came to her powers.

Amy rubbed her face with her hand, looked at me, and whispered, "I think someone is after you. Something was after my sister too. She saw something so terrifying in her vision that she stormed out of here. She never drives after dark, so whatever she saw must have been so bad that she had to go see you."

"Do you have any idea who might want to kill her?" I asked, releasing my grip and folding my arms across my chest.

[152]

"No, not at all. The police don't have a description of the creature. They don't believe it was creature anyway."

"Why did you say creature?" I asked, shocked by her statement. I had thought that Amy was out of the loop when it came to the supernatural world, but maybe I was wrong.

"It had to be a creature. No human could to do what they did to my sister." We both started thinking. I felt uncomfortable about sucking her into this I, and I felt that the less she knew the safer she would be. I jumped up, ready to use my guests as an excuse to get out. She stood up a few seconds after I did.

"Amy I have to go. If you need help with the arrangements please let me know." I kissed her on the cheek then made my way to the door, hoping she would not ask any more questions. I also wanted to check the property; the fact that she'd ignored the noise in the back bothered me.

"I was hoping you would stay for a while," she said with despair.

"I'm sorry, but I have some friends waiting for me. I wanted to check on you and pay my respects." I said my goodbyes and used my supernatural speed to survey the area. Everything seemed fine, but when I started back to the car I had the feeling that eyes were watching me again. I jumped into the parked car, and sped down the road without saying a word to the elves. I was paranoid as I continued to shift my eyes on the road, and back to the rear view mirror to see if we were being followed. Elin was in the passenger seat peering at me while his brother sat quietly in the back.

"Are you okay, Sydney? How is your friend?" Elin asked with a worried tone. I didn't know what to say to him, so I simply shook my head. It was almost 4:30 in the morning and I wanted to hurry home. I didn't want Tristan to be alone in the house after Luna was found dead. I explained to them what had happened to Luna and expressed my concerns that someone—or something—was following both her and me. Maybe they had been right when they told me not to leave the house. Who was I kidding when I thought tonight would be a normal night? I pulled into the driveway and we headed toward the house as fast as we could.

Chapter Seventeen

A s we flew up the walkway we noticed a black town car passing the house, and then turning down another street. The suspicious vehicle made me think twice. We scuffled quickly inside the house.

"That was the same car that I saw outside of Amy's place," I said softly, closing the door behind me.

"Why didn't you say anything?" Elwyn asked as I tossed my jacket on the coat rack and kicked off my shoes.

"Someone was listening out there. My brother and I sensed magic in the air coming from something we couldn't recognize," Elin added.

"I guess my powers are still iffy. Why didn't I catch the odor?" I asked.

"Maybe they have it masked so you can't detect what they are," Elwyn stated, shrugging his shoulders.

"Only angels have the power to mask their scent," I said to the brothers.

"That's not necessarily true," Elin purred.

"Where is the vampire?" Elwyn wanted to know. I pulled out my phone and sent Tristan a message. Seconds later he texted me back saying, that he was in the woods behind the house checking things out before he went down for the day. It was almost five; I knew if anything happened Tristan wouldn't be any good to me once the sun came up. Thank God it was winter and there were fewer daylight hours. The sun wouldn't be up for a little while longer, so it made me feel better knowing that Tristan had at least an hour or so before he really felt the effects of the sunlight.

After the initial survey of house and property, Tristan reported that everything seemed to be fine. He eventually went down for the day and I left the elves in the living room to play on the laptop and lounge around. I had learned that elves have strange sleeping patterns. They can go for days without sleep and feel no negative effects from it. Weird, but cool, I thought to myself. Since I had showered before the club I didn't need to take another one. I changed out of my designer outfit and threw on one of my lounging suits, the black velour one with a hood and side pockets. I threw my dark hair up in a low pony tail.

The light pounding of rain on the window calmed me as morning approached. The day was going to be a gloomy one. I sat on the bed and enjoyed the serene sound of the rain. Carefully putting on a fresh pair of thick white socks, I slipped into my house boots. I double-checked the tightness of my dagger strap, sighed deeply and curled into a fetal position. I finally drifted off to sleep.

The sound of thunder woke me up in a panic. I jumped up from the bed, and turned on my table lamp. I glanced out the window to see that it was still very dark and dreary, and rain was pouring down. The trees swayed from side to side against the forceful winds. A chill went up my spine as I gazed out at the angry precipitation.

The nap hadn't made me feel any better. My room was silent, and my thoughts were on Luna. Tears streamed down my face all over again. All I wanted was the comfort of my mom and dad. I wanted to embrace them, feeling the love we had for each other and enjoying each other's company.

I didn't want to be alone, so I wiped my face with my hand and started downstairs. I thought I would keep elves company. A haunting vibe engulfed my spirit as I completely maneuvered my body through the dark hall. The entire house was way too quiet. I kept my back against the wall as I made my way down the steps. The house had gone cold and didn't feel like my home anymore.

I took one step at a time and made it to the final step. I pulled out my dagger so quickly I didn't realize the speed of my movement. I crept through the house holding it down close to my side. As I walked I almost slipped on a slick substance. I balanced myself up to avoid the fall, but I tripped over something lying in the middle of the living room floor. Using my power, I focused on my ability to see through the darkness. My eyes suddenly illuminated a blue florescent hue, and I saw that the obstruction on the floor was a body.

It was one of the elves, and the slick substance was blood. I had never seen the blood of an elf before. From the look of it I knew that the blood was magical. It was the color of silver and shimmered. The wound was deadly, and I could see that the elf was fading away. I checked for any signs of life when I knelt down on the floor. I brushed his silver hair out of his face to reveal which brother it was. Elin, the younger of the siblings, was gone—dead. I shook him with great force making myself believe that he wasn't gone. My eyes were burning from the tears. There was nothing I could do. "I'm so sorry you had to die because of me. I'll kill the bastards that did this to you," I promised, kneeling beside the corpse. I blew a kiss down at the body then looked around to see where my enemy was hiding. I popped up, calling for Elwyn as I mourned the death of his magical brother.

Elwyn didn't answer my call, and I feared that something had happened to him too. I desperately wanted to run downstairs to wake my vampire friend, but I did not want to risk his life. He was gravely weak in the day and I couldn't have any one else lose their life because me. Fear gripped me as I scanned the room with the light from my eyes, and noticed another body near the steps of my dad's study. "Elwyn!" I screamed as I ran over to him. He was badly injured and had to feel the effects of his deceased brother. He had been beaten, and slashed a few times with some kind of blade. I felt that his essence had been weakened. Elwyn moved slowly, and was lying in a pool of his blood. I was afraid, but had to act fast.

I magically summoned the first aid kit and tried my best to tend to his wounds. I worked fast trying, to remain calm. The slashes were deep, but not deep enough to be fatal. I cleaned his wounds and stopped his bleeding. A sigh of relief escaped my lips when I saw that he was stabilized. I didn't have time to go in the basement and check the fuse, and I didn't want to leave his side, but I got up and opened the door to see if I could spot the intruder.

The cold damp air whisked into my house. I peered down the street and noticed that the few homes that were on my block where dark as well. The power lines must have been down because of the storm. Closing the door, my angelic vision caught a glimpse of something moving. I turned my head to see what it was, and my head snapped back as a hard hand landed across my face, knocking me down. Seconds later a foot forcefully pushed into my ribs. I was on the ground next to the front door. Whimpering in pain I called out for my guardian angel. Thick grubby fingers wrapped around my neck as my body was pressed against the wood floors. They were trying to choke the life out of me.

"Fucking Bitch! You think you can run from us?" a jagged voice said to me. The blows had weakened me enough to make the light from my eyes diminish. My attacker had let go of my throat, and pulled me into a sitting position, then covered my mouth with duct tape and bound my arms and legs. I tried fighting him off, but couldn't find the strength. I felt the circulation in my extremities slowly fade, making me feel claustrophobic. The presence of another creature was also in my home. I closed my eyes focusing on the dark vibe, trying to determine what they were. They were both demons, and they grunted in pleasure as they watched me squirm.

They hoisted me up and tossed me in a van. My first instinct was to use my power to astral project but, I was too weak to. Sleepiness entranced my whole body, but I fought through it. As the vehicle set in motion my body began to recharge.

The weakness I felt was replaced with great strength. Surges of electricity jolted inside me. Feeling like I had been shocked with a defibrillator, I embraced the energy that was given to me, and broke the tape that bound my hands and legs so I could move freely in the back of the van. The vehicle stopped abruptly, and I knew it was time for me to face the demons that kidnapped me and killed my friend.

My body slid forward when the driver threw on the breaks. I wasn't afraid when I heard the demons heading toward the side door. I breathed deeply as the door slid open, and moved a few inches back, positioning myself to strike. I was able to see the dark, cloaked, creature. I held up my hands against my chest with my palms facing outward. My power emanated from the palm of my hands, striking the demon with a blaze of light so powerful that his essence was swallowed whole and exploded in the light. I smiled over my triumph, but I realized that the other creature would soon come for me. I jumped out of the van and moved slowly around the vehicle. The terrain was very muddy and the environment dark and damp.

The power within the land was thick in its presence and from that moment I knew I wasn't in the Earthy Realm anymore. My eyes turned on their automatic glow, almost like a cat on the prowl at night. The demon was near, but I was ready. I felt confident in my power so there was no reason for me to back down.

Moving over to the back of the van I maintained my focus. I turned my head to the right as my senses caught a glimpse of evil. The demon was very powerful. I took a couple of steps closer to the thick trees, and he came out from the shadows. The huge foggy shape of the entity towered above me. We were standing about 20 feet apart. The sound of a fierce gorilla resonated deep within his throat.

Without delay I shot beams of light at the creature using the power within my hands. He retaliated by throwing small balls of fire at me. I created a force field by holding my right hand up above my head and curling my fingers like a claw, and the fireballs bounced off of the shield into nothingness. I had never dreamt of being involved in battle like this, but I got the strange feeling that I had used this power before in some other time or place.

I kept my arms up in position and as I suspected, his power was no match for mine. I continued to thrust the beam of light at him and when it finally made contact, it sliced through him like a hot blade, piercing through his cloak. That should have been the end of it, but there was more to the demon than I thought. After going back and forth for what seemed like an eternity, my powers wounded him enough to bring him down on one knee. He must have had some kind of protection barrier around him as well; because his foggy essence had diminished. The wounded demon had exposed gashes that revealed worms and maggots crawling from his face. The cloak he covered himself with was torn in areas where my magic had struck him. The light was deadly to him. Using both of my hands, with one final push of momentum my light penetrated his entire body and engulfed him instantly. He screamed with immense pain and was destroyed by the light. The beam retracted, returning to its resting place within me.

I made a run for it using my angelic speed. I didn't sense any type of portal that would lead me back to the Earthly Realm, but one had to be around here somewhere. If I had used my astral projection abilities to get here, it would have been easy for me to go home, but this time I had been dragged here in my physical form against my will. A gravitational force began to pull me to the North East. Unable to resist the influence I ran faster through the dense forest. The clamor of the wooded area vibrated with unknown threats. As I swiftly maneuvered my body to dodge huge trees and bushes, I realized where I was. I was back in the dimension of Kalaston, the dimension of The Fallen. Then I realized that I had been pulled in the very direction that I didn't want to go.

I found myself at the border of the Castle. There was no turning back. The last time I was here I was held as a prisoner, but the angel vamps hadn't seen it that way. I escaped at the first opportunity, and now that I was back, I didn't know how Hera was going to receive me at this point—especially since she sent the wolves and demons to recapture me, all which were now dead.

As I drew closer to the castle, something struck me with a mild force. I wasn't injured, but I had to reduce speed. I looked over my shoulder and saw shadowy creatures all around me. My vision slowly withered with distortion, and I could no longer focus on the creatures that guarded the castle, so I stopped dead in my tracks and rested against a tree. I tried to catch my breath, but I knew that panicking wouldn't help my cause, so I relaxed a bit and thought about how I was going to take control over the situation. The blurred silhouettes of the shadowy creatures crept closer.

"Welcome back, My Lady. We knew you would not forsake us," a deep muddled voice said to me. "We're here to guide you back into the castle."

"Thank you sir, I was hoping I would be able to find my way. This is my first time here in this form," I said, pretending.

"I understand. Your chamber awaits, but first you must go through the transition." I cracked a nervous smile and tried my best to play along. I hoped that wouldn't be a mistake. Still unable to see clearly, I had no choice but to follow them. I didn't want to ask any questions even though there were quite a few buzzing in my mind. One of these creatures had done something to me so that I wouldn't be able to see what was going on. I could just obliterate them with my power of light, but I nixed that idea since I was out numbered.

We made it inside; the presence of evil was prevalent with a strength that almost made me gag. I hadn't noticed it in the atmosphere before. I knew we were walking down the long hallway. There were several guards in the hall, misty figures that kept their backs to certain doors and were a race of creature that was new to me. We continued walking. I heard the sound of a heavy door creaking open, and I was instructed to hold on to an iron banister. We were going down the winding iron steps that led to the dank dungeon with the grisly corpses and human captives! What did these creatures have in mind? What were they planning to do to me?

I couldn't help but feel on edge about what was to come. As my feet touched the hard concrete, the deathly odor took my breath away. I could hear the faint sounds of whimpering and crying off to the sides of the dungeon. The pain of the humans hit me like a punch in stomach. I had to get them out of here. I avoided looking up. Despite the fact that I could not see well, just knowing that the skinned bodies and pools of blood was near sent a mix of negative emotions through me.

Caught up in the fear and pain of the captives, I eventually realized that I was alone. The misty creatures had vanished, but my vision hadn't improved, which frightened me. I figured that whatever they shot me with was some kind of serum or magical charm. I hoped that I would grow immune to things like that someday. Sometimes I felt that being part human made me weak.

I still had many questions for Angelo about my heritage. I missed him terribly, and wondered how the meeting was going with the Arcs or if Angelo was aware that I was in trouble.

The sound of footsteps caught my attention, and I spun my head in the direction from which the noise was coming from. Whatever it was, it was breathing hard. I feared for my life and didn't know what to expect. My back was turned, I stood there frozen, then sensed that he was a magical creature. I felt the light touch of his fingers brush against my face and eyes. A sigh of relief escaped from my lips when I realized that he wasn't a threat to me.

[158]

"Please sir, will you help me?" I brought my voice down to a whisper but the echo still hummed throughout the area.

"I will. They are coming. Be strong, My Lady. I will not leave your side, but they will kill me if they know I am here with you." The sound of his familiar voice made me relax for a second, but before I could find out who was with me, he retreated deep into the darkness as a band of visitors entered the prison. As the heavy iron door opened I crawled on the ground to get away from the door, and pressed my back against the cold wall waiting for what was to happen next.

The putrid aroma of the council members reeked of malice and deceit. They were all a bunch of blurs to me. I sat with my knees up to my chest as Hera's hand extended toward me. The angel vamps were moving about the area, eventually forming a crescent around my body.

"My fellow members of the Fallen, gather closer. The time has come for us to reclaim what is ours, to lead the humans back to the days of old." Hera raised her arms up as she spoke, her voice gaining intensity. "I give you all formal permission to drink the blood of life and light from our sister. This donor is free and willing!" she continued. All of the twelve fallen angel vampires hissed at me. The whites of their fangs penetrated through the blackness. These creatures were fiercer than I had realized before.

They each knelt down taking turns to drain me of my angelic blood. The piercing of my flesh caused me great pain. My blood ran down various points on my body, and I felt disgusted, dirty and violated. I silently prayed for refuge. I was losing a lot blood and fast. Drifting in and out of conciseness I felt myself grow weaker by the minute. The Fallen soon vanished and then someone came for me. I felt that he was holding me in his arms. He carefully patted my face to keep me awake but I could not push through the ordeal. The creature that so willingly tried to help me was unknown. The room faded away as I lost consciousness.

I awoke back in the chambers that I had occupied on my last visit here. I emerged from the bed to see that I had company in the form of a man kneeling beside me. Still very woozy, I touched my head and patted my body down. I was still wearing the ragged, blood-stained clothes I had on when I was attacked, and the material stuck to my skin. The creature beside me had on some kind of armor with a black hood covering his face, but I knew his scent. I carefully pulled the hood back to reveal his face. I had never seen Lothos in this manner before. The angel rose, standing before me. His eyes stared into mine as his luxurious hair flowed down his back.

"My Lady, you will make a full recovery." He took my hand. I could not take my eyes off of his beautiful features.

"What happened to me, Lothos? Did they...?" I asked with a weary look on my face.

"They tried to."

"They think that the nature of my goodness is only in my blood." Lothos nodded at my statement. "They're preparing for something."

[159]

"Yes and that is why I have to get you out of here," Lothos said.

"Thank you for saving me. It was you that held me in the dungeon. You never left me." I squeezed his hand lightly to show affection. Resting his right hand on my shoulder he gave me a slight smile. "I can no longer run away from this," I said. "I'll do whatever it is that they ask of me." My voice was bleak and empty.

"What? What are you saying?" Lothos asked, glaring with great confusion.

"I'm fine. I don't need saving." I said as my voice changed, and Lothos' confusion turned into worry. He dropped my hand, stood up and took a few steps back from me. I moved towards the armoire and viewed my hideous reflection. I looked like a woman that had been raised from the dead, literally. Trails of blood dripped down my legs. I thought about bathing in the Silver Spring. All I wanted to do was clean myself up.

In an instant I stripped off my clothes and stood naked, gazing at the mirror. Entranced by an energy force, I studied the bite marks that were all over me. I felt hollow inside, like there was some kind of void in me. Lothos just stood there in silence, perplexed. He couldn't explain what was happening and neither could I. Despite my terrible appearance, my hair was silky and shiny. My facial features had increased in beauty and the color of my eyes had changed again. This time they were lavender. My eyes had changed color so many times that I could not remember what color they originally were. Lothos turned his head while I looked at myself.

"Sydney. What are you doing?" He asked me. Turning my head from side to side I opened my mouth to reply but then closed it at the last minute. I thought about crying but held the tears back. Moving robotically, I found myself in the shower. Time seemed to have stopped while I lathered up. A mix of blood and soap went down the drain as I washed away the evidence of the Angel Vampires wrath. I realized that as the warm water hit the open wounds they slowly began to close on their own. Exiting the shower feeling refreshed, I tossed a robe over me and walked out the washroom. Lothos had never left. Standing by the large canopy bed he clutched a metal object. I assumed it was a sword of some kind.

"Tell me what you are thinking. You are really making me nervous." The skin on his forehead wrinkled as he spoke.

"I am going to give them what they want, which is me." I took a deep breath to let the words flow. I felt annoyed with him.

"Why? Do you want to be one of them? Do you want the humans in the Earthly Realm consumed by the darkness?" Lothos snapped with conviction.

"Lothos you don't have to stay here. They will be coming for me." I continued blinking sincerely. Lothos shook his head in disbelief and then straightened his face.

"I am so sorry that I could not stop the draining." He was rattled with grief but I had no reason to be angry at him. His eyes told me that he wanted to say something else to me but he bit his tongue. Rummaging through the wardrobe I came across a long crimson gown with

[160]

accented rubies and red pearls. The gown had a dropped waistline and a full length skirt. I pulled it out. Admiring it on the hanger I knew this was the dress I had to slip on.

"Why would you choose that gown?" he asked with a twinkle in his eye. Feeling possessed, I ignored his question and pretended that he was not in the room. I slipped into the gown and sprayed on some perfume.

We both looked at each other suspiciously. I wanted to know what he was thinking. He moved so quickly that I couldn't process his speed. He grabbed my cheeks with both hands and placed his soft lips on top of mine. Our lips lightly touched. I felt the sensation of static tingling on my skin.

"You have not lost yourself," he said. "I know what you have been through. I will follow you wherever this journey may take you. You have the heart of a pure angel. The light within you is greater than anything I have seen in a nephilim." I slowly pulled away from Lothos. Looking down, I touched my lips with the tips of my fingers. "Listen to me carefully," he continued. "The angel vamps tried to drain you of your humanity. It is the first step to making you one of them. I can tell that they failed in their attempts." Once again I didn't reply to his remark. I knew that Hera had something in store for me; I just didn't know exactly what it was. What I did know is that I had to obey my calling.

Before I could instruct Lothos to leave, there was a knock on the door, followed by a cloud of red sparkled mist that formed before my eyes. Seconds later a small card emerged from it and I caught the stationary before it hit the ground. The card was an invitation to a ceremony. When I told Lothos what it was his whole demeanor changed. He became nervous and I sensed a speck of fear within him. This was my invitation to let the darkness in. There was nothing else to say. Lothos stormed out of my room as swift as a rush of wind. While I waited to be summoned, I paced back and forth trying to maintain the confidence I had within myself to be able to face the true destiny that lay before me.

I found myself on the edge of the entrance into the deep forest. I observed the two moons in full view and stared at the unique constellations that were no longer alien to me. Moments later, Hera, the Guardian of Spirits and leader of the angel vampire Council, appeared with her entourage of fallen angel vampires. A surge of vitality overcame me when I saw them. I shuffled my feet to keep from being thrown back by the force, and balanced myself.

The mixed breed of angel vampires lined themselves up in single file. They all wore long draping velvet cloaks that were as deep and black as a raven's feathers. The paleness of their blank faces appeared ghostly to my sight. I noticed that near the end of the line were two elves, a fairy, a human and an angel. I recognized the angel. Lothos stood in line holding an object, just clinging to it enough to conceal it from my view. I hadn't realized that Lothos would play such a prominent role in this. He was wearing a dark cloak like the ones worn by the others. Hera grabbed on to my arm. I glanced over my shoulder to see what state the human was in, but couldn't see her. I tried to remain calm and stay focused.

[161]

"Lady Gaia, you look stunning," Hera said with a deceitful tone and a sparkle in her eye. Her eyes turned bright. I smiled and nodded with grace. I didn't remember ever having been called by my middle name. We led the assembly of the council members deep into the dark forest. The only light that guided our way were the torches that four abrasive werewolves clutched tightly in their claws. The creatures marched in front of us. I recognized that one was Uran, Hera's protector. Walking into the unknown made me feel anxious, and I experienced an explosion of scattered visions: warrior angels, The Fallen and a dead Earth pierced my conciseness. My time was drawing near.

The fierce elements of the deep forest came to an abrupt end when we approached a very large clearing. In the center of the clearing was a giant pyramid constructed out of limestone and granite. It was an exact replica of Egypt's Great Pyramid. My mouth dropped at the sight of the colossal structure. Even though it was well hidden I couldn't believe I hadn't noticed it from a distance. The terrain surrounding the pyramid was a flat concrete surface. Large stone megaliths were neatly scattered to form a circle around the perimeter. Thousands of steps led up to the entrance, which was well guarded by monstrous werewolves. The two creatures clung onto spears that were about seven to eight feet long. These wolves did not look like typical werewolves; their faces were disfigured resembling some kind of mutants.

The convoy soon came to a halt and I saw that the angel vamps were situating themselves to form a circle. The human I had seen near the end of the line was being led to the middle of the circle. Distraught, bleeding and in pain, her nude body was oozing with the wounds given to her by the vampires. Her hands were bound with a rope and her legs were shackled with a device that made her walk like a zombie. Hera gestured for me to move deeper into the circle and stand next to her and the sobbing girl.

I looked over my shoulder to take a peek at Lothos. He was positioned outside of the circle holding a medium sized dagger that was half wrapped in a blood red satin cloth. His legs were widely parted and he had a very serious expression on his face. Zeus approached the center of the circle, moving like a warrior god toward us. He was tall with platinum shoulder length hair and handsomely chiseled features, and his presence stirred something uncomfortable in me. I shifted my weight off of one leg and on to the other when he entered my personal space. He looked at me with his eyes narrowed, magically positioning the lighted torches around the girl and myself. I could not help but keep my eyes fixed on him as he retreated back to his place. The fire that surfaced from the torches was wild and out of control. I could see that the young girl was growing more nervous by the second. I shifted my eyes back on to Lothos without anyone noticing. Not once did we make eye contact.

My heart raced. It didn't take a rocket scientist to figure out what they wanted me to do. Hera raised her hands above her head.

"My gods and goddesses, the time has officially approached for our sister to become one of us! In the blood is power and within that power comes immortality and dominance over the Earth!" Hera motioned for Lothos to come into the circle. He approached slowly, carefully minding his steps. She met him half-way, gently taking the dagger from his hands. Lothos took several steps back into his original position, and briefly met my eyes. Out of nowhere a golden

[162]

goblet transpired from the palm of Hera's right hand. It had symbols carved around it that I couldn't identify. They looked like the ones I'd seen before written on the walls of my mother's room at Loving Hills. The goblet appeared to be an ancient relic, and I wondered if it could be the Holy Grail, the cup that so many people had been searching for throughout history.

Hera made her way around to all of the angel vamps, slicing deep into their flesh with the dagger in her left hand and collecting the blood into the goblet with her right. I just stood there in silence peering at the nasty wounds with no real reaction. The poor girl trembled and wailed every time the dagger met someone's flesh. I exchanged another look at Lothos and saw his eyes flicker for a split second. Once Hera was done with everyone, she then signaled for Zeus to step into the circle. He took the dagger and sliced the skin on her forearm. The blood freely glided down her arm and into the collection with the other blood as Zeus held on to the goblet with one strong grip. Zeus then gave the cup back to Hera and returned to his place. Hera approached me and lifted up my right hand; I felt the sharpness of the blade meet my palm. My blood then dribbled down into the goblet to fuse with the blood of the fallen.

"You must now spill the blood of this willing donor, and then take in the blood of the Council of the Gods. Once you have done this, all that is left is the fall from Earth." She intoned. Hera stood next to me looking into my eyes. Her bright smile morphed into a wicked grin. Feeling the wound close in my hand, I looked down at my healed palm. She told me to take the dagger. I obeyed her, and nodded to signal that I was ready as the girl screamed more franticly. She knew she was going to die.

"This has always been your destiny, My Dear." Hera whispered in my ear as I held on to the dagger. Leaning over and kissing me on the cheek, her cold lips stung my skin like dry ice. My disgust for the dark creature rumbled in the deepest part of my spirit. Facing the girl, I moved in slow motion, extending my arm up high. As I tightly clung to the weapon, I thought about my own dagger.

The air around us grew dark and misty, and the winds in the forest increased to storm gusts. The lights on the torches blew out and the sounds of thunder rumbled in the far distance. I extended my left hand and it tingled, growing numb, and glowed so brightly that it nearly knocked the angel vamps down on the ground. Looking up I realized that the hilt of the Dagger of Doshon was now in my grasp.

Before Hera could use her speed to move out of the way, I twisted my upper torso lowered my arm down, planting the blade of my dagger directly into her heart. The girl screamed loudly and Lothos ran over to me, making it before the angel vamps had time to retaliate. I pulled the pure silver blade of my dagger out of Hera's soulless heart. The goblet fell to the ground and Hera's blood dripped down onto the concrete. I watched Hera closely observing her eyes turn into onyx holes. Her skin withered and her flesh disintegrated into bits of ash and was swept away with the winds. Hera, the Guardian of Spirits and the leader of the angel vampire Council, had been completely obliterated. She was now an eternal part of the darkness.

As Hera's essence faded away, each of the angel vamps dropped to the ground, clutching on to various parts of their bodies. Their distress was quite evident. At the moment of her demise the ground beneath us shook. The creature responsible for destroying my family and killing my friends was truly dead in every sense of the word.

Lothos positioned himself directly in my path, still trying to protect me. I stood in the spot where Hera met her death and the dark skies opened up above me. Out of the opening fell a star. The brightness of it nearly blinded me as the power within the star settled in me. I was consumed by the star's light, and my body reacted with an intense tremble. Hera's angelic powers were now mine.

Flames of electricity encased the entire grounds surrounding the monoliths. Out of the electricity came a pulsating light from which seven extremely tall angels surfaced, along with a smaller angel. They all had silvery wings protruding from their backs. The Great Seven, also known as the Biblical Archangels had made their presence known.

The Angels were like giants among us, they each had to be about seven feet or taller. Their wings of glory expanded with grace to the width of between twelve to fifteen feet. Dressed like gladiators and covered with golden cloaks, they each had a weapon of their own to wield that was unique to their individuality. The smaller angel was Angelo, of course. He had kept his promise.

I glanced at Angelo, trying to hide my happiness. He stood with the Arc's, and they gleamed with immense splendor, in positions that read war, they were ready to defend me. Lothos bowed to show respect for the Great Seven. I followed his lead and bowed as well.

The angel vampires rose from the ground and lined up, exposing their fangs and claws. The wolves stood by their side. Uran snarled, showing his fury over the death of his beloved. The elves and fairy had vanished during all of the commotion, avoiding any type of casualty. The demeanor of the angel vampires grew extremely hostile.

"Look what you have done, you loathsome girl!" Zeus stated with a devilish rumble.

"She has weakened the collective, my brother." Poseidon roared as he stood next to Zeus, holding his trident. I was well aware of how deadly Poseidon's weapon was, but despite its power I was not threated by him. Poseidon's flaming red locks flowed down his back. His saffron eyes glowed with rage.

"The servants of the ultimate power are not welcome here in this realm," Demeter chimed in, as her short wild yellow hair got caught up in the wind.

"You Fucking Half Breed Bitch! You will pay for this, whore!" Hades bellowed. His ice cold eyes rolled in the back of his head, changing to the deepest black. He stormed toward me but could not penetrate the force field that the Great Seven held up with their power.

"How dare you speak to her in that manner?" Lothos yelled. "You are nothing but a dark angel, an element of the darkness. She is a being of light and represents everything good on the Earthly Realm. You hate and despise her because of her goodness, you evil bastards!" The wrinkles in his face tightened as he articulated my defense. Lothos really meant what he said. He had my back in this and had showed me time and again.

Angelo emerged from the assembly of angels to stand next to me. He gripped my waist, and I instantly felt safer.

One archangel stepped forward. "Enough," he said. "We may go where we see fit. You are the soulless ones, the ones condemned and consumed by the darkness. Your plan to bring down the Earthly Realm will not come to pass." He was the most beautiful of the archangels. His hair was jet black and long enough to touch his hips. His eyes were silver, and his skin was illuminated. His jawline was strong and well-defined and his eyebrows were broad with a light arch. The air of this archangel was imperially divine.

"We want the girl and we will have her," Aphrodite said, softly narrowing her yellow eyes at me.

"This is not over!" all the angel vamps hollered in unison as they spun around with abnormal speed, rotating into a pitch black, ashy substance. They disappeared into the black elements that devoured them.

Angelo embraced me tightly. The departure of the angel vampires did not put my mind at ease. Something inside me was unable to break the tenseness within. The Great Seven took a few steps toward me, lowering their wings and putting their weapons down. The divinely handsome one approached me directly.

"I am Michael," he said with a serenely divine accent. "These are my celestial brothers, Gabriel, Raphael, Uriel, Requel, Saragael, and Remiel." He motioned to each angel in turn. I acknowledged them by inclining my head to show them respect, and I gleamed at Michael, captivated by his presence. I stared at his features. His hair was silky, and his pale complexion gave off a magical glow. I had never seen anyone's skin so smooth and beautiful. Standing there drinking him in, I was over taken by his ethereal essence. The angels' golden breast plates shone brightly. Their long cloaks floated in the captured breeze. The Arcs gladiator gear suited their angelic personalities.

"The purity and goodness of your heart gives off its own illumination," Michael said to me. "Your strength, resilience and faith in the ultimate power of good will most definitely be rewarded. I truly admire everything about you, Sydney." Michael spoke with a formidable pitch in his throat. I batted my eyes gracefully in response.

"We have officially granted you our protection," Raphael said, walking up close with his arms swinging by his sides. His long cloak moved with his body. He smiled, his full lips poking out a bit.

"The Fallen will stop at nothing to be the higher power and have rule over the Heavens and the Earth. Pandora's Box must not be found and opened. The fury within the box would be devastating to the Earthly Realm," Gabriel articulated clearly with an airy manner. I batted my eyes as I noticed his attractive body.

"Why was she given the box if she can't harness its power?" I asked.

"Your mother is not the only one that can harness its power," Michael answered. "The box was constructed for her to wield for the benefit of the Fallen so they could transform into the ultimate evil. Your mother was never evil. She was deceived into becoming a fallen angel. Hera and the other false gods tricked your mother into being one of them.

"You never knew this," he continued, "but your father had a rare disease. He was slowly dying and in constant pain. He tried to keep his practice functioning for as long as he could. Even though it was forbidden for angels to love humans, the angel vamps promised to make your father immortal in exchange for your mother's powers." I listened to what Michael had to say, and for the first time realized that my mother would have given up everything—even her immortality—just to be with my father.

"But the box was constructed eons ago, what does the box have to do with my father?" I asked.

"Before your mother fell from grace, she was once a guardian angel. Guardians of the nephilim and guardians of the humans are different. They come from two divisions of guardian angels. Pandora was originally a guardian of humans, but she fell in love with your father. It hurt her to see him suffer. Her love for him soon began to overpower her emotions and she confided in Zeus, which was a big mistake. You might not know that each council member helped to create Pandora, and gave her a special power. She felt that they all owed her happiness since all the council members were responsible for sharing their powers with her. They are all bound to each other, and have a supernatural connection." I was intrigued to hear family's past.

I did not know my father had been ill. I never realized that the false gods were all related in one way or another. I am a part of them; maybe that was why Zeus kept looking at me strangely. Michael continued his explanation.

"The Fallen Ones approached your mother and agreed to combine their powers to put your father's spirit under a spell. Pandora was afraid to lose him, afraid to live her lifetimes alone. Your father has lived hundreds of lifetimes. Each time he dies he is later reborn back into the world, always meeting your mother and living a life with her. The false gods promised to break the spell and make him completely immortal, so your parents could live forever in one lifetime, but only if your mother agreed to help them formulate the fury and the box. Your father spent each lifetime learning to be a doctor with the hopes of helping humans and finding a cure for his disease."

Michael paused for a moment, and continued, "The Fallen Ones promised your mother the freedom to live with your father in any dimension they pleased as soon as the construction and contents of the box were complete. However, there was a complication: Reincarnation is forbidden among humans. When the Ultimate Power of Good discovered what your mother was doing, He banished her from His Grace and stripped her of her guardianship, throwing her angelic essence down to Earth. So before your father died naturally during your lifetime and the spell could reactivate, the Council teamed up with the Circle of Destiny and sent Demas to kill your father. The Circle of Destiny put an enchantment on your mother so she wouldn't remember her life as an angel and her treacherous ways against them.

I listened carefully as Michael explained my family's past in great detail, trying to process it all. "You were the gift that your parents were blessed with in the last lifetime they shared. The Fallen did not know about you until recently. Your mother believed that going into hiding would be enough for her and your father to live as regular humans, and at the same time conceal and protect your existence. It lasted for about 25 years. Your guardian has protected you well," Michael concluded with a somber tone.

I was shocked at the thought that I almost broke a rule by bringing Christine back from the dead. I don't understand why Angelo and Gilad would allow me to make an attempt to do such a thing knowing that it was forbidden. I had to admit, though, that I had ignored several warnings.

"Even though the angel vamps didn't know about me, you guys did. You knew that the angel vamps would eventually learn about me. That was why you sent Angelo to protect me when I was a baby," I said. Michael nodded.

"That is true, but usually nephilims get their guardians by the time they turn 12, but your powers were active right after you were born. You are like no other nephilim we have encountered." Michael gestured to me by extending his right hand.

"Who was my father?" I asked with a quaver. Michael shifted his gaze around and then refocused back onto me.

"Your father was originally human, but from a time when the world was very different. He was the great Egyptian physician and architect Imhotep." When Michael spoke I felt a lump in my throat.

"How could this really be true?"

"Believe it, because it is true," Michael replied. "I know you have heard this so many times, but your parents did everything to protect you. Don't be crossed with them. It was for your own good. They love you very much."

"You mean loved. A part of me is human and it's not so easy for me to let this go. Everything I knew about my life wasn't even real." I made every attempt to not let my temper get to me in front of the divine assembly.

"I understand that learning the truth is hard for you, but try to understand your parents reasoning behind the decisions they made. The love they have for you is all around you. I sense it; I am surprised that you don't since you are in tune with your identity now." The end of his sentence implied my angelic heritage.

"Did my father have memory of his past lives?"

[167]

"Yes. The spell allowed him to remember everything except the experience of death. Once he reached full maturity, he proceeded with his life's work as a physician." Gabriel interceded.

"I must add that your mother was against what the angel vampires were planning to do with the box. She knew their plan because she was invited to be part of it. After she found out about the accident she thought she was being directly attacked, and she was right. Pandora hid the box in an undisclosed location before the Circle of Destiny cast the spell on her. Once the Council learned about you, they figured that they could entice you to join them, and that you would be able to find the box so they could execute their plan of destruction." Michael voiced with deep clarity.

I stood there under the stars in front of the angels and the quiet nude girl and Lothos, trying to process it all. "Listen, we understand what the human experience means," Michael said. "It's too much to handle all at once. We want to ease your pain. Don't say anything else. Let us do what we have come here to do." His eyes softened as he brought his voice down to an echoed whisper. I inhaled allowing myself to settle down. The conversation was so intense, but I needed to hear everything.

I looked over towards the girl. Lothos had released her bound arms and legs and covered her up with something. He carried her off to the side. Completely weakened by her devastating experience, she sobbed in disbelief and pain. Angelo joined them, preparing to do his thing.

The Great Seven gathered in a huddle around me. I stood in the center waiting for what they were going to do. Their wings extended, almost interlocking like pieces of a puzzle. One by one they bowed their heads and released a flow of energy and electricity. The huddle glowed like the moon and the energy radiated into me. I started to tremble and, felt myself levitating within the circle. Seconds later my feet descended back on to the ground. Feeling limitless, energetic, and humble something was different about me. Their angelic light diminished and the angels broke their embrace around me, taking a few steps backward. I glanced over to peer at Angelo and Lothos with a new perspective.

"You are like no other nephilim that we have come into contact with," Michael repeated. "We have given you the power to heal. Someone will always be with you to protect you. Your mother will be fine. Now go with your guardian to your mother. We will be in touch." Michael smiled with presence.

"Thank you, Your Grace." I uttered with a smile.

In an instant the Great Seven had departed in an explosion of light. I ran over to Angelo and Lothos to check on the girl. Now dressed, she was slowly regaining her senses. By the time I got to her she was already in the process of healing. I knelt down and touched her head.

"I was dying," she said, still shaking.

"Yes you were. I'm so sorry about all of this."

[168]

"I know it wasn't your fault. You came back to save me."

"I heard you when I was locked away in that creepy room," I told her.

"Josephine, let's get you and the others out of here for good." I said, helping her up to her feet. I hesitated for a moment and thought about how I had known her name.

Angelo was right when he said that it would be difficult to save the human captives. Using his angelic gifts, he sent Josephine back to her home, but not before he altered her memory about recent events and the things she saw. He recruited Lothos, Tristan and Elwyn to help rescue the humans. Each of us had a job in helping to restore their health and deliver them out of the situation. Angels are beings of mystery and wonder. Angelo had the power to touch the humans in ways that would help them get over their traumatic ordeal. He removed the tragic experience from their minds, spirits and emotions. Josephine's experience had been completely erased. I wish someone was able to do that for me. With every new discovery came a new hurt, a new pain. I understood that deleting the experience was the only way for the angelic community to be safe and the only way that the exposed humans had the chance of living normal lives. It would be devastating if the humans came back to Earth faithless.

Chapter Eighteen

I hadn't been back to the Earthly Realm for 48 hours before I found myself at the Loving Hills Mental Rehabilitation Center. It was a rainy midmorning, and I had no recollection of what day it was. The sands of time no longer had any effect on me.

I felt different as I walked down the long halls of the hospital. The atmosphere around me gave off a thick and desolate feeling, and the usual bustle of the hospital had been long lost and was replaced with a quiet subtleness. I loosened my scarf and unbuttoned the first hook of my rain coat as Angelo and I headed to my mother's room. A knot of anxiety pulsated in my back as we drew closer, and I held tightly onto Angelo's hand. I found it difficult to concentrate on anything.

When we reached the entrance to her room, I caught the essence of energy surrounding the door. There was a force field of protection blocking it. Placing my hand upon the energy, I sensed that someone was in her room. This was the power that came from the archangels. I glanced at Angelo before I wrapped my fingers around the knob. He nodded and I opened the door. My heart pounded hard when I stepped into the room.

The woman known as Pandora by the Greeks and the Egyptians was hovering in a corner with her face pressed into the wall. I was shocked to see her using her powers. I didn't even realize that they were still active. I caught the essence of another angel, and I turned my head around swiftly to see who it was. A figure shimmered, emerging from the wall. A broad shouldered, blond, hazel-eyed, angel approached me. Dressed in leather pants and a chain mail top with ankle silver-buckled boots, he gleamed at me cautiously. An expression of surprise crept into my face at his unexpected entrance.

"Angelo! I'm so glad you guys finally made it!" he said. "It's good to see you both. Sydney, hello, my name is Lars. It's nice to finally meet you. I'm sorry that it had to be like this." The chipper tone in his voice faded by the time he finished his last sentence. I shook my head in response and extended my hand to shake his. I greeted him with the same grip that I saw Angelo use when he greeted Tristan. I wanted to show them that I knew how to fit in with other enchanted creatures.

"It's good to meet you. I want to thank you for what you are doing." Angelo had told me a little about Lars, but that was all I knew about him—very little.

"I heard what you did. The buzz is that you are one bad-ass chick." Lars said with a thick grin. I smiled in response and glanced at my mother. Something told me that I was ready. I walked to where she was hovering. For a split second my mind went blank. I tuned out Angelo and Lars and whatever they were saying to each other. I thought Angelo said something to me, but I wasn't really sure. It was like I was standing in the room alone. I felt the presence of emptiness.

"Mom?" I said with a tremble. "You have to come down," I told her softly. I turned around and saw that Lars had blocked the window in the door. This scene would be hard to explain if a doctor or nurse walked past and saw her like this. I told Angelo to stand guard while I got her down. The moment Angelo stepped out of the room, I rose up my arms carefully. Concentrating down deep in my psyche, where my power was, I brought it up, allowing light to flow from my hands and on to my mom. I intercepted her power and was able to bring her down to the floor. She didn't resist. I allowed my light to fade as her feet touched the floor, then glided over to her, placing my arm around her skinny shoulder, I guided her over to the bed and we sat down. Lars looked on with nothing to say, his face expressionless. I could see Angelo moving in front of the door. I heard him talking to a nurse, purposely delaying her entry.

Easing off of the bed, I knelt down facing my mom. I laid one hand on my mom's head and the other on her thigh. Focusing intensely, I thought about the concept of restoration. Both of my hands tingled and grew numb as I released my power. My light flowed from my hands, brighter than I'd ever seen it before; I saw my mother's essence change. The power vibrated within my soul.

For the first time I realized how powerful I had become in such a short period of time. My energy felt extremely electrical, almost like when the Great Seven gave me the ability to heal. This was what it was like to really heal someone. Eventually the glow of the power and energy subsided. My mom's head rolled down the moment my light vanished. I stood up with her; supporting her by the shoulders. She raised her head slowly and her eyes met mine. I felt incredibly good at that moment.

"Sydney," she called with astonishment. Tears streamed down my cheeks. Just to hear my mother's voice was music to my ears.

"Mom!" My voice trembled as I collapsed into her, wrapping my arms tightly around her neck. I felt like I was getting a piece of my family back. An empty void had been filled in my heart. We released our embrace, and Mom touched the side of my face as I did the same to her.

"Now that you know what you are and who you have grown to become, please forgive me and know that I love you with all of my heart. My daughter, I realize that you're hurting, but now it's time for you to heal." Her wild matted hair was now long straight and smooth. Her eyes were clear, hazel with an angelic sparkle to them. Mom's skin radiated, displaying a thin luminosity. She hadn't looked like this since I was a little girl.

"Mom... I..." My voice trailed off as I noticed my mother's façade began to change. Her cheekbones reshaped, turning slightly triangular. Her eyes sparkled with a red yellowish hue. I narrowed my eyes and took several steps, backing up slowly as she changed. This did not look good.

Lars drew his sword but I threw my left hand back, signaling him to not strike my mother. She bent down, and letting out two yelps, sprung long, dark, grey wings from her back. The hospital gown was violently torn when the wings protracted from her flesh. She hollered an awful, unrecognizable sound, and she flapped her wings fiercely causing me to retreat further, moving closer to Lars. Her face pulsated with great rage.

I froze with shock when my mother plunged through the large window, and flew out toward the horizon, heading west.

Angelo was no longer able to deter the nurse or doctors, and they all exploded into the room. His eyes widened as the hospital staff looked at the big hole in the window. Huge chunks of glass were scattered all over the floor. I didn't even have time to make up a story. I was totally shocked and couldn't find any words. I couldn't react.

Angelo threw up his hands. His face had a million questions etched into the frown lines of his forehead and around his eyes.

"What happened?" one of the doctors asked incredulously. Shaking my head, I told the truth. I said that she jumped out of the window. They all ran out the door. I heard the doctor tell a nurse to dial the police. My body shook with anxiety.

"What did you?" Angelo asked accusingly. His face was convulsed with terrible fear and anger.

I searched for the words, and all I could say was "I…"

"Please tell me that you didn't heal her! How could you? She has the darkness in her!" Angelo's anger was so intense that I felt the ground rumble under my feet.

I started to explain, but suddenly realized that I wasn't meant to heal my mother. A new fear arose within me. The fact that Pandora was fully restored with darkness in her frightened me on a whole different level. She harbored a deep dark vengeance that was ready to explode.

Pandora was prepared to seek war against the Council or join them in their efforts to rule over the dimensions. The struggle for this realm to survive will continue. Overcome by the emotions of what I had unleashed, I realized that I had caused more damage than I could handle.

About The Author

LaTaeya Lane has been writing since she was seven years old. She began jotting down phrases and themes, later turning them into poems and short stories. Writing became such a passion that she became the junior and senior editor of her high school newspaper. She wrote her first novel at age sixteen.

Lane entered several creative writing contests and won a few of them. Always captivated by the supernatural and elements of fantasy, Lane was inspired to write a series of books that focused on going beyond the boundaries of life and imagination. "Swept into the Darkness" is Lane's first published book.

Lane completed a degree program in Liberal Studies and resides in New Jersey with her husband Leo and son Lucian. "Dark Betrayal" is the next book in the Chronicles of Celestial series.

www.ingramcontent.com/pod-product-compliance
Lightning Source LLC
Chambersburg PA
CBHW081147170626
46809CB00010B/3114